THE FOREVER ONE

THE ESCORT SERIES VOLUME 6

N.O. ONE

Cover design – N.O. One

Editing – Encompass Press Ltd

Published by N.O. One

The Forever One, N.O. One – 4th ed.

ISBN-13: 978-1-917471-05-3

THE FOREVER ONE

FOREWORD / WARNING

Before you continue...

The Forever One is the sixth volume of a series of six.
It is graphic and morally on the fence, containing extremely sensitive material that may not be adapted to your needs. If you need specific details of things involved, please visit our website for a list of warnings.

www.author-no-one.com

If you're okay with all of this, just remember... we warned you.

On the plus side, the lead female is strong and proud and these men come with a fire extinguisher.

If you're still reading after all of that then, by all means, sit down, relax, and enjoy the filthy, bumpy road ahead.

To reiterate:

!! If you have triggers, please do not continue. This is not the series for you. !!

Seriously, if you don't want all the angst and smut with some suspenseful darkness thrown in for good measure, stop reading.

To all of you who began with The Rich One, strapped in,

and trusted us on this rollercoaster of a ride.

We see you.

We appreciate you.

Thank you.

Chapter One

Enzo

The first sign that shit went wrong is the taste in my mouth as consciousness begins to tap at my frontal lobe. My mouth is pasty with an aftertaste of copper, which tells me I've got blood in or around my mouth. The salty, almost soapy taste at the back of my throat tells me even more. I was drugged, probably with some kind of Benzo. If I had to guess, I'd say liquid ecstasy fits the bill.

I'm lying on my side—the pressure along my ribs impossible to ignore—on cool, uneven flooring like an unfinished basement or a cabin exposed to the outside forces of nature. Keeping my eyes closed, I concentrate on any sounds I can recognize, but there are none.

No breathing, no rustling of clothing, and definitely no talking.

Slowly and carefully, I open one eye, hoping not to alert anyone who would be watching for me to wake up.

It takes everything in me not to flinch at the bright slash of the sunbeam coming through the window angled somewhere above me.

I see no one, hear nothing.

Taking in a deep breath, I concentrate on the recent events that could have brought me here.

What do I remember last?

With the drug still lingering in my system, I'm not surprised that my short-term memory is complete shit right now, but I have to try to figure out where I am and what the fuck happened.

As soon as I lift my head, a searing pain almost paralyzes me. Moving my eyebrows up and down, I can feel the sticky substance that's pulling on my hair. Blood makes the most sense. My arms are tied behind my back so I can't verify my theory, but it would explain the pain.

It's like I got pummeled with a baseball bat. Or maybe sucker punched by an irate Godzilla.

Taking another deep breath, I open both my eyes and look around as much as possible.

The pain is almost unbearable, but I have to try. I can't just lie here and rest forever.

My last memory is in the warehouse.

Marco's with me and so is J. We're planning the attack against the Ambrosios.

River. She arrived shortly after.

Then all Hell broke loose from an ambush.

That's all I know for now.

I think about Madelina, who is probably worried sick about me. She seems flighty and carefree but my girl has empathy to infinity. She worries for those she loves and even though she won't admit it, I know she loves me.

Marco will find a way to get to me, he's got the resources and the will. We're closer to brothers than colleagues and Marco *always* fights for his family.

Gathering all of my strength, I grit my teeth and lift my head to figure out where the fuck I am.

Stone walls, stone floors, a wooden table to the side, and a massive oak door right in front of me.

It smells like goats or pig shit. Maybe both.

Fuck, where the Hell am I? I know this isn't The City, that's for damn sure.

Looking around, my eyes land on a lump just behind me.

Tall, dark, and familiar.

He's lying at an awkward angle, his face flat against the stones below, his shoulders pulled back from where his wrists are tightly tied at the small of his back.

A pool of blood below his head and shoulder tells me I may be too fucking late.

Marco is here with me and from the eerie quiet in the early morning light, I'm afraid to even voice it in my head.

His chest seems still. His breaths aren't wheezing. His life doesn't feel present.

Fuck.

The last thought that crosses my mind is that I'd rather die than explain to Madelina and River that I couldn't do my job.

Save Marco.

Chapter Two

River

Everything is numb. My surroundings are inconsequential. But I know I can't allow myself the time to wallow in my own pity. It might be the sensible thing to do, giving myself the space to think logically and work through some of my emotions, but I can't.

My emotions are my fuel.

I'm working on pure instinct. Which is why I'm trusting this J woman who was at the warehouse... with all the bodies... the blood... Bruce...

A shudder runs down my spine at the thought of the warehouse. No one should ever have to witness that monstrosity.

Parking Marco's Earth-killer—the car he and Enzo took to the meeting—in front of our home, I turn off the engine and take a deep breath. I now need to break the news to Gabriella and Lina. None of this makes any sense. Even in my head it sounds so unbelievable. Like, what the actual fuck?

Marco and Enzo have been kidnapped by a rival mafia family and Bruce was shot in the head.

Yeah, that sounds like normal news to give a person.

Stefano startles me and I nearly throat-punch him the way Lina taught me before I realize it's him opening the car door.

"Signora Mancini, come on inside. Signorina J has called and I have informed your sister and mother-in-law. I will take care of the car and there is a strong coffee waiting for you in the living area, along with the other ladies of the house." He ushers me out and I remain silent, nodding my thanks and hoping he knows how grateful I am for him.

What I expected as I walked into the living room wasn't Gabriella pacing across the floor on the phone, her tone harsh as she speaks Italian to whoever is on the line. Without pausing, she approaches me, her free arm held out wide to grab me and pull me in. She holds me tightly, squeezing all her love and reassurance into the hug before I kiss her cheek and move away so I'm not disturbing her call. It seems important.

I sit on the sofa next to Lina, who is obsessively watching her mom with wide, blotchy eyes, her elbows resting on her knees as she leans forward. She puts an arm around my shoulders and brings me in closer, just holding me. I return the half-hug, kissing her on the head and reveling in the comfort of the moment, but it's not enough.

My mind is whirring with options, outcomes, and obstacles—none of them are things even remotely in my usual wheelhouse.

Lina's body shakes next to me as her mom's voice gets louder to whoever she's speaking to and I squeeze her tightly. "We'll find them, Lina. I promise, we'll get our revenge on these motherfuckers."

She sniffs and wipes at her eyes, nodding slowly. "We... we should make a list."

A list? That actually sounds like a great idea. My focus immediately clings to this task as I pull my cell from my pocket and open the notes app. "Let's do it then."

Lina looks up at me, a slight twinkle in her watery gray eyes. "Fuck, yes. Ambrosios need to be at the top of that list."

"Yup, the woman at the warehouse, J, said this was on them." I give the note a title—People Who Need to be Unalived—before typing the Ambrosios as number one.

"J will be beating herself up about this, I know it."

"You know her?"

"Of course I do. She's like an adopted cousin, and definitely the crazy one no one messes with. We're lucky she's on our side."

Crazy is an assessment I'd have to agree with, but in a good way. In the kind of way that is totally going to play in our favor for whatever fucked up shit we're going to have to do to get our men back. J's heavy breathing and blood-covered body were frightening when I first saw her, but her eyes showed me such kindness, it was difficult to doubt her intentions toward me.

"Okay, girls, I have news. Are we ready?" Gabriella has finished on the phone and now all her attention is on us, her hands on her hips and her chin high, like the regal mafia wife she has always been.

"Si, Mamma."

"We are."

Lina and I answer at the same time. I shouldn't be surprised by the strong and powerful stance Gabriella has; she is a formidable woman, despite losing her husband a short time ago.

"After speaking with my friends, I have found some sources. The Kastellanos assisted the Ambrosios logistically on this. They were going for you, River. Right now, the fact that they have no idea who you really are is on our side. It does beg the question, why? But my belief is that it's about power for them. It always is. They need Marco to marry Elizabeth, and they need you out of the way to do it." She rubs at her forehead in agitation, taking a deep breath before continuing. "They did it once before, when you were still known as Volpe to the families. The Kastellanos took the blame, but the Ambrosios were responsible. With you and your family gone, they were able to move in and take Naples. It originally belonged to your family, but they wiped them all out... or so they thought. It's a good thing your parents kept your brother concealed at the time. Not taking him to your grandparents' party that night was one of the best things they could've done."

My mind is blown by the information coming out of Gabriella's mouth. Things from my past are beginning to piece together, but not quickly enough. Trying to figure out all of that is—frustratingly—not the first thing on my mind. However, I do have another name to add to our list. *Kastellanos.*

"Okay, so I'm going to be asking about all that some more when we've got the guys back. For now, do we have any kind of plan? People we can call for more help, information... anything?"

A small smile graces her lips as she assesses me with a little pride in her eyes. "Yes, we have people. You can't be the wife of a don without learning a few tricks along the way."

"Apologies, signore. Lady J is here to see you. Shall I bring her through?" Ever the silent ninja, this man.

"Yes, please, Stefano. Thank you. You can come and join us too if you'd like. We need all hands on deck here."

He gracefully nods his head before leaving the room, returning moments later with J in tow. It looks as though she's had a shower and changed her clothes. Instead of the blood-soaked outfit she'd worn at the warehouse, she's now wearing tight black pants with buckles on the sides, a deep-pink plain top, and a black leather jacket. She's also a girl after my own heart, because the black shit-kicker boots she's sporting have a three-inch heel I'd be proud to wear. Her blonde hair is still damp, scraped back off her face into two french-plaits.

"Mrs. Mancini. I'm so sorr—" J approaches my mother-in-law with her shoulders drooped, only to be cut off when Gabriella marches forward and grabs her by the shoulders, bringing her in for the same mothering hug she gave to me.

"Do not apologize, *mia cara*. I have everyone on standby. Our first task is to find them."

Mrs. Mancini is a boss-ass bitch, and I'm in awe of her right now. The strength this woman holds in the face of such travesty is awe-inspiring. I want to be her when I grow up—minus the dead husband. I'd very much like my husband to stay alive and I'm praying to all the gods I know of to help make that happen.

I feel like a fish out of water with all of this. My eyes are burning, my head is pounding, and I have no idea how to handle this. I may have been born of this world—which is a shocker in and of itself—but I didn't grow up in it. I knew what I was getting myself into with Marco, but I think I was fooling myself with how fucking serious and huge it all is.

And now some jealous fuckers who want *power* have taken my husband from me, my soul mate, my twin flame. I know that's what he is. And I didn't tell him how much he means to me. What if I never get the chance? Why did I let us go to bed angry last night? If I get him back... no, *when* I get him back, I'm going to make him promise me that will never happen again. Going to bed angry is the worst. What if he thinks I don't love him, that I don't care? What if it's already too late?

"River!" Gabriella's voice brings me out of my mini-spiral. She's crouched in front of me, her hands on the sides of my face, and once she sees she has my full attention, she continues. "Listen to me, *cara*. You need to think and act like the queen you are, like a leader." J, Lina, and Stefano remain silent while I get a well-needed talking to. "We have people, lots of people, and they are all loyal to my son, which means they are loyal to you. Use them, use their knowledge, and let's focus on getting those boys back home, shall we?"

I nod, taking another deep breath before composing myself and clearing my throat. Gabriella is much like her son, I can tell she needs my words. "Yes. *Sì*." She smiles at my use of the small Italian word—baby steps. I can totally do this, I've basically trained myself for this in a way. I've seen Gabriella do it, and it's as easy as breathing. I slide on my mask, only this time, I'm not Rose, the escort.

I'm River Volpe-Mancini, the mafia queen.

"Okay, Stefano, I know you're Marco's *guy*, so are you able to track their phones? If not, what else can we use? Because I know for sure that you would never let them out there without some kind of back up." Stefano is an anticipator, and in the months I've known him, he always knows exactly what is needed and when, prepared for every situation exactly how he should be. If my people-reading skills are serving me well, then I know this man has plans A-Z for every circumstance.

"Si, signora. You know me well." His mouth moves up into a knowing grin. "Their cells are off, gone. The Ambrosios' crew at least have a little sense, I suppose. But Enzo is chipped. I already have my software working on finding him. It's an old system, we didn't think we'd ever have to use it after installing it years ago. I'm sorr—" His slightly bowed head isn't what I want to see, he has nothing to be sorry about.

"I won't accept an apology, Stefano. It is what it is. It's not like kidnapping is a regular occurrence. Can I ask why Marco wasn't chipped too?"

"Grazie, signora. The chip was a trial run, we'd never used it before, so Enzo volunteered. He'd said it was best for him to do it because if someone ever got hold of the system, they'd find Marco in a heartbeat, and that he was always with Marco anyway, so it worked."

Yeah, it kinda does. Fucking Enzo. Always looking out for Marco. In the few sessions he helped me with my self-defense, I could just hear the dedication to my husband in his voice. If this works, I owe Enzo a lifetime of gratitude. Well, I owe everyone in this room the same thing, but I'm not dwelling on that now. I have to focus.

Lina gently rubs my back as I stand, looking down at her with a strong nod and a wink, letting her know I've got this—even with the tears still burning behind my eyes. Her reply is a ghost of a smile as she straightens her back, readying herself—she is a mafia princess after all. She's grown up around these people, these dangers, and while she may have been sheltered somewhat, I know she's a powerhouse—that much was evident in our self-defense sessions after she told Enzo she'd take over my training by herself. I've learned that, as well as dance and hairdressing, Lina's got a few other amazing skills.

"Okay, one second." Everyone stays silent as I type onto my cell, adding to the list Lina and I started earlier.

It may seem inconsequential, but I need this.

People Who Need to be Unalived

Ambrosios

Kastellanos

Elizabeth? - Find out if she's a lying bitch or not first.

Eleanor? - Because she's creepy af and friends with Ambrosios.

Whoever killed Bruce.

"J, would you recognize who that is if you saw them again?" I point to the last one on my list, showing her my cell so she can read what I'm asking.

"Yeah, he's currently in an incinerator after being cut into pieces. Don't worry, Boss, I got him good." The glimmer in her eye tells me she enjoyed it too, and I don't blame her for that. I think I would've enjoyed flaying whoever laid their grubby hands on Bruce.

"Okay, I'll cross that one off my list then."

Having something to hone my focus on is helping.

Stefano's phone pings just before a faint knocking sounds from the hall and he silently leaves the room, cell in hand, gesturing to one of the guards to follow him. We're all on high alert, wondering who the fuck would be visiting. Anyone who ever comes into this house is already here.

Shortly after, Stefano is back and before he even has time to announce the newcomer, Elizabeth fucking Ambrosio shoulder checks past him and rushes toward us like she's family. With sorrow swimming in her eyes, she's the picture of worry and regret. Either she's genuinely pained by what's happened or she's a damn good actress.

J growls beside me, Lina stands with her hands fisted at her sides, Gabriella raises a regal eyebrow, and my anger flares.

Storming toward her, I grip her throat and push Elizabeth against the nearest wall. She holds my wrists but doesn't resist, defeat clear in her eyes. She is on my list, but she's also question-marked because I'm not going to blacken my soul by taking my revenge on an innocent person. Although her innocence is yet to be proven, the fact I'm unsure of her involvement is keeping her alive. For now.

My anger is a living, breathing thing inside my body, and thoughts of killing people don't seem as abhorrent as they once did. It's as if my Volpe mask has some kind of haze over my brain, allowing me to turn off the humanity switch. But River Fox still lies underneath and I'm willing to hear out the red-headed bitch in front of me.

"Give me one good reason not to kill you right the fuck now." My tone is full of venom, filtered only by my clenched teeth.

Her eyes are wide and she is having difficulty speaking through my grip on her, but I'm not letting up. Not yet. Bitch can struggle.

"I-I-I know"—she fights to swallow as her eyes begin to bulge—"how we can fix this."

CHAPTER THREE
RIVER

I guess we now know why Stefano's chip isn't giving us a signal. We waited for a couple of hours trying to triangulate Enzo's location, but the device wasn't made for long-distance.

And by long, I mean, really fucking far away.

Like, four thousand miles away and across an entire ocean.

That's right, Elizabeth confirmed that they were taken to the outskirts of Naples and that she was expected to fly out within the next day.

"They'll want to prepare a ceremony for you and Marco." Gabri's words physically make me sick, but I push that shit down because... what, now?

"Ceremony?" I spit the words like they're acid on my tongue.

Gabri turns to me, her soft gaze like a mother's caress, and reaches out to comfort me. "The Ambrosios will no doubt be prepared for just about anything. But the good news is that if they want Elizabeth to leave now, it means Marco is still alive." Those four words gift me the ability to draw oxygen into my lungs. She's right, why would they want her there if he's dead? This whole fucking scheme is a ploy to forcefully join their two families through marriage. Apparently, I put a dent in their plans.

Well, by the time I'm done with them, they'll wish they'd settled for the dent because I'm about to total their lives like a tsunami on crack.

"Yes, but before we can proceed, they'll want to..." She doesn't finish her sentence, just darts her gaze to me before lowering it and sighing.

"Before they snuff me out?" I raise a brow and cock my head, daring her to say the words to my face. "Is that your job, Elizabeth?" Taking two steps toward her, I get right in her face. "Are you trying to befriend us? Give us crumbs of information so that we feel comfortable enough for you to kill me and get away?"

From the corner of my eye I see J step closer just as her hand reaches under her leather jacket, pulling out a huge fucking gun. I wish I could say my mask is on and that's the reason I don't even flinch when J points the end of the barrel right at Elizabeth's temple.

Maybe I've watched too many mafia movies. Or maybe my imagination isn't wild enough to understand the thousands of layers that exist within a mafia family, but whatever it is, I'm gradually becoming numb to the violence. Violence these motherfuckers brought to my doorstep.

The rules. The traditions. The power that goes along with a simple name. None of it makes sense, yet I get it. I get it and I won't fucking let go.

"On your orders, Boss." J's words almost make me smile, which is admittedly fucked up.

With horror written all over her face, Elizabeth shakes her head vehemently. "*Mio Dio*, no. I could never… I would never… I'm a pawn in all this, just like you."

Elizabeth's words only spur J on as she brings the gun to within an inch of our potential enemy's head.

"That's where you're mistaken, *bella*." Gabriella speaks and my shoulders automatically square off. A few weeks ago, Lina explained that the word "*bella*" is more often than not used, by Italians, in a slightly derogatory way unless, of course, they're saying "*Ciao, bella*." I imagine it's like a caress… with a razorblade. "River's not a pawn, she's a ruler. A leader. Your parents raised you to be a wife, but they didn't raise you to make life-or-death decisions." At my side, she takes my hand and squeezes it. "My son fell in love with a partner in all things, not a trophy wife. So, no, River is nothing like you."

I step back, watching Elizabeth to see if her façade slips at all, but it doesn't. She seems genuinely shocked by my accusations and more than a little sad by Gabri's assessment of her, but that doesn't mean she won't sell me out and walk away, either.

I kiss Gabri's cheek before burying my hands in my hair and turning on my heel. And so the pacing begins, back and forth, from one end of the couch to the other. I don't want to trust her, but she's the only person who knows how to find Marco and Enzo. At this point, I don't really have a choice but to—tentatively—put a little faith in her, even if it means I lose the game for myself. At least I'll die saving the man I love.

Jesus, did those desperate thoughts just go through my mind? If *Gone With The Wind* and *The Godfather* had a child, it would sound like me just now. Cliché as fuck.

"Fine. Let's stick to the plan." I pause then turn my sharp gaze on Elizabeth. "Cross me and I will slit your throat."

"I'll help her." The unwavering strength in Lina's voice gives me a rush of adrenaline.

"We have a deal?" I'm steady now, both of my hands are pressed against the back of the couch and my eyes are narrowed, fixed solely on Elizabeth.

"Si, we have a deal." She bows her head, almost in deference, then turns and walks to the door, J escorting her out of the house.

This is it. It's all we can do for now as we wait for our pieces to fall into place. Hopefully, they'll fit perfectly and we can get my husband and Enzo back home where they'll be safe.

"*Cara*, you need to rest. Soon, they'll be calling you. They'll want to get you alone and you will need to be alert. Go, sleep, rest. Dream of Marco and how perfect life will be when you're both back on your thrones." Except, I don't care about the throne or the power. I just want Marco back home, driving me crazy and giving me orders he knows damn well I won't follow.

We hug like a mother and daughter, when Lina joins us, our circle is perfect.

A family of strong women ready to scorch the Earth for a small taste of revenge.

"Come on, let's go to my room. I won't be able to sleep alone." Lina takes my hand and we both pad our way up the stairs with the weight of our legacies pressing down on our shoulders.

As we lie on our backs, both wide awake, we don't even pretend to rest. I don't know about Lina, but my mind won't stop tormenting me with images of Marco suffering, screaming. Being tortured the way I know he's tortured others who have hurt me.

"They're okay. I can feel it." Lina's voice cracks on the last word and I don't have to look over at her to know tears are freely falling down her cheeks.

"Me too. Me too." I reach out, my hand squeezing hers as we give each other some much-needed comfort.

"Enzo would never let anything happen to Marco." The conviction in her voice reassures me, except my brain is taunting me, preparing me for the worst. I mean, what if Enzo was passed out and they killed Marco? What if Marco was shot and Enzo couldn't get to him? What if he bled out on the flight over to Naples?

What if…?

"Stop, River. You can't let the negative thoughts overcome you. If you don't believe they're alive, we'll never get to them in time." I snort at Lina's words as we turn our heads to look at each other.

"You sound like Petal." At just the mention of my sister-in-law, a sob escapes my throat and my body breaks like a two-hundred-year-old dam that's been beaten by the water.

"Shh, they're okay. They're okay. They have to be."

I don't know how long we lie there holding each other, reassuring each other, but at one point I fall asleep because the next thing I know, Gabri is waking us up with urgency in her voice.

"River. River, wake up."

My eyes fly open, my brain trying to refocus on whatever news she may have. Lina snaps awake too and we both turn to Gabriella as she wraps her hands around mine.

"The Ambrosios are on the phone. They want to speak with you."

CHAPTER FOUR
RIVER

"**I**s that Marco's little whore I'm speaking to?"

The bone-chilling voice of Ugo Ambrosio makes me want to reach through the phone and strangle the fucker. I've never met him, talked to him before, nothing, but the disdain on Stefano's face as he handed the phone over to me was clear. We hold no love for this man.

"You are speaking to Mrs. Fox-Mancini." I almost went with Volpe, but something in the back of my mind said that was a bad idea for right now. That little nugget is something I want to save for when I see this cunt in person, let him know his family screwed up when they didn't actually take out the whole Volpe line.

"You really are a disrespectful slut, aren't you? How dare you sully a good Italian name by adding your own to it, as if you even have the right, American whore."

Obviously I can't see him through the phone, but I can feel the corners of my mouth tipping into a small smile at how angry I seem to have made him over a name. I want to shout at him, yell obscenities until I'm blue in the face, but I also know that a man like this won't be bullied into giving me information. He has to believe I'm compliant, weak, willing to do whatever he pleases, and feel as if he is in complete control of the situation. From just the few sentences he's spoken to me so far, he's an easy read. So, with a deep breath, I prepare myself for the job at hand.

The job of a lifetime.

Breaking this motherfucker, his family, everyone involved in all this shit, and finding my man.

"I assume you called for a reason, Mr. Ambrosio?" I am the picture of calm, apart from my shaking hands as adrenaline courses through my veins. Luckily, he can't see that.

"Yes." He laughs. "I assume you're missing a husband, Mrs. Mancini?" As he's on speakerphone, Gabri, Lina, and Stefano can hear everything he's saying, and considering the actual Mrs. Mancini—not Fox-Mancini—is standing right there, after having lost her own husband a short while ago, well, that comment from him hit harder than I think he'd intended.

Gabri sniffs quietly, wiping at her eye before seemingly steeling her own spine against the whole situation.

"Enough of the games, Mr. Ambrosio. Ugo. Whatever. Just tell me what you want. Where are Marco and Enzo?" Maintaining my calm façade isn't easy, but I'm a goddamn professional at it.

He laughs down the phone again. "I was hoping a little whore like you would be up for some fun first." He takes a long, deep, annoyingly loud breath in, before exhaling on a bored sigh. "You have forty-eight hours to get to Naples. I will send you a burner phone to take with you and you will send a message to the number saved when you arrive. Once there, you will await further instruction."

After Elizabeth's revelation, that was the plan anyway, but I really don't understand what they want with me. It's weird, man. Fucking weird.

"Okay, when will I get the burner phone?"

"Soon. Make sure you're alone. You don't want to know what will happen if you're not." He laughs again but it's not a nice, kind laugh made from joy, it's evil. Pure evil. "Oh, you female Mancini's are becoming quite renowned for losing your men to us. This is all just so fun. Hey, do you want to know a secret, little whore?"

The nickname he has taken to using for me grates on my nerves and I can't help grinding my teeth as I respond. "Tell me."

"You're not the only Mrs. Mancini we have stolen a husband from." His cackle flows through the phone just before he ends the call.

Moving my head up to look at the other people in this room, I'm not surprised to find their faces in as much shock, pain, and torment as my own. Something crosses Gabri's eyes in that moment, and I know vengeance is on her mind. The Ambrosios are somehow responsible for Papa Mancini's death. They have Marco and Enzo, they murdered my family for power... and Bruce, there was just no need for what they did to that little fluffball... these fuckers have got a whole shitstorm coming their way.

I move toward Gabri, standing by the window in Marco's office, and wrap my arms around her, embracing her and offering comfort in the only way I know how.

"Mamma, we'll get them. Okay? We'll get those fuckers and make them pay a thousand times over." Lina joins in, making it another group hug, something I am savoring, gathering my own strength from these powerful women I get to call family.

Gabri sniffs then pulls away with one simple nod of her head. "*Si, cara. Si.*"

"River, the last of the capos have arrived. Shall I send them to a room until morning?"

I hadn't realized J was still here, but I guess if the capos were all on their way over, then it made sense that she stayed. I also hadn't realized any others had already arrived while Lina and I were sleeping.

"No, can you get everyone gathered in the living room, please? I'd like to be comfortable while we do this and I can't do that surrounded by the scent in this room." It smells of vanilla, all Marco, all mine... all gone.

"Sure thing, Boss."

I swear she's been taking ninja lessons from Stefano, because she's gone from the doorway within the blink of an eye.

This all feels a lot like a bad gangster movie. The capos with all their nicknames, which have taken me the last couple of hours to remember—not that I'm ever actually going to call them by those names. Eddie "Snake-Eyes" Borelli, George "The Butcher", "Babyface" Tommy...

I mean, who comes up with these? They're not exactly original.

Saying all that, J's nickname is amazing. I'd totally call her Shadow if she'd let me. Apparently, she hates it, but it's for jobs and people who need to stay afraid of her.

After what seems like weeks, but has only been a mere couple of hours, we have a kind of plan of attack in place. Our main issue is getting everyone over to Naples without detection and having no idea what sort of man-power the Ambrosios have.

Luckily, Marco has a private plane, but only one. And it's not big enough for the army of people wanting to help.

"Ooh, Tyler. Tyler is a rich bastard. I bet he has a private plane." Lina's excitement is contagious, and it just might work. If he's willing to lend us his plane without asking too many questions. Which I doubt. He's almost as much of a control freak as Marco, he'll want to know all the details. But we need it, we need *him*. I'm not above begging if it means I get my husband back safe and sound. Fuck my pride.

"Okay, ask him. See what he says. We really need it available within the next few hours if that's possible."

"Yes, ma'am." Lina salutes me with a playful wink, walking off to make her call. I shake my head at her antics. She's trying so hard to be okay, to act as though nothing is phasing her about this whole situation, but I can see it. I know she's struggling just as much as I am. It would seem that using a mask to hide real emotions isn't as uncommon as I'd once thought.

These Mancini women are warriors and I can't let them, or my husband, down.

"Okay then, Ray, you're the underboss, have I remembered that right?"

"Yes, ma'am." He nods his head respectfully, a small smirk playing on his lips.

"Great, well, I need you to arrange eyes on Elizabeth as she travels to Naples. And figure out where the fuck Eleonor is. I don't know why, but I don't trust her, and she's got some odd connection to the Ambrosios. We also need eyes on the Greeks, and as soon as we get people over to Naples, we need the Ambrosios watched."

"On it, Boss. Elizabeth is already on a flight, my guy sent me word about half an hour ago. So far, the information she gave us checks out. I'll make sure everything else is done." With that, he picks up his cell and leaves the room, tapping furiously at the keys before bringing the phone to his ear.

The other people left in the room are silent, waiting for their next instruction. Much different from half an hour ago when we were all arguing about the best course of action. In the end, I put my metaphorical foot down and demanded they actually listen to my ideas. J was the first to follow suit. I mean, I get it, they're all actually quite sweet with how they're trying to protect me and the other two Mancini women in the room, but they also need to understand that we're every bit as capable as they are.

Okay, so I'm not exactly experienced in all things mafia, but I don't need to be. I read people, I read situations, I can foresee outcomes that others blinded by a fighting instinct may not. I'm a bad ass bitch.

"J, I know most of our people are heading to Naples, but are there any that you would trust with your life...?" I pause, taking another deep breath before finishing. "I need eyes on my family in Staten Island. I don't know how much the Ambrosios know about me, and I need them safe. My sister-in-law is pregnant and she and my brother are just the kindest souls..." A tear falls down my face at the thought of my family.

I know they wouldn't condone what I'm doing, but they'd be damn proud of me for my strength. I'll keep my promises to them about no more lies and I'll tell them a very watered-down version of what's happening when it's all over, but until then, they need protecting.

"Of course. I'll call Harris. I trust him and his partner, Sam, with my life." She nods, and immediately begins calling whoever Harris is.

The heavy weight somewhat lifts from my shoulders knowing they will be safe amid all this bullshit and non-fun fuckery.

"Okay, I think that's everything. I guess I better go get changed and pack my bag."

Gabri smiles warmly at me, opening her arms for a final hug before I leave the room. I wrap myself around her, reveling in all her motherly glory before pulling back to kiss her cheek.

"*Cara*, there is one more thing you should know before you go."

"Oh?" I'm not sure I can take much more. I'm about to travel on a private plane, alone, to Naples, to face an insane family of people who think kidnapping and murder is a perfectly okay way to live. I'm also aware of how that thought refers to my own husband and his men too, but I can only see them as the good guys. I know how much good they do for the city.

"The Ambrosios' soldiers... there may be a few still loyal to the Volpe name. The Volpe were in power in Naples before the Ambrosio's took over. You might be able to use that. I know you've been a Fox your whole life, and you weren't brought up in this world..." Gasps sound all around me with that revelation and when I turn to look at their faces, all I see is a shock swimming in their eyes. I suppose there's going to be some explaining to do at one point, but now is definitely not the time. My attention swings back to Gabri when her last words fill me with pride. "But, my darling girl, you were always destined for it."

Chapter Five

Marco

The hard slap of cold water jolts me awake. Coughing as I practically choke on the drops that I've inhaled down the wrong pipe, I realize that the water is the least of my problems. By contrast, the searing pain in my shoulder pushes a growl from deep inside my chest. My teeth are locked, grinding hard enough that I'm afraid I'll break a few along the way.

Where the fuck am I? What the Hell is going on?

Panic rises up my throat as bits and pieces of my memory come running through my brain like an eight millimeter film reel.

Shoving River into the bunker.

Running out to help Enzo and J.

Shooting my way through the increasing number of enemy bodies.

The bullet to the shoulder. *Well, that explains the white-hot pain.*

Then nothing.

Again, I'm choking on my panic as I wonder where River is. Where Enzo is.

I don't need to open my eyes to know I'm not home. The fucking smell of this place is the only clue I need. Goats or pigs are my first thought, but the smell of piss is quickly becoming number one on my list of culprits.

Groaning when I try to move, I'm aware that I'm tied down to a chair. By the feel of it all, I'm guessing rope at my ankles and at my wrists behind my back. That's why my shoulder is fucking killing me. The position is putting way too much fucking pressure on whatever wound I have there.

"Wake up, you filthy American!" Another bucketful of water lands on my face and I fight not to drown.

"*Ti ucciderò.*" And I will. This motherfucker will be the first person I kill when I get my hands free.

"Not before he kills your wife." My eyes fly open and the movement makes my entire body convulse with pain. Pain from my shoulder, pain from the ray of sunlight that directly hits my right eye from the small window at the top of the wall in front of me. I blink, momentarily blinded, as I grit my teeth once more to regain a semblance of control.

The man laughs like watching me suffer is better entertainment than Monday night football. He leans down and whispers—no, taunts—in my ear. "Maybe I'll fuck that whore pussy of hers first, si?" I don't even think, my body just reacts as my head rears back right before I headbutt this asshole hard enough to make me see stars.

I know I'm in no position to attack, this guy could be capable of a hundred things that would keep me away from my wife, but my primal instinct is to cause pain to those who threaten her.

For my efforts, I get the grip of his gun across my cheek and I know I'll be sporting a swollen eye in mere minutes. As my head snaps to the side, I see Enzo. He's barely in better shape than I am and I'm guessing he mouthed off too, if that broken nose and swollen lip is any indication.

We lock eyes and, without a single word, try to communicate. But my brain is slow, rattled, my entire body surviving on just the adrenaline coursing through my veins.

His eyes dart to the door, which means there are more men outside. He narrows his gaze at me, which warns me to keep my mouth shut if I ever want to see my family again. *Fuck.*

Just as I take a deep breath to ask what's happening and who this guy is, the wooden door flies open and in walks Ugo motherfucking Ambrosio.

Of course, it's him. Of course, this tiny little gnat is the reason I'm tied up and bleeding with only a makeshift bandage slowing the blood as it soaks through my clothes.

"Well, well, well, it's about time, Marco. I was afraid you were going to miss the show."

I don't speak, letting him take the stage while I try to learn what's going on. However, my hatred shines through my narrowed glare.

"Now, be a good little body and keep your mouth shut."

I take it back. The first person I kill is this piece of shit. I should have done it weeks ago. Months, even. Hell, I should have killed him *years* ago when he was promised to Lina, but decided he wanted to fuck half of the Napolitan female population before being tied down to "some American pretending to be Italian." His words, not mine.

I watch him carefully as he takes his phone out from the inside pocket of his jacket and dials a number. It only rings once—the sound is thankfully broadcast via speakerphone—before the most beautiful music in my world soothes me from my flesh to my soul.

"Speak, motherfucker." I'm so relieved to hear her voice, strong and even, that I don't even react to her use of the curse. We'll have to establish moments where her use of colorful vocabulary is appropriate.

"*Tsk, tsk, tsk.* You are in no position to make demands." Ugo frowns, probably not understanding why she's not respecting him and his commands.

"Well, the way I see it, you're the one who wanted me here bad enough to kidnap my husband, so spill. I'm here. What now?" God, I love this woman, but her words put me on high alert. She's here? Where the fuck is here?

I turn to Enzo and he mouths, "Italy."

Goddammit.

"I think he's bluffing." It's Enzo's turn to go completely still, his calm and even demeanor vanishing after just four little words from the woman he loves.

"Who is that?" Ugo is now pacing in front of us, his temper rising. "I told you to come alone."

"Like I would be that stupid. Seriously? Did you think I would fly half-way across the world to show up, conveniently alone, on your home turf without some assurances of my own? Jesus, you really are a stupid motherfucker." Christ, she's going to get herself killed.

Enzo grunts beside me as the gorilla from earlier gags him with some disgusting-looking cloth, but I see the venom in his eyes knowing Lina is about to put herself in danger.

It's obvious he wants to hurl obscenities at these pieces of shit but, right now, it's impossible, so he settles for glaring at me like all this is my fault.

"Someone will meet you at the airport and bring you to me." He spits his words out like speaking to her is far beneath him.

If only he knew.

"Nah uh. I'm not going anywhere until I know for a fact that Marco and Enzo are alive and safe."

There's a pause as Ugo taps his thumb on the side of his phone, contemplating his next move. For some reason he wants her here and I don't fucking like it. It doesn't make sense. He could just use a sniper, kill her, and I'd be a widower. Yet, he's putting this whole elaborate plan into place because he wants her here.

Why?

"Fine." My eyes snap to his and I snarl as he puts the phone to my mouth and whispers, "Tell your whore you're alive." Oh, Ugo. Every word you say is another bullet I'll bury in your body.

"River, don't you fucking dare come here. Go back to New York where it's safe." I say it quickly, trying to put as much strength as I can in my voice, trying to make my words sound even and my body in control. Except it comes out like a croak, where only one word out of three is actually audible.

"Marco? Baby, are you okay? And New York is exactly where you got kidnapped, so no, it's not fucking safe."

"You and Lina go back to New York right n—"

Ugo backhands me hard enough for a burst of blood to explode in my mouth as I bite the inside of my cheek on contact. Goddammit, she's stubborn. But I hope she's not suicidal because coming here alone—and bringing Lina isn't exactly coming with reinforcements—is the most reckless thing she could ever do.

I make myself the promise that if we survive this, I will lock her up in a gold prison and make sure she's never able to put herself in danger, ever again. Although, technically, I'm the one who's been kidnapped.

"He's fine, but he won't be for very long if you don't get your whore ass over here. Do you understand? And Lina? I'm looking forward to seeing you again." There's silence, like Ugo's words have paralyzed River's vocal cords.

"I'll be there, but, Ugo?"

He hesitates, but this parasite is too curious for his own damn good. "What?"

"I'm going to enjoy slicing your balls right off and shoving them down your throat."

I grin at my wife's words just as Ugo growls and throws the burner phone against the stone wall of this disgusting little barn.

My wife is perfect and as soon as we get out of here, I'm going to make it my mission to tell her that. Every. Fucking. Day.

My strength is coming back, fueled by River's energy, but it's quickly snuffed out as Ugo approaches me and, with the barrel of the gun, pushes against my bullet wound. Hard.

Hard enough that the pain shuts everything down and my world goes black.

Chapter Six
River

What I'm doing may make me a dumb bitch—flying to Naples to deal with some mafia shit because my husband has been kidnapped is certainly not something sensible people do—but here I am, with Lina and Tyler, waiting to be picked up by 'the enemy', ready to be whisked off to some secret location.

Fuck, it all sounds ridiculous, even inside my own mind.

Tyler can suck a dick for all I care too, because I was supposed to be coming here alone. My back-up, consisting of J and her Reapers and some of Ray "The Stinger's" men as well as George "The Butcher" and his soldiers, are all flying into Naples as soon as they can. Some are using Marco's private jet, and others are using Tyler's, which is the only reason he's here. The bastard tricked me into bringing him and Lina and I foolishly trusted his help came without strings. The strings being they were coming with me.

Although, when Lina had asked for his help, she forgot to tell him that she wasn't a part of the whole plan to come here, insisting she was needed. And, of course, Tyler wasn't accepting that the woman he has taken such a liking to was putting herself in danger. Not that it's a danger he understands. He still seems to think that if he throws some money at the situation, everything will be fine.

So, here we are, at the airport like regular tourists—minus the luggage—waiting for Ugo's men to pick us up and take us to wherever it is they want me. He told me to come alone, and I tried so hard to make that happen, knowing Marco and Enzo were at risk if I did anything other than what I was instructed. But, stubborn men, and stubborn Italian women—Lina—are difficult to get rid of. Plus, Tyler had a good point when he reminded me that this Ugo dude clearly wants me for some reason, so he was likely to allow me to bend some rules to some extent. And a businessman and a salon owner-slash-dancer aren't exactly seen as a threat to the average bear.

Stefano has given J everything she'll need to track my phone, so she knows where everyone needs to head once their planes arrive in the next half an hour. We didn't want to leave too much time between us arriving and them, mainly because we've got no idea what's going to happen when we get to where we're going. The sooner help can arrive, the better it will be for all of us. I'm well aware that I'm so out of my depth with all of this that I'm almost drowning in fear, but I refuse to let the fear beat me into submission.

This is one of those push-the-emotions-down-and-deal-with-them-later moments.

"When are they supposed to be here?" Lina's voice is quiet, but it's not timid. She knows I'm not happy with her for putting herself in this situation, but if the tables were reversed, I'd have done the same thing.

"No idea. Cunt-face just said he was sending someone to meet me at the airport." My hands are in the pockets of my lightweight black jacket and I can't seem to keep my feet still, tapping them side to side in agitation. I hate waiting.

"Don't worry, ladies. We'll get this whole thing sorted out in no time. The Ambrosios are businessmen at the end of the day."

Lina scoffs. "Tyler, baby, I love you, but you have no idea what you're stepping into. You should probably wait here until everyone else arrives." She wraps her arm around Tyler's waist and snuggles into him, as if he's about to bow to her request. *Not if I know anything about Tyler Walker.*

"Not a chance, Gumdrop. But nice try." He smiles and kisses her head and a pang of jealousy, or more like longing, flitters through my insides at the image. I miss Marco and the way he holds me, the way he loves me.

A few large buses pass by, along with a variety of taxis, all picking up various groups of people. It feels like we've been here for hours, even though it's only been about fifteen minutes. A quick glance at my phone tells me it's only eight in the morning yet the scorching sun rays make it feel like midday. I wish we were here for a relaxing vacation, instead we're walking into the wolf's den willingly. I fear this whole experience may tarnish my memory of what is surely an incredible city.

"Ooh, is that it?" Lina points to a shiny black Mercedes slowing down as it approaches the curb of the sidewalk we're waiting on.

"I guess so." Another one pulls up behind it and I can see at least four large men sitting in there, all with nasty scowls on their faces, completely ruining the beauty of the morning.

Elizabeth climbs out of the back of the first car, bodyguard in tow, and her strained smile tells me she's finding this as difficult as I am. Especially after our conversation only yesterday back in my home in New York.

She gestures toward the car, encouraging me to get in, only slightly surprised by my extra additions in the form of Lina and Tyler.

"He can go in the other car. He's not going with you two." The bodyguard looming behind Elizabeth steps forward and grabs Tyler's arm, pushing him into the car behind ours.

Tyler begins to say something, but quickly stills as the man whispers something in his ear. I can't see his face, but I can only imagine what was said to make him stop talking or struggling. He wasn't supposed to be here. And I can do fuck-all about how he's being handled because I need to be compliant for now. For Marco.

Lina and I slide along leather seats into the back of the Mercedes and Elizabeth gets in next to us, her bodyguard goon slamming the door closed behind her and climbing in the front seat. As soon as his door is shut, the driver moves off toward wherever we're going.

"How was the flight?"

Elizabeth asking this means everything is in place and she has given Stefano the location details for J, George, and everyone else to find us—our fail-safe in case my phone was lost or stolen for any reason. Inside, I'm smiling. Step one of our plan is going well so far.

"It was good, there was no turbulence." To anyone else's ears, this is a boring small-talk conversation, but this answer has just let Elizabeth know that everyone is in place on our end as well, all ready to go. We discussed all of this before she left for her own flight to Naples.

"Marco and Enzo are still alive." Elizabeth's voice is soft, but her tone changes when driver-goon looks at her through the rear-view mirror. "And they will continue to be if you do as you're told." I see the apology in her eyes and I'm praying to all the gods that I'm right to trust my gut with her.

The car slows to a stop in the middle of nowhere. Literally, we are surrounded by nature. It's beautiful, but I have a feeling this wasn't part of the plan because Elizabeth tenses up beside me.

"Aldo, what's going on? Ugo said to pick them up and bring them straight to him." The guy Elizabeth calls Aldo has opened the back passenger door and he's peering in with a sadistic grin on his pale face, his greasy dark hair badly in need of a trim.

"We had different instructions, Signora. Everyone, out of the car. Now."

Confused, I follow Elizabeth out of the car, gripping Lina's hand behind me. The car behind us containing

Tyler has stopped too. Thank the gods we know where he is.

"Turn around and put your hands on the car."

"What the fuck, Aldo?"

He grips Elizabeth by the chin and brings his face down to hers as she practically growls at him to let go.

"These are my instructions. Be quiet and let me do my job, *Principessa.*"

I grit my teeth at the order, but, for now, I'm willing to comply. We knew that this was a possibility. Hence our fail-safe with Elizabeth. Just now, though, we're relying on her more than I had wanted to.

Lina does the same, quietly doing as he asks, allowing the dirty fucking creep to pat his hands around our bodies for hidden weapons. He finds our phones and nothing else. His hand moves round to my breast, and he squeezes once, fueling the anger inside me, then he does it again, so I cough before thrusting my elbow backward into his stomach. He doubles over, removing his slimy grip from me with a grunt.

"Whoops. Sorry."

"I'll fucking sho—"

"Aldo, Ugo wants her unharmed. He'll have your head if you do anything and you know it."

Elizabeth to the rescue. Aldo slowly lowers the gun he pulled from his waistband, after aiming it at my head. I must admit, I definitely had an 'oh shit' moment, but my life didn't flash before my eyes and I know now isn't my time. It can't be.

I'm curious as to why we didn't see anyone get Tyler out of the car behind us, but I'm not asking this douchewad any questions. And after the unexpected stop, I don't think Elizabeth will have any answers for me either. I just hope he's okay.

Lina is stoic beside me for the journey and I know she's doing what I am; preparing herself for the shit storm we are inevitably about to face.

The cars finally pull up outside a country farmhouse. It's a typical Italian villa surrounded by farmland and a couple of barns. It should look beautiful, but there's a dark aura surrounding the property, like nothing good ever happens here.

Elizabeth squeezes my leg to get my attention before her door is opened and her eyes are wide, like she has something to tell me, but can't say the words out loud.

She's looking from me to the house, and shaking her head in disbelief. A sense of dread fills me. If I'm reading her correctly, this isn't the original destination. Which means our *fail-safe* plan has failed—which is fucking ironic—and the army of people coming to be our backup and basically get us all out of here alive... won't be able to find us.

The lead in my stomach is heavy as I exit the car and I want so badly to tell Lina to stay. Don't get out. I've got us into some shit and I'm not sure how to get us out of it. I thought I could be some big bad mafia queen, but I've fucked it all up at the first hurdle.

As Lina steps out of the car, I grab her hand and pull her close to me, whispering, "Never forget, I've always got you. Whatever happens."

She nods. "Same, girl."

"Come on, what is this? Get them inside, Aldo." An overweight goon from the car behind us saunters past, a cigarette hanging from between his lips.

"Where's Tyler?" I'm asking no one in particular, but I know Aldo heard me when he begins snickering like the Beavis he is.

Before he answers, Lina gasps from beside me, drawing my attention to a lump on the ground beside the other car. It's a Tyler-shaped lump. He's close enough for me to see that he's breathing, which is the first thing I look for before allowing panic to set in.

"What the fuck have you done to him?" Lina's voice is full of anger and she squares up to the giant cunt that is Aldo. He's got at least three feet on her, but that doesn't stop her.

"Oh fuck off." Aldo hits her across the head with the butt of his gun, knocking her out cold.

I just about manage to catch her before she hits the concrete and I glare at the motherfucker.

"Aldo! What the Hell was that?" Elizabeth's usually calm tone is high-pitched, almost on the brink of losing it.

"Boss didn't say anything about harming this one." He chuckles, hooking his arm through Elizabeth's and turning to walk inside the weird barn-thing at the side of the house as I gently lie Lina down. She's coming to already, thank the gods.

No, I'm not having that.

I move to get up, but I don't get very far before my arms are grabbed from behind.

"Get your fuc—" I'm cut off mid-yell with some disgusting material forced between my lips. It's pulled so tightly, it's uncomfortable and a little painful to move my mouth to form words. Inside, I'm yelling all the curse words ever invented, while outside it sounds like a lot of muffled screeches as I'm dragged along into the barn where Aldo went.

I can see another couple of goons dragging Lina along behind me. She's struggling against them as much as I am, but it's no use. They now have us gagged and bound by the hands. I try kicking the thugs holding me, but they each manage to avoid it by dropping me on the spot before picking me up again to continue.

Once inside the building, I stop struggling, because my attention and focus is on one thing only: Marco.

He's here. And he looks like utter shit. There's blood all over his shoulder, his face, he's bound and gagged, and his eyes... I've never seen such a look of horror as he watches the goons throw me to the floor next to Lina. He and Enzo are on their knees, tied to a stable door at one end of the barn, hay and animal shit all over the ground.

"Well well well, finally, she has arrived. I told you to come alone, did I not, little whore?"

My muffled response just makes him laugh.

"Oh, but you did bring a treat. Hello, Lina." He moves to Lina beside me, putting his face into her neck and taking a deep breath. She flinches away from his touch and I don't blame her.

"Tie her over there. We'll hand her over to her new owner tomorrow." His attention moves from Aldo back to Lina. "Daddy's got himself a little fun to have first."

I watch Lina's eyes widen as she tries to move backward, away from the monster who has just gripped her throat. The once silent room is now full of muffled shouts and screams, from Marco, Enzo, me, and worst of all, Lina.

"Hold her legs down." Two more goons appear, each holding one of Lina's legs down, leaving room for Ugo to get on his knees in between them as he undoes his zipper. She's on her front, and I stop watching what Ugo's doing from where I've been tied, pulling at my restraints to get to Lina and finding it impossible. The ropes are burning my wrists, but I won't stop trying. I focus my eyes on Lina, because right now, she's facing me, the guys are just behind her, watching from a different angle.

I see the moment Ugo does the unthinkable, and even gagged, the scream that comes from Lina is one I'll never forget. Tears fill her eyes with every movement, and they fill mine too. The hurt and pain she's going through is incomprehensible.

It goes on for far too long and I've managed to block out the sounds of the room, focusing on Lina, sending every loving piece of energy I have her way. We will get vengeance for this. We have to.

Her eyes are torn away from mine and Ugo has her by the hair, dragging her over to Enzo. The sick fuck.

I can't see Marco in this position, but I can hear his growls promising death. Lina's eyes are now on Enzo's, her face close to his, and he's struggling with all his power to get free. Blood is beginning to pour from his wrists, but he just can't get close enough. His eyes are on Lina, unmoving, and it's obvious he's ready to die to make sure Lina survives this.

"She was supposed to be mine, did you know that?" Ugo's voice grates on my every nerve as he pants with every breath, watching and loving Enzo's reaction to what he's doing to Lina. "But I never got the chance to taste her. I guess it's never too late, is it?"

Lina's scream pierces through the air and Enzo's eyes widen, expressing every ounce of his agony. He's helpless, but he continues to growl and grunt and make himself bleed as he tries to escape the ropes holding him down. The barn door he's tied to shifts a little, but not enough as Ugo's frightening grunt of pleasure echoes around the room before he stands, zipping himself up.

Lina is left on the floor, her jeans around her ankles and her panties torn, hanging off of her waist as she lies in the filth, curled up in a ball. Her eyes are still on Enzo and she reaches out to him. He does the same and their fingers are so close they're almost touching when Ugo grabs her hair and pulls her up and over his shoulder.

"That was fun. Thanks for the treat, Whore. Aldo, lock 'em up." He leaves the barn with Lina struggling against him, even now, but I don't get to see the outcome since Aldo is suddenly in front of me. He grips my cheeks and growls a deep, disgusting growl before licking the side of my face and untying me.

My burning eyes find Marco's tear-stained ones as I'm dragged out of the barn, kicking and screaming, trying to tell him *I'm sorry.*

I love you.

Please forgive me.

Chapter Seven

Marco

The room is eerily quiet. No more cries, no more screams, no more threats echoing from these four stone walls. My throat is on fire from my fruitless efforts to yell at and intimidate that motherfucker.

Still tied to the barn door, my head hangs low with the weight of my shame, of my uselessness. A sob rakes through my body, the sound foreign to my ears.

What the fuck just happened? How did we get here?

Lina. My beautiful, carefree Lina, will never be the same and I don't know how I can save her from those unforgettable minutes she just endured.

I can hear Enzo sniffing and I don't need to look to know he's still lying in the same position as earlier as he watched the love of his life lose her youth. He hasn't moved since they were dragged away by the hair and taken to I don't fucking know where.

And River. Fuck. The guilt she no doubt feels is going to eat her up for the rest of her life. I'm livid with River for bringing Lina, even though my rational brain tells me she probably didn't have a choice. Lina may be happy and fun loving, but the Mancini stubbornness gene did not skip her. Still, my capos and my mother... how could they not keep her back in New York? It seems so fucking simple to me.

Heads are going to roll for this.

If I get out... no, *when* I fucking get out of here, every person who had a hand in this tragedy will die.

Every single one. From the pilot of the plane to the drivers of any of the cars. Hell, I might just slit the throats of their cooks and their fucking Nonnas if I hear they were involved in any way. And the guy who was holding River back? Yeah, he's going to lose those meaty hands he used to fondle my wife. I'll cut those off first, then I'll shove every one of his fingers down his throat and let him choke on them.

My breathing begins to pick up with the rage that slowly builds from the pit of my stomach to the hammering organ in my chest. Good, I need this fire to burn deep so I can be the leader I should have been weeks ago. Instead of trying to maintain the peace, I should have chopped off heads and asked questions later.

Lesson learned; I won't be making that mistake ever again.

The door to this godforsaken barn slams open but I don't lift my head, instead I watch through my eyelashes as a brick of a man takes one bucket and splashes me over the head and back. I'm disgusting, I can smell the days of filth sticking to my body and no amount of water will take that away, so I don't even fucking bother.

The guy does the same to Enzo, who doesn't even move, just keeps lying there like Lina is still facing him. Fuck, he's been through so much, how is he going to survive this guilt? The same guilt that's feeding my fury.

My gag slides off somehow and I just bend my head lower to make sure this asshole doesn't notice. Enzo and I need a plan and in order to make one we need to speak to each other.

"We have a special guest, need to get you nice and cleaned up." He tells me this in Italian and it takes everything inside me not to tell him to fuck right off, to tell him he's not going to live long enough to appreciate the fact he's on the wrong side of the war.

When the idiot walks out of the barn, I wait a few beats until I hear a car door followed by the turning of an engine and tires running over the gravel.

"Enzo."

Nothing.

"Enzo, look at me." I'm pulling at my restraints but fucking Hell, whoever tied them knew what they were doing. My skin is burning from the push and pull of the rope scraping into my flesh over and over again.

"This isn't going to help Lina. You need to—" Enzo's entire body turns and the violence etched across his face makes me pause. His gag is hanging around his neck and his teeth are so tightly gritted I'm surprised he hasn't snapped off his jawbone. But his eyes? Holy shit. I've never, in all the years I've known him, seen him lose control, but in this moment, the beast that has always resided inside him is out and seeking vengeance.

Good, but without a plan it won't do us any fucking favors.

"Why was she here, Marco?" The break in his voice is the only clue to his pain, all the rest is a mixture of hatred and condemnation.

"I don't know, but we're going to find out and heads will roll for this. They will pay, I can promise you this." My tone is even. It has to be in order to convince my right-hand man.

"Even if River is to blame?" His words bring with them my own rage as my body lunges toward him without my brain's permission, but I'm stopped dead by my restraints. I ignore the pain, it means nothing compared to what we just witnessed.

"That's what I thought." Enzo turns back into his earlier position like our conversation is over and he's got the answers he needs.

I'm about to tell him to focus on what we can do right now when the shifting of gravel grabs my attention.

"Focus on surviving this first, then we can count our losses." Enzo looks over his shoulder at me, our eyes boring into each other. The pain and the incredulity are dark shadows in the depths of his eyes, but Enzo is a soldier and he knows I'm right. Wallowing will help no one and our girls are being kept prisoner somewhere.

They came for us, it's time to go for them.

As footsteps approach, I return to my original position, kneeling with my head down, to wait for whoever it is that's about to piss me off again.

The door creaks open then slams into the wall. I watch through my eyelashes as city shoes step over the threshold and a sniff of disdain echoes through the rat-infested space.

"How the mighty have fallen." My head snaps up at the sound of her voice. What the fuck is she doing here? "But then, I suppose it's sweet irony, don't you think?" Eleonor Hunter or Reed or whatever the fuck she goes by these days, is standing in front of me, her heels trembling as they balance over the hay that's been strewn all over the ground. She's dressed like she's going to church, with a large hat and white gloves up to her elbows, but the sneer on her face is anything but holy. Why haven't I ever seen it? The devil inside her.

"What are you doing here?" I make the mistake of speaking, but it's like I'm missing puzzle pieces and she just doesn't fit with the rest of the image.

"Do you believe in karma, Marco?" Placing a handkerchief over her nose, she takes a step back from me as she ignores my question and just keeps on talking.

This time, I don't answer because I'm pretty sure it makes no difference. She's been holding on to something and she's traveled all this way to tell me about it.

I know she invited Elizabeth into her home, so it's safe to say she and the Ambrosios have something going on, but this? It makes no fucking sense.

Unless...

Does she know we had a role in her son's disappearance?

"You see, I believe we are dealt the cards we deserve. My husband's death was a direct consequence of the pain he caused us when he cheated on me." She gags a little, probably from the overwhelming stink of this place. "But my son? My sweet, thoughtful baby boy? Well, he didn't deserve any harm yet *she* hurt him."

I can respect the pain of a grieving mother, but kidnapping? Rape? No. I can't believe this woman would be behind all of this. "It's only fair I return the favor, don't you agree?" I raise my eyes to look up at her, *really* look at her, and I see it.

The evil.

The hatred.

The capability to harm. To kill.

"Who is *she*?" Deep inside I know who she's talking about, but I choose to ignore it because the idea that River is gone or has mere moments to live is too much for me to handle. I need that hope because, without it, I'm only left with soul-gripping fear.

"Oh, come on, Marco. You're a smart man, I'm sure you can figure it out."

CHAPTER EIGHT

RIVER

The light that once came through the crack at the bottom of the door has slowly disappeared as the hours have passed. The small window in the otherwise-empty room is blacked out, leaving Lina and I in darkness.

It's fitting, really. The darkness mirrors my emotions in this moment, and no doubt Lina's too. She's finally stopped shivering in my arms, and her breathing has evened out. I know she's not asleep yet, because her grip on my arm wrapped around her, holding her close to me, is as tight as it has been since we were thrown into this barren building.

The ground is stone, with some kind of animal shit and hay strewn all over the place. With no sunlight coming in throughout the day, it's permanently cold in here, but I can handle it a lot better than Lina can. Many nights spent sleeping outside, in tents, teepees... they've hardened me to low temperatures. So as soon as Lina arrived—too long after I did—in this building, room, whatever it is, with no clothes on, I immediately stripped and gave her mine.

At least I have underwear on, unlike my sister-in-law. My thin black jacket is useful too.

Lina resisted at first, tried to push my clothes back to me, refusing to take them, but it was a half-hearted effort, and thankfully my persistence won. She hasn't spoken a word, not as I helped her get dressed, and not as I pulled her into me, where we've stayed in silence ever since.

The guy Aldo had tie me up didn't do a very good job and it only took fifteen minutes to wriggle my hands and feet free of my bindings. Although, I've loosely re-wrapped them in case someone comes back in. I'm still trying to figure a way out of all this without getting us all killed, and kicking myself for how fucking stupid I was to think it wouldn't turn out like this.

Anger, grief, sadness, regret... there are so many negative emotions running through my veins that it's almost over-whelming. But for now, the only thing I can do is be here for Lina. Be her strength, her protector. I sure as shit have done a crappy job at that so far.

I should have been more forceful in saying no when she and Tyler insisted they came with me. Should have made her stay at the airport, even. But it wasn't my place to decide that for her. She has a reason for being here, just as much as I do. The Ambrosios have fucked with her and her family just as much as mine.

My conflicting emotions are at war inside my mind. I'm a peace-loving person, all this vengeance and bloodshed isn't who I used to be. But I was also very much alone. Existing day-to-day to simply work, anticipating the needs of others rather than doing anything of significance. A cog in the never-ending wheel of life.

Now though, I've found my true self. And I'm still the person I once was. I still love with my whole heart and would do whatever it takes to make my family safe and happy. But I'm also someone new. Someone stronger. And this time, whatever it takes to keep my family safe and happy is dangerous. It's fucking insane if I'm honest with myself, but that's what love is. It's dangerous, it's insane, and it's worth every second of heartache.

Lina stiffens in my hold as we sit, huddled together on the cold floor, and the reason becomes clear as the sound of someone unlocking the door becomes louder. Her grip on my arm around her tightens and I can feel her trying to control her breathing.

The stiff wooden door only opens a little, but I spot a flash of red hair before it closes again.

"River? Lina?" Elizabeth's voice is barely a whisper and I'm a little wary still as to whether or not I can fully trust her, so I keep my hold on Lina as I reply.

"Yeah, we're over here." My voice is croaky, my throat sore from all the screaming and yelling.

She comes closer, spotting us in the corner and kneeling in front of us.

"I'm so sorry." Even though it's dark in here, I can see the whites of her glassy eyes, but I'm still not sure if she's being genuine. "I didn't know any of this was going to happen. It was supposed to be simple; you'd show up, then he'd hand you over and let Marco and Enzo go free." She pauses and her eyes flick across to Lina before coming back to me. "My brother has gone crazy. I'm so, so sorry. Here, I brought you some water and a couple of ice-packs." She places a couple of bottles of water and ice-packs on the ground next to us.

A fire begins coursing through me. Elizabeth has been brought up in this world of mafia and madness, she's been trained to be the perfect mafia wife since birth, so believing that she had no idea that her brother was a crazy rapist fuck seems like quite a stretch. When I first met her, she came across as a manipulative bitch, but that changed with the more time she spent in New York. She actually became likable.

"Shit, River, where are your clothes?"

I narrow my eyes at her. *Is she serious?*

"My clothes, Elizabeth, are on the person who needs them most right now. Need I remind you that your brother is a fucking psycho. And are you really so naïve, that you didn't know what was going to happen?" My tone is laced with venom and I don't even try to hold it back.

"I-I-I..." Elizabeth takes a deep breath, closing her eyes briefly before opening them again. The atmosphere in the room changes and suddenly it becomes clear. "Okay, fuck it, I can't even pretend to like you at this point. I tried to be your friend before you die. At least Marco will still believe I was kind and helpful toward you before this. Should make him marrying me when you're gone a little easier, don't you think? For the record, no, I didn't know my brother was a full-fledged rapist. Didn't think he had it in him, to be honest. I wanted to keep Lina around, but Ugo got his panties in a twist about Lina going full-on slut, and well, she's not worth a thing to him now."

"Fuck. You." I grind the words out with as much hatred as I possibly can, not wanting to give away the fact that I could get loose at any time and finding it real difficult to remain where I am instead of throat-punching the bitch in front of me.

She cackles as she stands, saying nothing more before turning and walking out, locking the door behind her.

Ex-wives and girlfriends with a chip on their shoulder about me 'dating' their men seem like child's play next to Elizabeth. She's a conniving, manipulative fucking shit-stain on the Earth, and my first impressions of her were spot-on.

Always trust your gut, River. Big picture.

It dawns on me that I've been looking at this all wrong. Mr. Bobby once told me to keep my eye on the big picture, and I haven't been doing that. I've been focused on trying to fit into this mafia world and getting my own vengeance rather than making the mafia world fit with me. I'm a bad-ass bitch and I can figure this all out. I know it.

Lina's silent tears fall onto my arm and I squeeze her closer to me. "We'll get through this, babe. I promise you. We just have to be strong for a little while longer, okay?"

She sniffs and slowly nods her head, freezing and gripping my arm tightly when we hear a key in the lock again.

The first thing I see is an elaborate lantern of some kind, followed by someone I never expected to see again. Especially not here, in Italy. Although, it makes sense; Elizabeth was staying with her while she was in New York, so it stands to reason that Eleonor is involved in all of this somehow. And, of course she's carrying a fucking lantern, like the upper-class snob that she is, a torch simply wouldn't do. It lights up her features in a way that reminds me of a horror movie, casting shadows over her face that aid in her menacing glare.

"I've just seen your lovers." She laughs, a haughty sound, but I remain quiet. I have a feeling she's about to give me the whole big villain speech. "It's all worked out quite nicely, don't you think? It's managed to come full circle, with a little help from me of course." She begins to pace back and forth in front of us, and even though I have no idea what she's talking about, I keep my eyes fixed on her. "You really do look like the whore you are, don't you?" She sneers at me, sitting in my underwear, and I couldn't give two fucks. "My husband was not a loyal man, but he usually kept his exploits to the privacy of a hotel room, until he didn't. Until he decided to parade around a blonde whore at one of his business galas. Well, I couldn't have that, now, could I? My reputation would have been in ruins if he did it again or word got around. So, of course, he met with an untimely fate. Poor man committed suicide in his office.

Shot himself in the head." Her laugh sends shivers down my spine. This woman is fucked up beyond belief, and I'm confused as Hell. If anything, she should be mad at me for what happened to Nathaniel—although I'm not sure if she knows or not—but this thing about her husband is throwing me all off.

"What has any of this got to do with me?" I ask the question that I really need an answer to, because she is a whole bag of bat-shit.

Her laugh continues to go right through me in the worst way, confirming my suspicion that she is unhinged.

"What has this got to do with you? It has everything to do with you." She continues her pacing, pausing to find herself funny every few minutes. "You were the blonde whore my husband hired. Obviously, I know you're not really blonde, you were wearing one of those cheap wigs."

At the mention of my wigs, I feel a little sad over losing them all in the fire... the fire that happened the same night as Nathaniel... fuck, maybe I do deserve some of this woman's ire.

Karma's a bitch and all that, and she's not choosy.

"I looked you up, had a detective trail you, then told my son all about the wench responsible for his father's death. *You*. Of course, he wanted to help his grieving mother, so he helped me to formulate a plan. A plan to get rid of you, but it couldn't be simple. I wanted you broken first. I wanted you to feel all the pain I felt when I pulled the trigger on my husband, and my dear boy, Nathaniel, was only too willing to assist. Then Angelica came along. She was sweet, but she made my boy sloppy, made him forget what we needed to do. She had an accident too. Shame really, but it gave Nathaniel all the drive he needed to come for you. He has always been a mommy's boy, you see."

She's talking about him as if he's still alive, which means she can't know about that night in my apartment yet. Thank fuck. I don't imagine a cray-cray like this would let me live if she knew I'd killed her child. The whole thing with her husband though...? I barely remember him. I mean, I *do* remember him, and nothing sexual actually happened, but it's not my fault she's a fucking psycho and he didn't want her on his arm at the gala.

"It's a good thing I still have my Nathaniel. But after what you did, whore, well, obviously I'm not going to let you get away with it. Having connections to high-ranking mafia families comes in handy when you're in my position. The Ambrosios want New York, and they were so close... until my son failed his task and Mr. Mancini hired you. How you can carry on with this farce of a marriage is beyond me. They are a strong Italian family and you are sullying the name with your hippy-American DNA. The best thing for everyone at this point, would be for you to die. So, I help the Ambrosios get what they want by getting you out of the picture. The thing is..." She pauses, stops pacing and leans into my face. "I want you to hurt. To writhe in pain as your skin is flayed from your body. And I'm going to enjoy every moment of it."

Fuck, that laugh of hers is killing my eardrums.

She moves away and I internally kick myself for not just spitting in her face or trying to take her down now, but for one, spitting is disgusting, and two, I'm not rushing into this like I did by rushing over to Naples. I'm biding my time. For what...? I have no idea yet, but I'll figure something out.

It's been almost three days since everything went to total rat shit, I can handle a little longer.

"For now, I want you to rot in here and wait, in anticipation for what fun is going to come tomorrow. I *finally* get to watch you burn." She flicks her wrist out and something catches the light that I didn't see before.

A knife.

Sharp pain rolls through my face as the cunt slices the knife across my cheek, and I can't play helpless victim, something inside me flips a switch. Fury burns deep within my veins and I lift my arms over Lina's head, being careful to make sure she doesn't fall backward onto the hard ground in my haste, and I stand. The rope falls from my hands and Eleonor's eyes widen in shock.

I don't give her a moment to defend herself as I pull my arm back and swiftly throw my fist into her cheek. I get a sick sense of satisfaction as she wails in pain, but in my haze of anger, I forgot about the knife. I'm quickly reminded when I feel a sharp stab of pain in my arm before she spins on her heel and storms out of the room.

Two seconds later, the guard who tied me up before is back in the room, a torch in one hand and a slightly disappointed look on his face.

"Mi dispiace, Signora Volpe."

I freeze at the whispered use of my old family name, and I think he just apologized to me, but until I learn Italian, I can't be sure.

He doesn't give me a chance to speak, holding his finger to his lips as he undoes his shirt, then rips a strip of fabric from the bottom of his undershirt to wrap over the cut trickling blood down my arm. I stare in silence as he makes sure it's secure before gesturing for me to sit.

I do as he says, allowing him to loosely wrap the rope back around my wrists before he dabs more material over the cut on my face, because I'm finally beginning to see the light in this never-ending darkness.

The door is locked behind him as he leaves and Lina and I are left alone in silence once more.

Eleonor will get her wish tomorrow. She *will* watch me burn. I'm going to burn brighter than anything she's ever seen and fight back with everything I have.

For my family.

For love.

And that's more than that bitter old cunt will ever have.

Chapter Nine

Marco

I've lost track of the time in this place, especially considering I spent a big chunk of it passed out. Enzo is sitting across the room from me, staring straight at me, but I get the feeling he's not really seeing me. His eyes are nearly dead, devoid of warmth and wit, and I can't help remembering the first day he'd been brought to our home by my father. The first thing I'd noticed were his eyes. Distrustful, empty, hard.

I hate that he's retreated back to that young boy. The one who suffered more than any child ever should.

"Don't do that." The sound of his voice catches me off guard. We haven't talked about Lina yet and I figured I'd give him the space he needed while I tried to put all the puzzle pieces together to figure out who I'm killing first.

"Do what?" I keep my voice even. I need to bring him back to the present if we have any hope of getting the fuck out of Dodge.

"Try to psychoanalyze me." Even his voice is dead. No inflection, no anger or sadness. Just... nothing.

"I wouldn't know where to start." My brain has been woozy for a few hours now because of my wound and having my arms tied behind my back is only making it worse. Leaning my head back against the rough surface of the stone wall, I close my eyes and promise myself I'm only going to rest for a minute. Maybe even dream of the different ways I'm going to seek out blood-thirsty vengeance.

"If you fall asleep, you may never wake up, asshole. You know this." Fuck, he's right, but my lids are so damn heavy and the pain I've been fighting for so long is nearly impossible to ignore.

"I just want to rest my eyes." I can hear my own speech losing its edge, but his next words force me to snap back to the land of the fighters.

"I don't think River will appreciate coming all this way only to find out you gave up in a fucking pig sty. Never pegged you as a quitter."

"Never thought I'd be so happy to hear the asshole in you speaking again." My words are slightly slurred, but my brain kicks back into alertness when the door creaks open and a worried Elizabeth slinks in like she's trying to be discreet.

"Are you two okay?" She runs to Enzo, gives him some water and rubs some of the dirt away from his forehead and cheeks. He watches her, his dead eyes acutely fixed on her face, reading her every move like a hawk with a lie detector. I'm trying not to pass out, the only thing keeping me awake is my need to save myself so I can save River.

"Oh, Marco. I'm so sorry. I had no idea…" She glances at Enzo with a look of pity in her eyes, and he bares his teeth at her like a feral animal whose pups have just been threatened. "I just… here, have some water, you're burning up." She gives me water as well and wipes down my face with a clean cloth. Her next gasp jolts me awake again. "Your arm hasn't been cleaned or properly looked after? I think it's infected."

In my fuzzy head, I'm telling her a lot of things like, "No shit, Sherlock," but I'm just too tired to respond so I narrow my eyes at her, making sure to put every ounce of my anger into them.

"Of course it hasn't. Wait here." She stands, glances at Enzo then back at me again. "Right, right. I'm sorry, this is all just very disturbing."

"Why don't you just cut these ropes off and we'll take care of the rest?" Enzo voices exactly what I'd like to say, but I can't seem to get the words out.

"I..." She turns back to the door and waits for a second before she faces us again, whispering, "There are guards outside. I can't take that risk, Marco. I'm sorry." I open an eye and look at her. Really look at her.

She's perfectly put together, her dark-red hair pulled back into some type of bun at her nape, her makeup flawless. Her clothes aren't necessarily dressy, but everything north of her chest is perfectly made. My last thought before I pass out is that there's something incredibly suspicious about her.

When I open my eyes, the exhaustion is gone and in its place is only relief.

"River?" My voice is strong, exactly the way it should be.

"Were you expecting someone else?" I blink at the vision before me, her leather pants and halter top stirring feelings in me that need to be ignored for now.

"How did you get here?" I scan my surroundings. We're still in the disgusting barn, but Enzo is nowhere to be found. "Where's Enzo? Did you untie him?" River's laugh is like a balm to my soul. It heals all of my pain and gives me hope that things will be just fine, even if it's all going to end in a bloodbath.

"I didn't realize your fantasies included your sister's lover as a prop. I wonder if there's a name for that kink." I'm so fucking confused. What the fuck is she talking about?

That's when I notice the crop in her hand, just as she raises it to my chin and slides it down my chest.

My very naked chest.

"You look good all tied up, Husband. It makes me want to do dirty, filthy things to you." All thoughts of anything else fly out the window and my entire focus is only on her.

"I'm not a fan of being tied up, Tesoro. I'm the one in control. You know this."

"Not right now." Her crop slaps me on the cheek and I growl like a caged animal. "Hmm, I love it when you get feral, it always gets me so fucking wet." I pull at my restraints but the rope just bites into my skin, shooting an electric bolt of pain up my arms and into my shoulders.

"Come closer, Wife, so I can taste you. Prove to me how wet you are." River's playful *tsk* wreaks havoc on my body. I want her close, I need to feel her warm skin, feel her trembling body under my touch.

"We should do this more often, you know?" Her words confuse me at first until I realize she's talking about the dominatrix game she's playing.

"It's not my thing, Tesoro. It doesn't turn me on." River's eyes slowly trace a path down my chest and belly until she reaches my crotch, where my tented pants are calling me a fucking liar.

"Your dick begs to differ."

I grin and cock my head, my eyes drinking her in. "My dick gets hard at the mere mention of you, so it shouldn't be trusted with any type of decision making." Licking my lips at the sight of her suddenly getting undressed, I can feel my cock getting impossibly harder.

"I'm not going near that thing." I frown, raising a brow at her. *Why would she say that?*

"Are you planning on getting yourself off without me?"

River comes closer, her heat caressing my already-burning skin.

"I could, but I'd much rather use your face." Next thing I know, we're lying in our bed at home, the comforter soft and clean, my arms free from the ropes and my wife straddling my chest with her wet heat marking my flesh.

The moment her pussy covers my mouth, I devour her. I lick her folds, biting the plump flesh and kissing it all better. Raising my hands to her ass, I pull her closer and kiss her juices from deep inside her, delving my tongue in as far as it will go and growling at the taste of her. She's delicious, my very own addiction coating half my face.

The pads of my fingers dig into her ass cheeks as I separate them and push a finger inside her ass, reveling in the sound of her throaty moans dancing around my ears.

"Fucking you is the best part of my day." I'm not sure how I'm able to speak with a mouthful of her pussy, but as the thought enters my mind, it also fills my ears.

"Today is going to be a special day, indeed, Marco. One you'll never forget." She sounds so clinical, so determined. It's strange, to say the least.

I try to pull her off me but I can't. I have no strength, my fingers barely able to latch onto her. I'm practically choking on her pussy and any other time I'd be loving the feeling but right now, something feels off, not palpable somehow.

"Come on, Marco!" River's words are accompanied by a slap to my face and I'm not sure what shocks me the most; her slap or the actual pain on my cheek.

"What the fuck, River?" I reach out and grab her around the neck, squeezing harder than I probably should, but it all feels off. Her neck isn't the smooth column that I remember. The width is bigger, the smell of her skin missing the sweet hints of jasmine.

"Get him off me!"

My eyes snap open and everything delicious about River is replaced by nothing shy of a nightmare.

My head swivels and all I see are the stone walls of my Medieval prison and instead of choking River, my fingers are wrapped around some guy's throat, my head at an awkward angle as it leans back over the chair, hair dripping wet.

"Marco, let him go or I'll have to tie you back up again." The familiar cold pressure at my temple tells me I've got a gun to my head. Snarling at the man, and at Elizabeth as she rubs my hair dry, I release him and smack the gun barrel away from my face.

"What the fuck is going on? Where's River?"

With a threatening glare, Elizabeth forces the guy to back off. "I can take care of this." Her words grate on my nerves and make my skin crawl just as I begin to get my bearings back. Enzo, still sitting on the ground, narrows his eyes, trying to tap into some kind of conversation with me. But fuck, my mind is too weak, the throbbing pain keeping me from concentrating.

"She's fine, I think." Her sweet tone isn't as meek as earlier and there's something off about her demeanor. "But for now, you just need to concentrate on us." As she runs a comb through my hair, I apply pressure to my shoulder, wincing, but not struggling from the pain, my arm is still throbbing but I'm not blinded by it. The sling, though, is new and holy shit, I'm wearing a fucking tuxedo?

"It's your big day, Marco. Or should I say, big day… again?" Motherfucking Ugo walks in with his father, Giuseppe, in tow, and I bolt from my seat, lunging at his throat, my teeth bared and begging for bloodshed. Before I can even make it to him, I'm clotheslined at the throat and slammed against the wall, a gun pressing against my forehead for the second time today.

"I will fucking slice you open from one end to the other, you piece of worthless shit." At the sound of Enzo's voice, my head snaps to the other side of the barn, making my fury rise. It takes no less than two burly henchmen giving it their best to hold Enzo down. My second in command may be smaller in size, but his fury is bigger than us all.

"Here's how it's going to go." Ugo's voice rings out and I swear to fuck it makes my blood boil. "You will both calm the fuck down or else Lina will be the least of your worries. Although, she wasn't all that good, you know? A bit of a dead weight." Enzo and I both lunge again, our target standing confident and at a safe distance. One guy clocks Enzo in the back of the head with the butt of his gun while two others force me back to my chair and, despite the fight in me, lack of consistent nourishment has me at a disadvantage. The asshole to my right makes quick work of the rope and all too soon, I'm a prisoner again, my hands tied to the arms of the chair and my ankles bound together. Baring my teeth at Ugo, it takes every ounce of my willpower not to lash out, reminding myself that I have no idea where my sister and my wife are being held prisoner, so I need this fucker to talk. I need to leverage his narcissism to get information.

"You've got me, Ugo. Let River and Lina go, they're of no use to you."

Pushing his hands into the pockets of his pristine slacks, he cocks his head and raises a brow at me like I'm a little slow and not functioning on all cylinders.

"You're right, River means nothing to me. In fact, I wanted her dead, but you know what a drama queen Eleonor is? She wanted to make this a big show and, since we needed her cooperation, well, here we are." He nods to the guy beside me, who leaves my side and begins to follow

Ugo out. Watching his every move, I don't miss the wink he throws his sister and the tiny uptick of her lips.

The bitch played me. She played us all.

My eyes search out Enzo's, the savagery behind his dark orbs a clear sign he saw the same exchange as I did.

Change of plans.

"Elizabeth," I whisper my words, my tongue darting out to lick my dry lips. "Could you get me some water, please?" I soften my gaze for her, like we're still on the same side, using my charm to trap her into my web of wrath.

"Of course, Marco. What was I thinking?" With Ugo gone, we're here with two guards. Any other time, Enzo and I could have taken them out. The bigger they are, the easier it is to put a bullet in their small brains. This situation, however, is less than ideal. Although Elizabeth is playing the game, her sharp scrutiny tells me she doesn't trust me. Smart girl. I will end her the first chance I get.

She walks back with a glass of fresh water she poured from the tap in the wall. Leaning my head back so she can help me drink, I tap my tongue hard enough against the rim of the glass to spill the contents all over myself.

"Fuck, I'm so sorry." I gasp before sucking air through my teeth and closing my eyes as tight as possible. This is my only chance, I can't fuck it up.

"Are you okay?" Elizabeth places both of her hands on my cheeks, her face close, too close for my liking. "I've got pain medication, but you have to wait another hour before you can take it." Christ, she's a good actress.

"I'll be fine, I just moved too quickly so my shoulder is killing me." Opening my eyes again, I look everywhere but at her, playing the part of the dutiful prisoner.

"He's got your binds too tight, I told them to be careful." Her words are muttered but I hear them loud and clear. I won't get another chance. The guys are talking about football, or soccer in the States, about the fact that Italy's national team isn't rousing any emotions so they're only betting on the league teams. This should keep them occupied for a while. I look to Enzo, knowing full well he's been watching me, and when my eyes dart to the two guards, he immediately gets my message.

"It's fine." I suck in another breath and it's all I need to convince her.

"I'm going to loosen this rope, Marco, okay? I'm trusting you." Our gazes meet and I fight the urge to bite her face off. Instead, my lips curve into a docile smile for her benefit only.

"I really appreciate it, Lizzie." My coup de grace has its intended effect. I haven't called her that nickname since we were teenagers, before I met River. Before I fell so hard my entire world turned upside down.

"Oh, Marco." She concentrates on the knot and no sooner than it's loose enough to allow me to move, I'm pushing her off and grabbing her by the neck, pulling her into my chest. On the other side, Enzo slides his legs beneath the men's feet, sending them pummeling to the ground. Quick as a viper, he grabs the gun that slides across the ground and shoots both men, one bullet in each head.

Elizabeth screams but I cut off her air, squeezing her throat hard enough to kill her. I ignore the burn in my shoulder, push past the searing pain traveling down my arm, and whisper in her ear.

"Where. The fuck. Is. My. Wife?" I loosen my grip just enough to allow her to speak. Elizabeth turns her eyes to mine, the gentle light in them gone, replaced now by evil.

"She's right here." We all turn to the door as it slams open like a fucking Shakespeare play with all the dramatic entrances, and there she is, the love of my life.

River's eyes search me out, scanning me from head to toe as I do the same to her. She's bleeding, cut up, and looking worse for the wear, but when our eyes meet, I know. She's perfect. A warrior ready to go to battle or die trying.

"*Tsk, tsk, tsk.* So much violence. Did you have to kill my men?" Ugo's voice grates on my every nerve, so I squeeze his sister's pulse point with the little strength that's left in me.

"Let her go, Ugo, or I swear, as God is my witness, I will end your sister." Ugo laughs and it doesn't bode well for me. Or anyone else for that matter.

"Eleonor, I think your presence is requested," Ugo calls out behind him, and not a second later, Nathaniel's mom steps in, a gun in her hand, raised just high enough to point at the back of River's head.

"I was going to make her suffer. Record it so my baby boy could see that I always have his back, but you're all annoying me and I'm bored of this whole situation."

Wait, did she just...

Blinking in disbelief, it's all the distraction they need to turn a nightmare into a horror scene.

"Say goodbye to your precious River."

The echo of a gun firing is the last thing I hear before all Hell breaks loose.

Chapter Ten

River

The click of the gun sets off a barrage of sounds all around me. I can pinpoint where each one is coming from, the people I love are so ingrained into my soul that they're right here with me in my last moments.

An ear-piercing scream shreds through the air from Lina, Marco's throaty howl rocks me to my very core, and Enzo's silent, wide eyes are like laser beams through my body as he raises his arms, gun in hand. In the back of my mind, I also hear Everest, Petal, and Kai, their voices like comforting whispers as I accept my fate. There's nothing more I can do now, and I mouth 'I love you' to Marco, my vision blurred through unshed tears as I lock eyes with my husband for the final time.

His face is the image of pain and vengeance as he pushes Elizabeth to the side by her throat and charges toward me in slow motion. More shouts and yells come from the others around the room, followed by gunshots, and I watch as Marco practically flies through the air as he jumps over fuck knows what to get to me.

Wait a minute...

Gunshots...

All this, *after* the click of the gun at my head...

"What is wrong with this—" Eleonor's voice is clear behind me and as soon as her frustrated tone begins, a surge of hope shoots up from the pit of my stomach and I spin around. My fist connects with her nose and blood spurts everywhere with the sound of her bone cracking. I quickly pull my arm back and go in again, this time aiming for her throat—which is open wide as she tilts her head back and holds her face.

She goes down like a sack of bricks, but I don't have time to bask in the fact this bitch finally got what she deserves.

"Ugo, three o clock!"

A heavy weight pushes me down beside her before I can figure out what's going on and a hint of vanilla tickles my senses. Gunshots are going off all around us, but all I can concentrate on is Marco above me. The relief in his eyes is like a drug and I never want to leave the safety of their warmth as he takes in every inch of my face, as if he's cataloging each and every new mark.

"*Amore mio.*" The word is whispered over my lips, and my heart soars.

Marco makes me feel indestructible but I know we can't keep lying here and ignoring the chaos surrounding us. It *feels* like a small lifetime, in reality it's only a few short seconds before Marco's lips are on mine. It's not a soft and sensual kiss, either. It's hard, rough, and he's giving us what we both need to get through this together.

"Ti amo, River."

"Ti amo, Marco." And I do, with all my heart. I'm never going to let my fear of the unknown stop me from saying what I feel for this man again.

His eyes light up like the shine of a thousand moons and his growl vibrates through me before he rolls off, grabbing Eleonor's gun from her still body.

"Stay down, Tesoro. We'll finish this."

After checking the gun, taking the safety off that Eleonor had left on—rookie move—he places a chaste kiss against my lips and moves to a crouching position. Then he joins in the gunfight, wincing as he uses his wounded arm to throw my vacant chair to the side.

I swear there weren't this many people in the barn before I hit the deck. The space is filled with bodies, the noise quieting down as people fall to the ground one by one.

At some point, Enzo must have been freed, because he's currently back-to-back with Marco as they beat the crap out of seven men at once. Guns have been discarded in favor of fists and knives.

From my position on the floor, I look around for Lina, who is exactly where she was left before this all started. Huddled in a corner of the room, surrounded by a wall of men not allowing anyone near her. Then I spot J and I realize our people must have arrived at some point.

They found us.

That thought almost breaks me and I struggle not to let the tears fall out of pure happiness. Lina's safe. Marco's going to be safe. They found us.

Okay, lying here on the ground isn't going to help anyone. My face hurts and my body aches, but I need to get to Lina. She may be safe and surrounded by our people, but she's also alone. Slowly getting to my knees, the glint of a knife beside a bleeding corpse catches my eye and I grab it as I crawl toward Lina, trying to stay low and out of the line of fire. I'm not totally stupid, I know what my strengths are, and getting in the middle of a gunfight isn't one of them.

Tracking my surroundings as I creep across the floor is difficult with so much going on around me. Grunts and groans from the injured and those still fighting distract me enough that I jump and gasp as a foot on my back pushes me down, hard.

"Where do you think you're going?"

It's Elizabeth.

I look over my shoulder at her standing high above me, one foot on my back and her hands on her hips, one brow raised and a smug smile on her face as she bends down to grab what she can of my hair. Before she can lift my head even an inch, I swipe my arm out and slice into the back of her ankle with the knife I picked up. In the movies, it looks a lot easier than it is. The resistance caused by the bone and flesh is almost jarring, but I put all my strength into it.

Her scream is like music to my ears and she lets go of my hair at the same time as she drops to the floor.

"You bitch!" The words are barely audible through her piercing cries and I smile down at her as I get back onto my knees.

"Yes, I am. A badass one, to be exact. So, fuck you." I stab into her thigh, not daring to stab her anywhere more debilitating, although the sheer amount of blood seeping through her linen slacks is alarming. I know death is all around us, but if I can avoid being the physical cause of it, then I will. The squelch as I remove the knife almost makes me wretch a little, but I refrain, trying really hard to maintain my composure as she continues to scream bloody murder.

Fucking drama queen.

Finally reaching Lina—the men surrounding her separated enough to let me into their little circle of protection—I bring her into my now-blood-covered arms.

"Lina, babe, we've got this. Okay?"

She nods slowly, almost frozen in time, with unfocused eyes just staring straight ahead. She's numb, probably in shock, and I get it. I'm not going to force her to get through this any quicker than she's ready.

One of the seven men in front of us goes down, quickly followed by two more, and another... and I'm frantically looking around to see where the shots are coming from as they begin shooting back.

Giuseppe Ambrosio is standing ten feet away, aiming his gun in the direction of the remaining men. Another one goes down and I know I need to act before his gun is pointing in my direction. I grab a gun from one of our fallen soldiers and aim as best I can in Giuseppe's direction.

Following the instructions Enzo gave me what feels like years ago now, I focus on my target's chest and exhale as I pull the trigger. I guess I need more practice, because it completely misses and one of the soldiers I recognize as ours yells out as the bullet grazes the edge of his arm.

"Sorry!" He doesn't hear me, but the distraction was enough for Giuseppe to now be a lot closer than before. He throws his gun across the floor and the murderous look on his face promises pain the instant he gets hold of me.

I pull the trigger again, realizing too late that the gun has run out of bullets, because he's now only a foot away. The remaining guards surrounding us are fighting off some of the Ambrosio soldiers, leaving this one on me. *Fuck.*

I scramble for another gun, but they're all too far away, so I grab the knife covered in Elizabeth's blood and thrust my arm up as Giuseppe reaches for my throat. The knife scrapes along his arm before he grips my wrist tightly in his hand, trying to force me to drop it as his other hand circles my neck. I have no time to make sure Lina is okay, but his focus is on me right now.

"You think I don't know who you are, little girl? I should have finished the job myself years ago. If only you'd stayed in your place, away from my world, my daughter would be married to the head of the Mancini family and the Ambrosios would finally have what they deserve. It would have been a matter of time before Marco met an untimely death, leaving New York City to us."

These things are always about power. Greed. Always *more*.

Interrupting his evil villain speech, because his grip is becoming uncomfortably tight, I heave my leg up as high as it will go, kicking him in the crotch and hopefully causing his balls to jump into his throat. He yells, loosening his hold on me, and I take the opportunity to jump on him, pushing him backward and straddling his chest. I don't give him a chance to fight back or myself a chance to think about what I'm doing as I slam my hand down into his neck.

His eyes go wide as the knife goes through his throat, his arms struggling underneath my knees to move me away as his body becomes weaker. Pulling the knife out makes me gag at the sound and the sight of all the blood and flesh coming from the fresh wound. He tries to speak, causing blood to pour from his mouth before his eyes begin rolling into the back of his head, his noises more garbled, but I don't stop. I plunge the knife into his chest several more times before he stops moving and before I can catch my breath, I see Ugo storming toward us with rage etched in his features.

Searching for a gun on a nearby body, I scramble to find something I can use because the knife I just used is slippery with blood. A shot rings out from behind me and I watch as Ugo flinches backward, a spot of crimson growing on his shoulder through his white shirt. I turn to find Lina with a gun raised in his direction, determination on her face as she pulls the trigger again. It would've gone straight through his head if one of his soldiers hadn't jumped and pushed him away. Then the coward runs. He fucking runs toward the exit, and Lina continues to pull the trigger, the clicking sounds of the now-empty clip causing her to scream in frustration.

There are no more gunshots and as I look around for Marco. I spot him next to Enzo. They're both throwing punches into Ambrosio soldiers who already look dead.

"Boss... Boss. It's over." J tentatively puts her hand on Marco's shoulder and he turns and almost punches her too, but she steps back quickly enough, her arms raised in surrender.

His eyes are wild as he searches the room. When they land on me, he immediately stands, stalking over to me like he's on a mission. We're both covered in blood and I'm not sure how much of it is our own. Hopefully not a lot. He grabs my face in his hands and pulls my head against his, claiming my lips in a searing kiss before resting his forehead against mine.

"Let's get out of here."

CHAPTER ELEVEN
MARCO

It turns out the Volpe name solicits unconditional love and devotion from the people of Naples and especially from the neighboring villages and towns. Before we left the farm where we were being held, loyal supporters who remembered how well the Volpe family took care of them rushed to help in any way they could. Our only request was for a few items of clothing for River. They didn't hesitate, quickly bringing her jeans, a tee shirt, and shoes her size. Without these brave people tonight, shit would have ended a lot differently.

The thought of what could have been has me flexing my vice-like grip around River's waist, pulling her flush against me while we ride to the hotel a friend of my mother's reserved for us.

"Hey." I whisper that one word into her hair, placing my lips at her crown and inhaling her scent. We're both being careful not to jolt our respective wounds and despite the fact that I was washed up, I need a real shower to scrub the stench of Elizabeth's hands off me.

The angry slash across River's face is a constant reminder of how close she also came to dying at the hands of those fucking psychos. Touching her, feeling her warm skin against mine, reassures me on a visceral level. She's alive and in my arms and, although I never lost hope, there were times in that dank barn that dark thoughts invaded my mind.

Thoughts of life without River. Of a life without her light. Of an existence without her soul-healing presence.

A life I refuse to entertain.

"Hey." Craning her neck back, she pierces me with those penetrating green eyes and despite the fatigue and the toll these last few days has had on us, her love shines through, which is more than I deserve from her.

"I guess a heart-to-heart is long overdue." I close my eyes, lips still resting on the top of her head when her sass lights up my nervous system.

"Oh, *now* he wants to talk."

I should bite that smirk off her face, or maybe lick it from her mouth all the way down to her pussy, but now is not the time.

"In my defense, I wa—" My words are interrupted by her palm slapping against my mouth.

"Marco Mancini, do not give me fucking excuses. There is no defense for your lack of good judgment. But..." She removes her hand and palms my cheek, her lips sliding across my hungry ones. "I'll let you make it up to me."

Oh, I like where this is going.

"You may be resistant at first, but I'm sure you'll enjoy it."

Wait, what now?

"Oh, Tesoro, it's impossible for me to resist you." My first warning that I was about to get punked was her throaty laugh bouncing around the confined space of the car.

"You say that now but you don't know what your punishment is going to be. Although, if I do things right, it's more of a reward." In the last three days, I've gone through the entire spectrum of emotions but the ominous way my wife is threatening me takes the fucking cake.

"River."

"Marco."

"What's the punishment?"

"I guess you'll just have to be patient, won't you?"

Yeah, it's still not a quality I possess.

I hand over a few euros to the driver—J made sure I had some on me just in case—and just when I thank him, he gives me a knowing look. The look all married guys share when they recognize a fellow husband renting out a dog house for the foreseeable future. It doesn't matter that he's Italian and probably didn't understand a single word we said, he can sense that I'm fucked.

In more ways than just one.

By the time we check in and make it to the penthouse suite, we're both back inside our heads, quiet and pensive. The click of the door behind us acts as a wake-up call, clearing the fog and forcing us to return to the here and now.

For the first time since the calm settled around us, I focus solely on my wife, my eyes taking in every scrape and bruise those fuckers caused. It takes every ounce of my self-control to push my hatred for them all down. I need to take care of her and by the way her eyes are roaming over my entire body, she's thinking the exact same thing. J had brought in a doctor, anticipating the need and wanting to keep it all on the downlow. I'm pumped up on antibiotics to fight off the infection from the bullet wound that went in one side and out the other, thank fuck.

"Tesoro, I need to ask you for a favor." Reaching out, I wrap an arm around her waist and pull her in flush against me once more.

"Anything." Our eyes lock and the sincerity and love that shines through in her gaze nearly breaks me.

"I know you are strong and thinking of a million things you can do to keep yourself busy but..." Careful not to hurt her face, I palm the back of her head and rest my forehead against hers. "Please let me take care of you. Let me bathe you and feed you. Bandage your wounds and heal the ones that no one can see. I'm begging you, Tesoro, please let me be your husband in every way that counts." I hope she hears the desperation in my voice, the crack in the syllables, how close I am to breaking down now that it's just the two of us and we're both safe.

"I thought you'd never ask." Our lungs empty out on an exhale, the stress of recent events taking a back seat so we can recharge in each other's care.

"Thank you." I push her hair behind her ear and kiss her forehead, lingering with my eyes closed for just a few seconds. "Okay, order room service and I'll run you a bath." Taking a step back, I realize my feet are like cement blocks keeping me close to her so I take a deep breath and reassure myself that she's safe here.

By the time the bath is filled with hot water, I turn in a circle, not quite sure what I'm looking for until my eyes zero in on the amenities box with a whole bunch of stuff in it. Small matching shampoo and conditioner bottles, round soap bars with the hotel logo, bath salts... I almost grab the bottle with the small pink rocks inside but think better of it. Salt and open wounds do not make for a good bath time.

Grumbling under my breath, I dig deeper into the box and find five tiny bottles of essential oils. I open the first one but quickly close it right back up. How the fuck is that supposed to be relaxing? It smells like someone shoved a eucalyptus in my nose and forgot about it for a week. The next one is patchouli. The only reason I know this is because Petal wears it like it's her natural scent. I love that woman but she's not taking a bath with us, is she? Maybe I shouldn't consider oil anyway. I've got a bullet hole in my shoulder and I'm pretty sure none of this is a good idea. But fuck it.

Making a mental note to make our hotels' amenities basket a fuckload better than this shit, I almost miss the round bottle sitting in the corner of the box.

Bingo.

Bubbles for the win. I try to read the instructions, this being a first for me and I have no clue at what point a bubble bath has too many bubbles, but, of course, there are none. I'm completely on my own. But I refuse to let my wife down. How fucking hard could it possibly be?

Water.

Bubbles.

Done.

I shake out a couple of drops but nothing happens. Frowning, I look at the bottle again, willing it to explain what the fuck I'm supposed to be doing.

"Food's here!" River's voice is much closer than I expected and when I look up, she's at the threshold of the bathroom. "Everything okay in here?"

"Yeah, of course. Just waiting for..." I look back at the water and still no fucking bubbles. I scowl as though that will make them magically appear. No such luck.

River walks in, kisses me on the cheek then turns the water on before kissing me again and walking out.

And just like that, those fuckers start popping up. Except now the water is threatening to spill over. Turning it off, I drain out a good amount before running it again and emptying the bottle into the water. I grin because I've made this bath my bitch.

"Bath's ready, Tesoro. Bring the food with you." When I step out of the bathroom, I watch my beautiful and slightly-broken wife pad her way to me as she carries a platter with various appetizers sitting prettily. My stomach growls at the scene, reminding me that I haven't eaten a real meal in days.

"Here, give me that." I reach for the platter but River scowls at me and shoos me away. "River, you promised."

"And you have a hole in your shoulder, Einstein. I want to eat this delicious looking food, not clean it up off the floor."

Fair enough.

Her sudden gasp has me turning on my heel and there, like an uncontrollable GoodYear blimp growing out of the fucking bath, are my bubbles. The fucking traitors.

Once I've turned the water off, I punch my fists on my waist and stare at the water as it licks at the edge of the ceramic tub.

"Yeah, we're gonna need a bigger tub." I love my wife but her sarcasm is not welcome, ever, if I'm honest. "Oh, don't be a grumpy grandpa. All your scowling isn't going to make the water go down, you goof. Just open the valve and watch it drain."

Arching a brow at her, I revel in the sound of her laughter dancing off the walls of the bathroom. It reminds me that she's here with me and we're both going to be okay.

"Sassy girls get their asses spanked, Tesoro. Is this your way of begging me?" The monster bubble dome, which is well above my head at this point, begins to lower as River places the appetizers on the side board once we're in the water.

We undress each other, careful not to bump into a bruise or wound. River raises her arms above her head and I let my fingers trail behind the tee shirt as I pull it up and over her head. Once I fling it to the side, I kiss her awaiting lips as I pop open her button and slide down the zipper of her jeans. I wince as I drop to my knees and place open-mouthed kisses on her exposed stomach, taking my time to cover her in my love.

"Marco?" I pause, raising my gaze to meet her mesmerizing green eyes.

"Yes, Tesoro?"

"You're on your knees again." Her words are just a breath spilling between her lips.

"Even when I'm standing, I'm on my knees for you."

Grabbing either side of my face, she pulls me up until our mouths are locked in a kiss that lets us dream of a time and a place where we don't have to deal with kid-nappings or daily violence. Our lips dance to the rhythm of our heartbeats, our tongues battling for control as we swallow each other's moans and revel in the perfection of this moment.

"Come, let's see how awesome this bath feels." I shed my remaining clothing and step inside, careful not to get lost in the white fuzz trying to swallow me up or slip on the smooth surface of the ceramic tub. We don't need another concussion, we just need some down time.

River swats at the bubbles as she settles between my legs, her shoulders shaking with the efforts to hold back her laughter.

"You're killing the mood. You know that right?" I lean back and curse when my nape hits nothing but air. I make another mental note to make sure our bath tubs at the hotel have a raised lip so our guests can rest their heads while in the tub.

"No, the Pillsbury Doughboy here with us is ruining the mood."

"Har har, you're just on a roll aren't ya? Well, I'll have you know that I've never done this before." I pepper kisses down the side of her neck, grimacing at the taste of lavender on my tongue and lips as I reach her collarbone where the water has settled.

"You've never taken a bath?" She looks over her shoulder at me and frowns, her gaze darting from side to side as she tries to read me. She's like a human lie detector, my talented wife.

"I'm a man's man. I take showers." I grin, waiting for her to assault me with her indignation.

"What the fuck does that even mean?"

I chuckle as I take her chin, turning her head at the perfect angle, and attack her mouth once again, my cock stirring behind her. The hunger I feel is reflected in her dilated pupils, heavy with lust, telling me she can feel my arousal at the small of her back.

It's a living, breathing entity, this lust of ours. It stays hidden behind our respectable personas but in the privacy of our little bubble, it takes up every inch of space.

Straddling my hips, River doesn't sink onto my cock. Of course not, that would be too easy, too anticlimactic. Instead, she slides her slick pussy up and down my dick, over and over again from tip to root. It's not the water and it's not the fucking bubbles, it's her natural lubrication easing her movements. The need to get fucked, to have me so deep inside her that it erases everything that's happened to us, is like a living, breathing beast. It replaces the memories that are plaguing her with something pleasurable, even if it's just for a little while.

My hands at her hips, I guide her pelvis, pushing her harder onto me so that it's almost painful, pressing my cock down as she uses it against her swollen clit.

"That's it, Tesoro, use me. Get yourself off for me." One hand slides up her taut belly to her plump breast, giving her needy nipple a pinch, hard enough to make her cry out. Continuing my path, I reach her neck and place my palms right beneath her chin and squeeze her tight enough to watch her pupils dilate and her nostrils flare.

Her hands are planted on either side of my shoulders, pushing against the lip of the tub as she takes exactly what she needs, circling her hips when she reaches my tip.

"You blame me, don't you, Tesoro?" I squeeze her tighter and revel in the fire that flashes in her eyes. River may put on a mask to hide her true emotions, but she can't hide from me. I won't allow it. Her movements become more erratic, more forceful, as if every inch she loses in control, she gains in her anger. Her well-placed anger. Because she should be furious with me. After all, my selfishness played a leading role in what happened this past week.

Gritting her teeth as she drills holes right through my skull with the force of her stare, I stare right back, unafraid of giving her my underbelly. She's earned it and much more. She is the only person on this Earth who's seen and felt and comforted my vulnerabilities but I need to show her she's got the power to either heal us or destroy us. For the first time since that fateful day in the café, as we ironed out the terms of our agreement, I'm truly giving her the reins.

"You should have told me. You should have trusted me—"

"I did. I do, River. I always have." I cut her off because she has to know that I've never trusted anyone more than her. Not even Enzo.

"You should have trusted me"—she repeats, completely ignoring my pleas, or excuses—"to be strong enough to hear the truth. You should have trusted me to know how powerful this thing is between us." Lifting one hand from the tub, she taps my chest, right where my heart is, then taps hers. "You should have trusted in us." There's a heat in her voice that tells me she's hurting, and it destroys a piece of my soul knowing that I caused this. Trapping her delicate fingers in my mine, I squeeze just enough to get her attention, to get her eyes on me so she can see my own emotions echoing hers. I bring her hand to my mouth and, without releasing her gaze, kiss two of her knuckles.

"I've let you down and I'm sorry." Then I kiss the pinky, my heart nearly beating out of my chest with the fear that I could ever lose her. "But I swear to you that I will make sure you never doubt my trust again." My lips land on the knuckle just above the sacred place where her wedding ring encircles her finger. "I swear to you on my vows."

I've seen her break down before because of my choices, but at this point in our story, I should have *known* better. I should have *done* better.

Tears swim in her eyes without falling. Taking a deep breath, she brings her mouth close enough for me to taste her, gently gliding her lips along mine from side to side. Our eyes are closed, our souls never closer than this moment.

"I should have trusted in us." I repeat her words, making them true in the small space between us. "I won't make that mistake again."

With that promise hanging in the air, River lifts her hips and buries my cock inside her hot, wet pussy. My home. My safe space. "We're not leaving this hotel until every card is on the table. Every truth told, every secret exposed. I won't live in the dark again, Marco. That life is over."

My hand releases her throat and latches onto her nape so our mouths clash together in a promise of eternity.

"*Te lo prometto.*" Even though she can't speak Italian, her body tells me she understands my promise to her.

Our kiss is bruising, desperate and violent, as our tongues battle against our raw emotions, our bodies rising and falling with every thrust of my hips. I'm following her lead when it comes to our rhythm, but River likes her pleasure with a dash of pain and I refuse to deny her what she craves most.

With one hand still clasped at her nape, I slide the other over her ass cheek and squeeze hard enough to elicit a moan that I'm all too happy to swallow. Our rhythm accelerates, her pussy growing impatient as she rubs her clit over my groin every time I bottom out. We're still kissing as though we're trying to make up for lost time, our need so desperate it's impossible to let go.

Releasing her hold, she plants her hands on my cheeks, her hunger intensifying as she bites my bottom lip, the taste of copper blossoming on the tip of my tongue.

Pressed one against the other, River's tits can't even bounce up and down but the hard points of her nipples are like diamonds digging into my flesh. She's so fucking close, I can taste her orgasm through our kiss but she needs the bite and I'm more than willing to oblige.

Releasing her nape, I run my nails down the length of her spine until I reach her ass cheeks, spreading them wide enough for my fingers to inch closer to her puckered hole. The water is getting cooler the longer we fuck and more spills over with every thrust of our hips. I couldn't give any less of a fuck than I currently do about the mess we're making because the more we ruin the floor, the closer we are to repairing us, our marriage. Our future.

I press both of my index fingers inside her ass and it's like a fucking detonator to her climax. Our mouths part, her eyes closing in ecstasy as I pull her closer and grind my groin against her sensitive bundle of nerves.

Watching River climax is a gift from the gods and, just as her first cry escapes from between her parted lips, I let it all go inside her. I come so hard it makes my vision blur with its intensity. Little stars dance at the corners, my hazy gaze fixed on River. Her head is thrown back, her face contorted, brows slanted, and then... magic. Her features relax, her muscles loosening as her body settles and her trembling stops. She crumbles into my arms and I ignore the wince from the sudden weight of her against my shoulder. I'll take a thousand jolts of pain just to have her languid in my arms.

We lie there long enough for the water to turn uncomfortably cold. Reaching to the side with River still wrapped around me like a little monkey, I turn on the shower nozzles and rinse the bubbles off her body. She moans into the crook of my neck as I grab the hotel's body wash and run the gel all over her shoulders and back then her ass and legs.

"Scoot up, baby. Let me wash your front." I try to untangle her from me but she just tightens her hold.

"Don't wanna."

"We'll be more comfortable on the big bed." At my words, she raises her head and opens one eye, playfully suspicious.

"We should probably have a conversation before you distract me with your big cock, again." I chuckle, my body relaxed but my dick still at half-mast and buried inside the perfect cocoon that is her pussy. To be fair, being naked around each other is always distracting.

"The question is, can *you* resist impaling yourself on my dick?" I thrust up to remind her that she's the one who had all the control earlier.

"Fair point." We both groan as our bodies separate and she lifts up and off my cock. A tremor travels from the base of my shaft all the way to my throat. Fuck, I love the feel of her. Now I'm just cold.

Making quick work of the lather, River takes my hands and spreads the soap on her fingers before running them all over my body. We wash each other in silence, cleansing ourselves of the Hell we just lived through, until her hand is on my cock, stroking from base to tip and back again.

My brow rises with a smirk firmly planted on my lips and it takes everything in me not to give in to the groan that wants to escape.

"What? Hygiene is important."

Little minx.

Once we're all cleaned up, I help her out of the tub, my head snapping to hers when I hear her sigh.

"What's wrong?" My eyes scan her body, her face bearing the marks of what that bitch, Eleonor, did to her. I wish I could kill her all over again.

"We didn't eat our food, now it's cold." Her pout reminds me of her age. She's so fucking strong and regal that I forget she's not far from my sister's age.

"Don't worry, it's just as good cold as it was warm. Besides, we can always order more." Wrapping her in a large, white, fluffy towel, I can't help but envelop her in the safety of my arms.

"Ti amo, Tesoro. Never doubt that." She sighs at my words and it's like a warm ray of sunlight has just pierced my heart.

"I never have. In fact, I was scared of how big it was. Your love, I mean." She looks up at me, her honesty and sincerity swimming in the depths of her gaze. "I was afraid of losing myself to..." She pauses, searching for her words. "I was afraid that your love for me would be so blinding that I'd lose myself, incinerate myself in it."

"I'm not sure how to take that, if I'm being honest." A pang of hurt and incomprehension has my heart rate racing.

"But it hasn't, Marco. It's only made me discover parts of me I didn't know existed. It's like, allowing myself to be loved by you has made me shine brighter instead of burn out."

I make my wife come twice more before she passes out sprawled over my chest with her thigh trapping my legs.

Tiny snores tell me she's deep in sleep and I wish I could shut my brain off and sleep with her.

But I can't.

I'm haunted by the unrelenting visions of the last few days. The blood, the pain, the violence and the lives I took with my bare hands, they flash on a continuous slideshow across my mind's eye.

On instinct, the muscles in my arm contract, pulling River closer to my chest, and easing my own torment. My lips rest against the crown of her head before I allow myself to go back to my thoughts.

God, I hope Lina will survive this. If I'm plagued by it all, I can't imagine what she is feeling. My chest aches for her, my eyes burning with guilt and anger because there's nothing I can do to make it better. Nothing I can say that could possibly help. The only silver lining is that Tyler was found with only a few bruises and a gash on his head. Had he died, we would have lost Lina forever. I spoke to him briefly after he was found in a nearby stone stable by one of our men. I don't think I've ever been so fucking happy to see him. Out of all of us, he's probably the least traumatized by the events considering he was passed out almost the whole time he was there.

I'm not as optimistic when it comes to Enzo, though.

The things he witnessed will haunt him forever and I pray to God that we'll be able to bring him back from the depths of the emotional abyss he's most likely throwing himself into at this very moment.

There's a reason he's always so detached, always the observer, always the protector, and it has everything to do with his past. So, not being able to save Lina from her fate will eat at him until there's nothing left to take.

Hopefully, they can all help each other to heal, Tyler, Lina, and Enzo. Be for each other what River is for me. What I pray I am for her. The breath in a world that tends to suffocate me. The light that pierces through the blinding darkness.

River stirs on top of me, bathing me in her warmth as though she knows I need to be reminded that we're in a cocoon.

"What are you thinking about?" Her throaty voice makes me smile.

"Everything. I can't get the images out of my mind." She rises on her right elbow and looks down at me.

"Did you just answer my question without deflecting?" Wide eyes stare back at me, her pupils darting from one side to the other.

"You asked, I answered. That was the promise, right?" My hand slides up her calf and stops at her thigh, squeezing enough to make her moan.

"Right. It's sexy as fuck."

I grin at her choice of vocabulary. My wife wants to play.

"Let's play a game." In a flash, she's lying beneath me, her chest rising and falling with her heavy breaths.

"Does it involve me coming all over your cock?" She smirks. "Or your face? I wouldn't be opposed to either."

I glide my dick between her already-wet pussy lips and run my tongue along the seam of her mouth.

"How about I make you choke on my cock. Would you like that?" I punctuate my proposition with a hard thrust of my hips, burying myself deep inside her welcoming pussy.

"Hmm, I don't know. What's in it for me?"

I bite her neck, indenting her flesh with my teeth as I plunge inside her twice more.

"Nothing. It's your reminder of how I feel about the language you use." I grind our bodies together, my dick swelling impossibly harder every time I bottom out.

"Well, my husband would never do such a thing. In fact..." She meets my thrust with a pump of her hips, rubbing her clit against me. "He would make sure I'm fully satisfied before he'd ever satisfy himself."

Fuck, I love this woman.

"He sounds like a good man."

"He has his moments." We forget about our conversation for a while, enjoying the reprieve of these rare moments of peace. I savor every stroke of my tongue across her skin and memorize every sound she makes.

In the end, all I care about is her. My wife. The woman of my literal dreams.

Keeping as much pressure off my shoulder as I can, I put most of my weight on my healthy side and pump in and out of River's snug little cunt, reveling in the sound of our sweat-covered bodies slapping together, the smell of sex making me hornier the longer I fuck her. We're moaning into each other's mouths, sucking on each other's tongues, biting whatever bit of flesh we can get our teeth on as our minds focus on one thing only: ecstasy.

The headboard plays a rising staccato against the wall as we gasp and groan and grunt the closer we get to orgasm.

"You come, Tesoro. Right fucking now."

"So..." she gasps, her body convulsing as her cunt squeezes the life out of my dick. Every muscle in her body is taut, her neck is straining and I can see her veins struggling not to pop out. "Fucking..." I cover her mouth with mine just moments before we roar out our climax, chests heaving and pelvises slapping together uncontrollably. "Bossy."

"You wouldn't love me any other way."

Chapter Twelve
Marco

Throughout the night, I have to pull River into my arms as she whimpers and cries out obscenities at her inner demons. Those same demons are the reason I can't sleep and every so often, my wife wakes and takes comfort in my love.

It's morning and we've showered, deciding we should finally get some food in us.

"You said something a while back about the first time you saw me. It didn't make sense then, but I'm guessing it will once you explain it to me." River is sitting cross-legged on the couch, a plate stacked with waffles bathed in syrup and whipped cream resting on her thighs as she cuts into them and takes a forkful into her mouth. I'm content just watching her stuff her mouth like a kid at Christmas as I sip at my espresso. I have missed real coffee and no matter how hard we try to make our coffee exactly the way we've had it served here in Italy, it just doesn't work out that way.

"You probably don't remember me, but the first time I saw you was like a brick house fell on my head." I take a sip and push back a chuckle at River's answering facial expression.

"Lovely. So, seeing me was like getting a concussion?" She's talking while chewing, whipped cream on her lips and waffle dough in her teeth. My gaze darts to her plate and there are a thousand things I'd rather be doing with her food and she picks up on it. "Down, boy. I need sustenance. You have to feed me if you want to keep making me come. It's the law." Cocking her head to the side, she looks like she's five years old with her bright eyes and goofy grin. My happiness is short lived, the gash on her cheek bringing my anger back tenfold.

"Does it hurt?" I nod to her cut, but she just waves her hand at me and pins me with her death glare.

"Do not deflect, Marco. I asked you a question and you're being all romantic about 'oh you hit me like a ton of bricks' blah blah blah." Her index finger points at my face and her lips pucker into a pout as she adds, "Spill."

Leaning in, I kiss the top of her head and rise to my feet. I'm going to need more coffee if we plan on emptying our bags right away.

"Our families had planned for us to be united. The two most powerful families in New York, one of which had a strong following in Italy, would be impossible to take down once united." I wait for the machine to fill the bottom third of my espresso cup with a ristretto before continuing. "My mother and your father were childhood friends. When he met your mother, he realized that he didn't want anything to do with the family business, the life. But..." Sipping at my coffee, I take a second before turning her entire world upside down. "In our world, you're either in or you're dead."

River's head snaps to the side, her eyes wide and her mouth hanging open. "You mean, it's like in the movies? If you want to leave, it's in a coffin?"

I shrug, "It's the only way to survive, to make sure those who want to leave can't talk."

"So, my father was risking his life every day?" She gulps a mouthful of waffles down, her happiness faded a little.

"Yeah, but our families understood and let it slide. The problem is that the threat of you taking over one day and forming this unbreakable alliance, well, it was still very much alive." River takes her plate and puts it on the coffee table before she curls up in my arms, listening to the story of her life. "Your grandparents had a huge party and they begged your father to bring you. At seventeen, you were close to being your own woman and able to choose your own path. They probably threatened him or promised him it would be the last time or something, I don't know, but he brought you to the party."

"It was the night of the accident." Her voice is barely audible, her hand on my chest and fingers curling into my cotton robe.

"Yes. You see, that night, my parents wanted me to meet you and see if we hit it off. I told them to forget it, I wasn't checking out a seventeen-year-old to see if I wanted to marry her. Lina was just turning seventeen and any man my age looking at her as a trophy wife would make me murderous."

"I don't think we stayed very long. I don't remember seeing anyone, really. I remember seeing my grandparents, but I wasn't allowed to speak to them much." I rub a soothing hand up and down River's arm, nodding at her comment, even though she can't see me.

"Your father probably made them promise not to, he didn't want you anywhere near this life. He was trying desperately to protect you."

Fuck, I understand his need.

"I guess it didn't work out the way he wanted."

"No, Tesoro, it didn't. You see, that night wasn't an accident and you weren't supposed to survive it either. When Nathaniel came to us with his plan to get revenge on you, I had an investigator check you out. At first, it was to protect Nate from himself. I thought if I could make you disappear, it would appease this crazy notion he had and we'd get our friend back. But the more he started digging, the more I realized who you were, and Tyler beat me to it. That fucker…" I kiss River on the top of her head, inhaling the scent of whatever essential oil she chose to use this morning. "Figured he could protect you by hiring you, keep you close, being the control freak he is." River glares at me with a raised brow. "More than me, yes. Trust me, he's not one to delegate."

"Fair enough. Continue, please."

"So, I had to bide my time, and in doing so, I dug up all the information I could, including the fact that your parents—and grandparents, for that matter—were a hit job and you were supposed to be dead, too. I don't know how you survived or how you fooled them into believing that you hadn't, but once you were in the system, they lost track. Or maybe didn't bother verifying if you were alive or dead. But here's the thing…" River looks up at me, eyes wide with curiosity. "At the time, no one knew you had a brother. Your parents kept that from everyone."

We stare at each other as River digests the information I just gave her until there's a pounding at the hotel suite door.

"Hold on." I kiss her lips, lingering and licking the whipped cream taste off her lips, reminding me of the things I'd love to do to her, when the knocking starts right back up.

"Ok, *arrivo, arrivo.*" I look through the peephole and sigh. Enzo in the morning, pounding on the door, is never a good sign.

"Come on in." I open the door wide and let my gaze roam his features. He's got bags under his red-rimmed eyes and his mouth is tense.

"The local capos want to meet River. They want to pay their respects and be given instructions for the future."

River sits up, kneeling on the couch and tightening her robe across her chest.

"How's Lina?" River ignores the urgency in Enzo's voice and goes straight for his heart. He takes a step back like he's been punched in the gut.

"I wouldn't know. She stayed with Tyler all night."

Chapter Thirteen

River

All this mafia stuff is getting a bit much for me, in all honesty. I mean, I'm trying really hard to adapt as quickly as I can, but it's fucking difficult. It's not happening as fast as I want it to and I feel like I'm on a never-ending downhill slope, picking up speed and shit as I roll head-first toward the lake waiting to drown me. Only, with Marco by my side, it's like I have a life-preserver, my very own PFD to help keep me afloat.

It's corny as fuck but I find myself grinning at the thought. Six months ago, I would have outright laughed at anyone who tried to tell me I'd ever find my twin flame. Because that's what Marco is, he isn't just my soul mate, we aren't just two souls extraordinarily linked. We are one soul, split in two, destined to be together for all eternity.

Just the idea of never feeling his breath on my skin, seeing his eyes glow with happiness, or hearing his laugh as it pierces my soul, hurts my heart like nothing before. All the secrets, lies, deceptions; they're inconsequential in the grand scheme of things. I'm not a dumbass who's about to run away at the first sign of trouble or from misunderstandings, I get his reasoning for keeping things from me.

I don't like the reasons, but I understand them.

Knowing that he fell in love at first sight all those years ago sends a thrill through me every time I think about it, causing my grin to grow wider as I stare out of the window of the car, watching the beautiful Italian scenery as it flies by.

We were destined from the start, and while that is something I would have refused at the time, I guess the universe and the fates had their own ideas.

"I hope that smile has something to do with me, Tesoro." Marco's fingers affectionately squeeze my thigh, dangerously close to my pussy, and I roll my eyes as I look at him.

His facial scruff is longer than he usually keeps it, and his dark floppy hair could do with a trim at the sides, but I won't complain at having more to hold on to. Right now, it falls into his steel-gray eyes as they hold my gaze, and I can't help raising a hand to gently brush it back with my fingers.

"It might be." I lift a brow at him and he grips my hand at his head before I can let it drop, holding me in place.

"It can only be me. I've only seen you smile like that when my cock is buried deep inside you."

Cocky bastard.

"Marco, baby, I think about a lot of things to do when your cock is buried deep inside me. Like my taxes... how I can improve the clu—" I squeal as I'm cut off by his lips on mine in a bruising kiss, and I give just as good as I'm getting. My tongue battles Marco's for dominance, tasting every inch of his mouth, and this, combined with his grip on my face, makes me want to fuck this meeting with the capos off and take my man to bed. Or be taken by him to bed. Either way, I'm not fussy.

We nip and suck at each other's tongues until finally I bite at his lower lip and pull away.

I know he's trying to help distract me from what's about to go down, and really, I still have no clue what's going to happen. I'm pretty much winging it, which is a first for me. I'm all about the research research research, give me all the information so I can make proper informed decisions. But not this time, it's all a little rushed and now my head's out of the clouds with daydreams, I really should think about what's going to happen when we arrive.

My emotions are all over the place; I'm up, I'm down, I'm in love, I'm scared shitless... even my thoughts are a jumbled mess of everything.

Marco must notice the sudden change in my mood and wraps an arm around me, bringing my head to rest against his chest. I lift my feet up onto the seat and lie all the way down, resting my head in his lap instead.

"If you were hungry, you just had to say, Tesoro." Marco winks at me as I stare up into his face and I grin back at him.

"You're a horn dog, Mr. Mancini."

"And you wouldn't have me any other way, Mrs. Fox-Mancini. Or is it Volpe-Mancini?" He's genuinely curious as he asks this and, truth be told, so am I.

But no, am I? No.

"Actually, I'd like to remain Fox-Mancini. It feels disrespectful to my parents to take away everything they tried to give me." Yeah, that feels right.

Volpe may be what I have always been, who I was always meant to be, but the universe had other ideas and I'm sticking to what feels good. Volpe is long dead. And with it, any claim the mafia thinks I have on Naples.

Marco continues to softly stroke my hair back from my face, massaging his fingers over my head with each movement, nodding in understanding.

"I want to give it all up."

Marco stills for a moment, processing what I just said before continuing with his movements and asking, "Give what up?"

"Whatever claim on Naples I have as a Volpe. So I think I need to know more about these capos and who would be the best person to take over. I can do that, right?"

"You can. But they may also need that confirmation from your brother. He is a Volpe too."

"What if they never find out about Everest? I mean, they still don't know anything about him, do they?" Shit, how could I have so easily forgotten my brother in all this?

"They don't as far as I'm aware, Tesoro. Don't worry, I can see it in your face. We can keep this from them. They never need to find out. Okay?" He leans down and kisses my forehead and I close my eyes at the soft contact.

"Okay. Then let's do that." I nod my head, almost to myself, convincing myself that I can do this. "Do you have any way of getting me some detailed research on each of the capos that I can read over in the next thirty minutes? Maybe I should delay the meeting? What if—"

I sit up, suddenly alert and realizing the gravity of the situation I'm actually in. How are these people even going to take me seriously? This isn't me.

"Oh God, Marco. I can't do this. I shot one of our own men in the shoulder for fuck sake." I know I'm spiraling, and yet I can't stop it. "Wh—"

"Hey, stop that." Marco grips my chin, careful not to let his fingers touch the wound on my cheek, and bores his eyes through mine. All I see there is love and understanding and utter devotion. If I were standing, the look would have the power to bring me to my knees. "You, Tesoro, are a fucking queen. In every way that is possible. You just need to trust in yourself and you can do anything you put your mind to."

"Does that mean I get to wear a crown?" His trust and belief in me are my superpower, and I know I'm being obtuse by ignoring everything else he said with my response, but this man gets me. It's an uncomfortable conversation and I'm doing what I do best... lightening the mood with obvious sarcasm.

His grin slowly grows and his grip loosens, his fingers now caressing the side of my head. "If you want to wear a crown, I'll buy you a crown." Marco places a soft kiss against my lips before pulling away and grabbing his cell.

"I can buy my own crown, you know."

He smirks at me, tapping on his phone before looking me in the eyes again. "I know you can buy your own crown, Tesoro. But I love providing for you. It's the caveman inside me. I'm never going to stop wanting to see the way your eyes light up when I can do that."

"Okay, Captain." I almost snort at his mock-amusement at what I call him, but his cell ringing saves him from replying.

"Si, Mamma... Si. Okay. *Ti voglio bene, Mamma.*" He holds the phone out to me and I raise a brow in confusion. "I texted Mamma. If anyone knows anything about the capos you're about to meet, it's her. She's been around these people since before I was even born."

This man.

He has just provided me with exactly what I need to make some big decisions and it's like nothing to him. Like a drop in the ocean.

He winks at me again, as if to say he knows what I'm thinking, and I smile, knowing I'm going to reward my husband with an epic blowjob before the day is out.

After speaking with Gabriella for twenty minutes, only five of which were discussing who should take over as the head don of the Naples mafia, the car finally pulls up to a hotel. A Mancini Hotel.

"Wow, I didn't realize you had a hotel in Italy. It's stunning!" I lean into Marco as we get out of the car and just stare at the tall building. It's as glamorous as his New York locations and I wouldn't expect anything less at this point.

"*We* have hotels in *many* countries."

"Okay, show off."

He chuckles beside me as I ready myself for what's about to go down. Not that I think I'll ever be ready for the unexpected, but I can at least pretend to be. I take a deep breath and stroke my hands down my sides, the soft material of the sheer shirt I'm wearing a little soothing against my skin. I make sure it's tucked into my cream-colored wide-leg pants and that I'm giving off the professional vibes I was aiming for. It's amazing how fast people can get you what you need when you flash a little money around.

We walk into the foyer, where J and a few soldiers I recognize from the fight are standing, presumably waiting for our arrival. She's dressed all in black, as usual, her cargo pants no doubt full of some dangerous surprises in case shit goes south.

She guides us through to a meeting room up on the second floor, where ten other people are already seated at a large wooden oval table in the center. I'm guessing these are the capos and their seconds. Gabriella told me there were five capos, two of which would be worthy to run Naples, so I search them out first.

One is a woman named Emilia La Rosa, mid-fifties, long graying hair, and full of all the elegance Gabriella described, but she also has a light surrounding her. The man sitting next to her is clearly her second and his body language alone tells me just how devoted he is to her.

Okay, yeah, I can do this. Reading people is my thing. I move my eyes over the room, which simmered down to complete silence the moment Marco and I walked in, and they land on my next possibility. Romeo Bianchi, slightly older than Emilia with brown eyes full of wisdom gained from age and experience. His second is rigid by his side, more out of fear of us than anything else.

I stand behind an empty chair and Marco stands behind me, my steady rock as I address the room.

"I want to begin by saying thank you." Marco repeats my words in Italian. They may all speak English, but I want to be respectful in their country, so I asked him to do this for me. "You all played a part in helping our people against the Ambrosios, and I understand how difficult it was for you to go against your leader... sorry, don. I'm learning more every day here, so please bear with me if I get the terminology wrong."

That seems to lighten the mood in the room a little, some of the tension suddenly lifted as Emilia stands, nodding respectfully to Marco before she approaches me, immediately wrapping me in her arms.

"I knew your grandma, she and I were good friends. In fact, Gabriella, your grandmother, and I used to get into a lot of trouble together in our youth." She smiles, laughing a silent laugh at the memory as another of the capos stands.

Two hours later, and I still haven't said what I came here to say. This really has been the meet and greet the capos wanted. They've asked questions, most of which answered with zero details—I can't trust these people with my life like I can Marco—and I've asked questions in return. In reality, my trying to rush things would probably have led me to making a completely different decision.

That universe, always putting obstacles in the way and making me think things through rationally.

"Can I just get everyone's attention, please?" The room quiets again and everyone takes their seats, myself and

Marco included. "While I have loved getting to know you all, and hearing stories about my family, I can't stay here in Naples. I can't run this organization the way you need it. It's completely a me thing. I'm just not cut out for this, I wasn't raised for this, and this isn't a decision I've taken lightly, because I'm aware of what is at stake to some extent. But I need to hand the proverbial reins over to someone who will cherish the opportunity. After a discussion with Gabriella, along with my own research,"—I'm technically not lying, but I want them to think my research involved a lot more than just talking with them for two hours and a chat with Gabriella—"I have decided that your new don will be Emilia La Rosa."

It was almost Romeo. It had felt like thousands of years of internal misogyny were pushing me to choose the man to rule the mafia family. Until, that is, my brain kicked me in the ass and pointed out that this woman has a presence only a leader possesses. Not only does she stand out in a crowd but she's regal and possesses a spine of steel.

The room bursts with excitement, rumbles of congratulations bouncing off the walls, and Emilia's face is almost stoic as she graciously accepts. Although I can see the slight upturn of her lips before she speaks.

"I will not let the Volpe family down. Grazie, River. Please know, we will always be here for you. It is what your grandparents would have wanted, so do not hesitate to call if you need anything at all. Okay?" Emilia stands as she speaks, her shock quickly fading as she assumes the power she will need to run Naples.

Whatever the fuck that entails.

"Well, there is one thing. Ugo and Elizabeth escaped. If you could keep an eye out and discreetly let us or our people know what you know, that would be super helpful. Thank you."

Marco chuckles beside me, knowing I'm feeling awkward as fuck with having to ask that question of the Naples mafia people after handing it all over to someone else, but we discussed it before we arrived. And it's something we needed to do.

Ugo and Elizabeth can't be allowed to get away with everything.

All I'm doing is giving karma a push in the right direction.

CHAPTER FOURTEEN
MARCO

I never thought I'd be so happy to leave Italy behind. Initiating my wife into the mile-high club for the better part of the flight may have had a part to play in that sentiment. Tyler, Lina, and Enzo flew out a few hours before us, leaving us a plane to ourselves. The staff didn't even bat an eye at what I'm sure was a boisterous flight.

Stefano had the house cleaned and ready for us upon our arrival, going as far as preparing a list of potential locations where he thought Elizabeth and Ugo might be hiding. We thanked him profusely and, although he tried his best to hide his emotions, I could see the relief at our safe return shining in his eyes. We briefly spoke about firing Justin and Aly for making a colossal mistake in allowing River to leave the house the day we got kidnapped. She was pissed, but in the end understood that it was better than the alternative. At least they still have their heads.

Grabbing the files, I guided my wife upstairs and let him know that we were not to be disturbed unless the world was on fire—and even then, I wasn't sure it was important enough.

A shower, a couple of orgasms, and ten hours of deep sleep later, we're digging into an elaborate breakfast that we both desperately needed in order to recharge. It's well past noon, but our bodies are still on Naples' time, which means bacon, eggs, and coffee are exactly what the doctor ordered.

"How's your shoulder?" We're lying in bed, sated and well-nourished, just taking advantage of these rare moments where only we exist.

"It's fine." I'm taking the meds the doctor in Naples gave me to minimize the pain, but the burn from the torn muscles and flesh is still omnipresent, albeit dull.

"You're a good liar, Mr. Mancini, but not good enough to fool me." Lifting her head from my chest, she places a soft kiss on my bandaged wound before straddling my face and giving me what I really want—her delicious pussy.

"If this is my punishment for lying," I thrust my hips up off the bed on instinct, all the while pulling her down over my mouth and licking up her sweet juices. "I think I'll lie all day long."

"Don't press your luck, Mancini." In a flash, her silky pajama top is flying behind her, landing somewhere at the foot of the bed, and my tongue is back where it belongs: inside her.

Eyes closed as my mouth gives and takes, I slide my hands from her hips to her ass and use it as leverage to fuck her harder with my tongue, topping from the bottom. My scalp stings as she tightens her grip on my hair, my lips throbbing as she rides my face and takes what she needs from me. What started as something slow and tender is becoming more and more torrid and rough.

Everyone deals with trauma in their own way and being that close to death has made us hungrier than we thought was possible. It's not about the orgasms—although, let's be honest, they're the perfect bonus—it's about the closeness, the connection we have that was almost taken away from us.

"Fuck, I love you, Tesoro." Ignoring the burn in my shoulder, I flip us around and grin at the scowl on River's face.

"Excuse me, I was the lead part in that show, Mr. Mancini." She's cute when she tries to fight me, her legs wrapping around my waist, trying her best to flip us back around.

"Shh, Tesoro. No one likes a diva." I plunge my dick between her swollen pussy lips as I lick a path across the seam of her mouth, reveling in her moans, knowing she can taste herself on me. "Plus, I have plans." Her pupils darken at my words, my hunger growing exponentially at the sight of her relinquishing her control to me.

I need it. Crave it, to be honest.

"That's my good queen." I fuck her hard and fast until she digs her nails into my back and slides them down my spine, avoiding the bandage all together. It should hurt, but all it does is make me harder, drive me faster in and out of her tight cunt.

Her body shoots off the bed with a cry that has my heartbeat thundering and the hairs on my arms standing at attention. It's animalistic, a lion's mating call, with wild eyes and curled lips. Fuck, she's beautiful when she's feral.

The vice-like grip her pussy has on my cock eases, but its hold was enough to keep my own orgasm at bay, thank fuck.

Reaching over to my bedside table, I open the drawer and take out the lube and her favorite vibrator. We'd bought it online one night, long ago. We were high on pheromones and she let it slip that double penetration was quite enjoyable, and since I would gladly kill any man who dared touch my wife in only the way I can, we compromised with a toy.

"Oh, I like the way you think, Husband."

"Think? Or fuck?" I pop a brow at her, knowing exactly how she'll answer as I squeeze the bottle of lube and spread it over the root of my cock. It's nice and snug inside her pussy and just as I pull out, I push her vibrator inside and turn it on to the minimal speed.

"Both." My beautiful wife is also my filthy queen. Perfection.

I watch her watch me as the toy keeps her buzzing and distracted while I push her thighs up and back, exposing her pretty little pink puckered hole. I prep her, pushing one finger inside, my eyes glued to her face so I can witness every emotion that flashes across her features, every moment of pleasure and pinch of pain. I want to see everything I do to her and for her.

"Don't you dare come without my cock inside you, Tesoro." Adding a second finger, I grit my teeth as my dick gets increasingly harder to ignore. Emphasis on *harder*.

"Then maybe you should hurry the fuck up and put it inside me." Her sass has no bite to it because she's too busy fighting off her impending orgasm.

"Always with the language." I grin. I love my wife's dirty mouth but to be honest, I'd much rather ruffle her lust-filled feathers. "You know how I feel about that." She doesn't have the time to respond before I'm pulling my fingers out of her ass and the toy out of her pussy.

River clamps her lips together, probably fighting the innate urge to tell me to fuck right off a cliff with my cursing obsession.

"What do you say, Tesoro?" I lick the vibrator from root to tip, savoring her taste as it explodes on my tongue. My moan is guttural, my pleasure deep and primal.

"What do I *want* to say or what do *you* want me to say? Two different things, Husband." She spits her words through gritted teeth with a snarky grin on her beautiful mouth.

"Hmm," I lick from the source, this time taking a second to tease her clit and revel in her body's immediate reaction, the trembling of her thighs, the clenching of her muscles, the groan that she can't keep locked up. "Whichever you think will allow you to come."

Growling as she narrows her eyes on me, I cock my head, waiting for her to apologize.

"I am *beep*ing sorry for getting carried away, *Husband*. I *beep*ing love you, but if you don't *beep*ing put your *beep*ing cock inside me right—" I slam her vibrator back inside her, the speed higher than before, hitting the button that makes the head of the toy move. Her gasp is music to my ears, but her cry when I finally push my cock into her ass is enough to make me come like a preteen.

"Fuck!" We both freeze as the head of my cock breaches her hole, my entire body begging for me to continue.

"Where's *your* punishment when you use that language?"

Speaking in between her gasps, I look up at her and grin. "*I'm* not a lady."

Even on the brink of orgasm, my wife is a proud defender of women.

"No, you're an asshooooole." Her words end on a groan as I turn the base of the vibrator to its highest setting just as I slam inside her ass. One of her hands flies up behind her, latching on to the headboard while the other clutches the sheets and makes a tight fist. Her entire body is taut, her chest arching above the bed, her perky tits on display and her nipples begging me to sink my teeth into their flesh.

And who am I to deny them?

Leaning forward, I suck one nipple then the other into my mouth just as I begin fucking my wife in earnest. She can't speak from the violence of my thrusts and she can't fight the need we both have for release so I decide to put her out of her misery.

Just as I pinch her nipple between my teeth, I press the vibrator deeper, my thumb grazing her clit as I watch her every reaction.

"Now."

That one word creates a butterfly effect.

River gasps, her muscles convulsing as she begins to come. I quickly pull my cock out of her ass and replace it with her vibrator as my mouth clamps onto her pussy and devours every drop of her cum as she shakes and trembles all over my face. Just as she begins to calm down, I wrap my hand around my dick and aim it right at her tits, my first spurt hitting her right nipple, then the left. I coat her skin with my seed, marking her with the pleasure she so often gives me.

Completely spent, I remove and disable the vibrator before covering her body with mine. We kiss for minutes in a languid show of post-orgasmic happiness, our tongues slowly dancing around each other, our lips swollen and wet.

"Tesoro?"

"Husband?"

"I love your filthy mouth."

"I know."

"Stefano thinks they're in The City? Could they be that fucking stupid?"

Sitting up against the headboard with River cross legged next me, I cock a brow at her in response. We're going over the files Stefano prepared, weighing which one seems more plausible than the others as we fill up with some healthy snacks we got from a kitchen run. The problem is, they're all possible scenarios. And yes, for the record, those two are stupid enough to fly back here.

"Narcissists feel untouchable so if they have something cooking here, they wouldn't think twice about returning to Manhattan."

"Right. Does that make us their main course?"

"Well, if that's the case, I refuse to be anything less than a T-bone steak, but yeah, we're probably high up on their to-do list." River rolls her eyes at my simile then grins like a naughty schoolgirl.

"Well, I'm the only one allowed to *do* you, so they're shit out of luck on crossing that item off their list." My head falls back on the headboard as a sudden laugh escapes me. This fucking woman, I swear to God.

"Okay, let's get back to work, my little sex fiend." Yeah, pot meet kettle and all that shit.

"Ugh, can we just pretend they're dead? I mean, they're not going to come after us again, right? We've got more security than the fucking president and the pope combined." She lets herself fall back onto the mattress, her arms up above her head and hanging over the edge.

"To be fair,"—I close one file and open another—"the Pope's Swiss Guard only has about a hundred men." River hauls herself back up, leaning on her elbows.

"Okay, first of all, Encyclopedia Britannica, that is not the point." Sitting back, she pauses with her brows pinched and her eyes unfocused. "Second of all, why would the pope's guards be Swiss?"

Slapping the file on my lap, I turn fully to look at her and grin. I love feeding my wife's curious mind, it satiates a deep, primal need in me. "Back in the fourteenth century, the Helvetians were considered fearless warriors and loyal to a fault so the pope hired them to protect him." A very long story short but I'm guessing she's not here for the history of the Swiss Guard.

"Like mercenaries." It's not a question so I just shrug because sure, that's about right.

"Taking the best men available to protect him while the Italian government protects everything around them." I look over at her and frown. She's lost in thought, her eyes darting from one side to the other like she's figuring out a complex puzzle.

"Yeah, something like that. Are you okay, Tesoro?" At my question, her pupils focus back on me and a Cheshire smile grows at the corners of her lips.

"So, we're the pope. We've got our detail in close ranks here at the house and our capos and soldiers out there in The City. What if we use those soldiers to close ranks and smoke Elizabeth and Ugo out from their hiding places? They can't possibly know who's made and who's not."

Staring at my wife, I take a quick mental count of the possible men and women out on the streets, think about how many we need working their sectors and how many we can afford to assign to seeking out the siblings.

"I'll have to talk to Enzo and the capos but yeah, creating circles of protection while pushing out the rats is definitely something we can try."

River grins at me, a proud glint in her eyes. "Maybe I'll get this whole mafia thing down one day."

"You're perfect, Tesoro." I wrap my hand around her throat and pull her to me, bruising her mouth with my lips and kissing the breath from her lungs.

"We'll get through this, right?" I hate the vulnerability in her voice. I want to take it away and bury it under a hundred miles of cement.

"Of course. Which is why I've decided to go after the Greeks. They helped Ugo and Elizabeth and they have to pay for the part they played in this whole thing." By the way her eyes shift from vulnerable to furious in the time it takes a bullet to fly through flesh, I'm guessing she's not happy about this news. Too bad, it must be done.

"Jesus fuck, Marco. Are you serious? Do we not have enough shit on our plate? Oh, sure, let's add the fucking Greek mafia war to our agenda. No problem, dude." She jumps from the bed and begins pacing from side to side, throwing ridiculous threats my way as her arms flail in the air. My gaze follows her trail back and forth, a smirk forming on the corner of my mouth as I think about how perfect this woman is for me, how lucky I am to have realized the importance of her in my life.

"Are you even listening to me? What the fuck, Marco?" She stops pacing, facing me now with her fists planted on her boy-shorts-covered hips.

"I bought a yacht for the fourth of July. I thought it would be nice to have both of our families together for the day and the evening. The fireworks are amazing from the water." Her frown deepens at my revelation and just when she's about to rip me a new one for ignoring her previous rant, I interrupt her. Again. "But if you want to stay home and pout, I'll ask Enzo to keep an eye on you." I'm taunting her now and by the way her eyes narrow and her jaw tightens, I'm guessing she's about to explode—and not in the good way. Too fucking bad, I won't budge on this.

"Marco! Marco!" At my mother's voice and sudden banging on the door, River and I both freeze, eyes wide and alert, heads snapping toward the bedroom door. Thankfully, we both dressed after taking another shower washing away our time in this little bubble of Heaven we created for ourselves since our return.

"Coming!" I jump out of bed and pull on a pair of sweatpants to hide my semi inside my boxers.

As I pass her, I grab River by the jaw and kiss her hard and fast, our eyes locking, this conversation on the back burner. When I open the door, I find my mother grinning with tears in her eyes.

"They've found Nathaniel!"

And we're back to reality.

CHAPTER FIFTEEN
RIVER

Not telling Gabriella about what happened with Nathaniel was a mistake. The woman has been through Hell these last few months and I know Marco felt like complete shit when he had to douse her happiness that he's *finally* been found. She completely understood and the fiery storm behind her eyes when Marco explained everything was clear. Luckily, it wasn't aimed at us.

The real shocker though—and it's something I'm having mixed feelings about—is that it's not Nathaniel's *body* that has been found washed ashore or at the bottom of a six-foot hole. He's been seen at the cemetery, walking around New York City...

Alive.

Stefano's research found a new grave site in the name of Eleonor Reed. Apparently he had an automatic search on her name for any new mentions and this popped up earlier today. So we're now in Marco's office and he insisted I sit in his lap so he could hold me through the conversation.

In truth, I'm not sad about it. As much as I resisted being basically coddled by him, I secretly hoped he wouldn't give in... and he didn't.

"We haven't been able to effectively track him to know where he is. There are eyes on any known properties, but it seems he is avoiding those. The only times he's been noticeably seen have been the cemetery and the lawyer's office for the reading of his mother's will. Other than that, it's like he is the ghost we thought him to be, Signore."

I fidget in Marco's hold, unable to stop the growing feeling of dread in the pit of my soul, but he just tightens his grip, making me relax into him as we listen to what has been found.

"I have some footage of the cemetery from this morning. I think you should see it." Stefano passes Marco an iPad, pressing play on the full-screen video.

My stomach drops and my heart leaps into my throat at the image. It's Nathaniel. His hair is a lot longer than I remember, and he now has a beard, but there is no doubt it's him. The thing that makes me hold my breath is the person next to him, an arm around his waist in comfort as he stands over his mother's fresh grave.

A grave I'm semi-responsible for creating. Okay, *mostly* responsible.

This can't be happening. It can't be a coincidence that he's suddenly walking around now that his mother is dead. And of course he'd be there with her. Why wouldn't he? Because life isn't complicated enough. It's not like we didn't just rid ourselves of one big bad or anything. Is he another big bad?

Well, *she* certainly is.

Her red hair is shorter, styled similarly to mine—which is just fucking weird—but it's unmistakably Elizabeth.

My eyes strain as they widen in surprise, my heart pounding in my chest as if it wants to burst out, and my breaths come short and fast, like even *they* don't want to be around me.

Soothing circles being rubbed into my thighs helps me become more present and I realize Stefano is no longer in the room.

"I've got you, Tesoro. Breathe for me." His chest moves deeply against my back and I try to match his slow, even breaths, closing my eyes and allowing all that he is to envelop me in his warmth.

After a few minutes, my breathing is back to some kind of normality and I groan at the feel of Marco's fingers massaging my scalp. His other hand is still resting on my thigh, dangerously close to my pussy, and I can't help grinding my ass against him for more. I need to forget again, just for a little while. Then I can try and process what was in that video and what it could mean.

"You're wearing too many clothes." Marco sounds as tense as I feel; we both need this.

"For once, Husband, you are right." I stand, pushing my ass into his crotch and arching my back for emphasis, before gripping the zipper of my knee-length pencil skirt and sliding it down. It gives Marco a fantastic view of my ass as I slowly reveal it, pulling my skirt down and stepping out of it. I leave my shiny black stilettos on, I'm otherwise bare from the waist down.

"No panties?" His low growl as he speaks still sends a shiver down my spine, a direct link to my tingling clit.

"I stopped wearing panties around you when you kept stealing them to carry around in your pocket." Turning to face him, I begin slowly unbuttoning my red satin shirt and the heat from his look alone is addictive. The way his lips upturn on one side, the crinkle in the corner of his eyes, the raising of that sexy-as-fuck eyebrow...

All that combined with his porn-worthy forearms peeking out below the rolled-up sleeves of his white shirt make this man irresistible.

I'd be doing a disservice to women everywhere if I didn't take full advantage of the way he's looking at me. It's like he wants to devour every inch of me.

"Now *you're* wearing too many clothes."

Marco grips the arms of his office chair as I drop to my knees, sliding my palms over his strong thighs. I unbuckle his leather belt and slowly pull down his black slacks, sliding his shoes and socks off as I go. Leaning over him, I gradually push myself up, making sure my breasts rub against his rock-hard cock as I unbutton his white shirt, leaving him bare chested for me.

My fingers trace over the script on his ribs, and the word *volpe* stands out again.

"What does this mean?" I'm still rubbing my breasts over his cock and he palms the sides of them as I look up through my lashes at him.

"'*Ciò che il leone non può fare, la volpe può.*' It means, *what the lion cannot manage to do, the fox can*. So you see, Tesoro, we were always meant to be a team. The lion needs the fox to defy a snare, and the fox needs the lion to fend off the wolves." I fucking love how he sounds when he speaks Italian.

"And you're the lion in this scenario?"

"Always."

Oh gods, yes. That growl.

He squeezes my breasts, swiping his thumbs over the peaks and holding them in place as he slowly thrusts his cock in between them.

My nipples are tight and my clit is pulsing, begging me for attention. But it can wait. I want to get lost in my husband before he gets lost in me. I kiss his stomach, nipping and licking as I go, wanting to taste more. I slowly lower myself, gripping his cock between my breasts for as long as possible, and he moans when contact is lost. It's quickly replaced with my mouth over his tip and take the time to lick the slit before sliding my tongue down his shaft.

I grip his dick in one hand and roll his balls together in the other before gently sucking them into my mouth, one at a time, using my tongue to add extra sensations. His hands are in my hair and his heavy breaths and soft groans encourage me to move my hand faster up and down his cock. Popping a ball from my mouth, I replace it with his dick, moving my tongue to add pressure down his shaft as I slide my lips over him.

"If you keep doing that, I'm going to come down your throat instead of into your delectable cunt." His words are so deep and breathy, and my pussy throbs with anticipation.

"How about both?" My words are muffled around him, but he understands as I begin to suck harder and faster.

His breathing is heavier, his groans louder, and his fingers dig into my scalp as he tries to control my movements.

"Oh fuck yes."

Warm spurts of cum hit the back of my throat and I swallow him down, moaning around him and making sure I get every drop.

"That pineapple Stefano's been serving at breakfast needs to stay. You taste fucking delicious, husband of mine." I smile up at him, my hands now on his bare thighs.

He grabs my face in his hands and pulls me up to meet his lips, tasting himself as his tongue explores my mouth.

"The only man's name I want to hear coming from these lips when you're naked, is mine." He punctuates his sentence with a slap against my ass, followed by a bruising squeeze as I straddle his lap.

His kisses turn frantic and he tweaks my nipple before encouraging me to rise so he can suck it between his teeth.

"Mmm, whatever you say, Sir."

The deep rumble that escapes his chest makes me smile as he brings my lips to his again, gripping my hips and moving me so my clit rubs against his cock. My wetness covers him and we're both fighting for dominance with our tongues, our hands gripping and stroking and rubbing every inch of naked skin.

His cock hardens again and I can feel his readiness nudging at my entrance.

I try to position myself over him, moving a hand to his shaft to place it where I want it.

"Not yet, Tesoro. I want to play some more." He tries to stop me, but it's too late. I've lined him up and I slam myself down so he's seated inside me. His growly breath is against my neck, tickling the short hairs and sending those delicious tingles down my spine again.

"Whoops?" I giggle into his shoulder and his grip on my ass tightens.

I lift myself up, slowly rolling my hips on the way, then sliding back down just as slowly. I manage to do this a couple of times before Marco takes over, using his hold on me to control my motions. Every time I come back down, my clit rubs against him, sending all those buzzing feelings through my body and bringing me closer to orgasm.

Each thrust inside me sends sparks through my veins and I'm already on the brink of exploding around him.

"Don't come until I say the word."

I almost squeal in protest, but he slams into me again and again and I'm practically losing my mind with ecstasy.

"Marco... baby... Please."

I don't know if it's the 'baby' or the 'please', but his thrusts become more insistent and I know he's close too.

"Now."

"Yes!"

My body is alight with flames and a rush of electricity spreads through me as I let go, allowing all the sensations to pour out in a wave of pleasure. His warmth coats my insides and our breaths mingle together as he kisses me soft and slow.

"I love you, Husband."

"I love you too, Wife."

There are several of Marco's soldiers dotted around the cemetery, watching over us as we visit Mr. Bobby's grave. I bought a peace lily plant on the way and have lovingly placed it between his and his wife's headstones.

"Do you want a minute, Tesoro?"

He may be protective and overbearing, but he also seems to know just when I need time to myself. I know he hates it, but he doesn't begrudge me of it.

"Please."

His grin is contagious and he winks at me, bringing my hand to his mouth and gently placing his lips against my ring finger in a soft kiss. It would be romantic as fuck if he didn't then suck my fingers into his mouth, biting down with a lusty growl that promises many orgasms for me when we get home.

He doesn't go far, walking over to stand with Sam, one of the only soldiers with us today whose name I remember.

I inhale deeply and return my gaze to Mr. Bobby's grave.

"Hey, Mr. Bobby. It's me, River." I sit down, and pull out the Thermos of coffee Stefano made for me, putting two cups on the ground and filling them up. "It's already Irish, just how you like it." I pick one of the cups up and clink it gently to the 2nd one before taking a sip.

"There's so much to tell you. I almost can't believe it myself, to be honest, but I took your advice, the whole big picture thing. I'm a legit business owner now, Rapture is now mine. And I'm actually loving it. It's hard work, but it's so worth it to see the smiles on my customers' and employees' faces, knowing I'm responsible for being a cog in the wheel that makes that happen. Ooh, and I finally chose. You called it. He infuriates me, challenges me, and surprises me every day in all the best ways." I have another sip of my coffee, holding the warm cup in both of my palms as I sit cross-legged. "What might shock you is my new heritage. Or I suppose it's old, because I've always been Italian… apparently. Yeah, I know. Shocker. I'm Italian! I haven't told Francesca. You remember her, right? Gods, I miss that pesto sauce she hid from everyone but her best customers." With a quiet chuckle, I let the recollection bathe me in the soothing memories of a time less complicated, for sure, but also more lonely. My free hand plays with the overgrown blades of green grass, a smile planted on my lips. "Anyway, she'd roll her eyes so hard at my lack of knowledge for her culture—well, my culture now, I suppose. I'm learning, slowly, but it's going to take some time, and I'm not going to lose the person I've become. Which is a mix of many things now. Honestly, I don't think there are enough hours in the day to tell you about everything that's happened, so I'm glossing over. You know, concentrating on big picture stuff." I laugh to myself and finish off the coffee, then pour the other one over the grass in front of me.

"The main thing, though—and I think you and Miss Josie would be proud—is I'm just trying to live a life of happiness, and now I have Marco by my side, my very own devoted partner. I never understood it fully before, but love is fucking beautiful, you know? I love my family, and I loved you *so* much, always will, but the love that comes from a partnership is something special. And I think that's maybe what you tried to teach me in your own way."

A tear falls from my eye and slowly rolls down my cheek and I wish so damn hard that he was still here to give me all his worldly advice. Although, I'm not sure how he'd take all the mafia shit, which is why I'm not mentioning it. I mean, he knows, of course, but I don't want to taint this special visit with all the madness.

"I'm going to make sure I visit you more often, hopefully things will calm down soon and I can do it without an entourage. But for now, I'm going to love you and leave you, Mr. Bobby. My friend."

I screw the cap back on the coffee and stand, closing my eyes and taking a moment to breathe in the air around me. There's something spiritual about being in a cemetery in the early evening dusk.

"Always looking at the big picture, Mr. Bobby. Until next time."

Looking to my husband, I smile at the intensity of his gaze and his worried frown disappears as he begins to walk back over to me, immediately wrapping me in his strong arms and holding me to his hard chest.

"Let's go home, my queen."

Chapter Sixteen
Marco

"That is not a boat."

I look over to River and squeeze her hand, crushing my lips together to avoid laughing at her outrage.

"And what would *you* call it?" I follow her line of sight as we stand on the top step of the dock where my new acquisition awaits us for this day of celebration. I figured it would be nice to watch the fireworks from the Hudson after spending the day relaxing with her family and mine.

"A planet destroyer? A gas-guzzling fish murderer?" She holds out a finger at me when I try to defend myself before continuing her rant as the crew pretends they're not amused by her antics. "Oh, a Pompous Ozone Sucker."

I wait, watching her brows furrow every time her gaze slides across the impeccable lines of our new yacht. She's not exaggerating its size, I may have gone a little overboard there, but my priority was to be able to fit everyone today without us being cramped on the decks. Who wants to watch fireworks from inside? No one, that's who.

"She's a yacht and she's going to be very useful in our future." With all the amenities onboard—swimming pool, jacuzzi, outdoor and indoor dining, a gym—I kept imagining all the ways I could fuck my wife throughout the tour. The upper deck with its massive sectional couch deep enough to fuck River from behind with the stars as our only witnesses is what sold me on it.

"*She*? Did you just refer to this hunk of metal as a woman?" Her fiery gaze bores a hole through my skull and I don't think she's ever been more beautiful than she is right now. With all her fancy clothes and well-learned class, it's in moments like these that I remember River's upbringing was a far cry from mine. In her soul, she's a child of the land, a believer in things like magic and karma. Most of all, she's a fierce defender of women's rights and me equating a thing to a woman may have put me in the doghouse. Again.

"Tesoro," I try my soothing voice, but it only makes her take a step back and cross her arms. "It's customary, like a good luck thing." I have no idea if that's true, but every person involved in the sale, including the crew I hired, refers to all yachts as 'she'. It would suck if this thing sank because I disrespected its existence.

"It's gross but whatever."

Leaning into her so my words are for her ears only, I whisper, "Your outrage makes my dick hard as fuck, you know that, right?" I bite her earlobe when she harrumphs at me.

"I was expecting something small." She's giving in, mostly because the deal is done and we are the proud owners of a Cloud Atlas.

"That's where you made your first mistake." When her head turns toward me, I take advantage of the moment and kiss the indignation right out of her.

"You're impossible, Mr. Mancini, and I'm still mad at you for wasting your money." The bite she had earlier has faded but her comment makes my jaw clench.

"*Our* money."

"Well, next time you spend *our* money," she stresses the word our like I'm obtuse before continuing her rant. "You should probably ask my opinion first." We stare at each other for a beat, our stubborn need to win this fight keeping us at a stand-off.

I don't roll my eyes at her but, fuck me, I really want to. Taking a deep breath, I eat crow for the first time in my life.

"You're right. Next time I want to make a big purchase, I will consult you." That was almost physically painful. "Now, let's take the tour, and as we do, you can think of all the ways I'm going to fuck you on *our* new yacht."

"You're impossible." The corner of her mouth ticks up and I know I've got her. Sometimes an apology can go a very long way, it would seem.

"Some of the positions I have in mind, up there"—I nod to the upper deck—"may very well be, but we'll have fun trying." I kiss this argument away, our lips fitting perfectly together as our tongues delve into each other's mouths.

As our crew captain gives us the tour and explains the different functions at the helm of the boat, River whispers in my ear. "Ev, Petal, and Kai are going to hate it."

I scoff. "Kai is going to love it. He's *maybe* a third hippie. The other two-thirds belong to capitalism. Trust me." Wide eyes and an open mouth greet me and fuck, I want to slide my cock between her lips and fuck her face. Maybe I'll cancel our plans and take the boat out myself so I can spend the day worshiping my wife's body and mind.

"That's a horrible thing to say, Marco. Take it back." I raise my brow at her because, seriously, Kai would be living the high life if he could, but his friendship with Everest and Petal is too strong for him to jump to the dark side. That said, I want today to be perfect and it won't be if I put my *dolcezza* in a bad mood.

"Fine, I take it back." River stares at me, her eyes roaming mine as she searches for my insincerity. Thank fuck everyone arrives at that moment, distracting her and saving my ass.

"Holy shit, that's a monster boat. I thought we were going on a dinghy."

I chuckle at Everest's naïveté. Have they even met me?

River looks over the deck and her entire face transforms into something so luminous it takes my breath away. I love how important family is to her.

"Come on, let's greet our guests."

An hour later, everyone is onboard and we're ready to head out for the day and half the night. River's family is here, including Freya, who decided to bring a date? What the fuck is wrong with that woman? Petal's concern when she saw River's wound was palpable. My sister and mother are here too, but Lina isn't her bubbly self and her clothes are a size too big from the weight she's lost since we've been back. Enzo has been a tomb when it comes to her and she won't talk to me about... well, anything. I've arranged for a therapist—fully vetted and researched to within an inch of her life—to come to the house once a week as well as being on call anytime Lina needs her. The problem is that patient-client privilege keeps me from knowing how she's doing. So, I do what I can by keeping her close or with Tyler.

Enzo decided he was staying on land, something about keeping an eye out. I know better. The idea of being trapped on a boat for an extended amount of time makes him jittery. I get it, for the sake of his sanity, Enzo needs to be in control of it all.

"Oh! What about Daisy?" River's got a martini glass in her hand, two green olives firmly pierced by a toothpick. I steal a piece of pineapple and pop it in my mouth, making her grin at me from beneath her eyelashes. I know what she's thinking about and it has nothing to do with the baby names she and her family are trying to narrow down.

"Daisy Fox? Are you fucking kidding me? That's worse than Daisy Duke." We all roll our eyes at Everest, who has pretty much vetoed every single girl's name we've suggested, but I have to agree, Daisy won't work.

"Sierra, like the desert. She would be calm and serene yet deadly for anyone wishing ill-will against her." I'm expecting my suggestion to be axed once again, but am surprised when the table falls silent, all eyes on me.

"Dude. Deadly? Careful, your mafia is showing." Fucking Kai thinks he's funny. Har-har motherfucker. Although, he may have a point.

"No, I like it." Now, all eyes are on Everest since he's been the toughest one to convince.

"Me, too." Petal pushes herself up to standing as she takes careful steps toward her husband until she's standing right in front of him. He bends over and places a tender kiss on her big round belly, and I swear to fuck my emotions almost get the better of me. It must be the salt and wind getting caught in the back of my throat and making my eyes well up.

"What if it's a boy?" River asks, and the baby name merry-go-round continues.

At lunch time, we all gather around the exterior table that has been prepared for us. It looks fancy, but I've ordered traditional Fourth of July foods like hot dogs and burgers, making sure to have vegan and vegetarian foods available, including gluten-free bread.

I'm thoughtful like that.

Somehow, I'm sitting next to Kai and we've both been listening to the conversations around the table more than participating, when my eyes land on Freya's hand. Her *left* hand with the wedding band still on the ring finger as she places it on her date's thigh.

As I'm bringing my beer bottle to my lips, I lean toward Kai and nod once to his wife. "So, what's up with that?"

"She's pissed because I won't sleep with her." He shrugs like it's no big deal. I know he only married her to help her with her medical bills and the whole thing is a sham, but still. If we're being honest, my marriage to River started out as a sham—or that's what she thought, it was very much real for me from the get go—yet I would have carved out eyeballs if anyone even looked at her the wrong way.

"It doesn't bother you that she's here with him?" I turn to look at him, weighing his sincerity.

"Nah, it is what it is and, at the end of the day, her treatment is over and our divorce is imminent." It's my turn to shrug. It makes sense. "Besides," he continues. "I'm biding my time until River realizes I'm her forever one." He has the good sense to grin like a kid who's just played an award-winning prank or else he'd be swimming back to shore.

I lean my full weight back in my chair as my gaze slides to my wife, who is having an animated discussion about the merits of turkey bacon versus the real shit. There are none, bacon is pig or else it's not bacon, end of.

"Didn't realize you were delusional." I did, but this conversation is fun.

"Mark my words, Mancini."

"I'd rather mark you between the eyes, Briggs." He chuckles like I'm joking. He should know better. Does he have any idea how easy it would be to sink him to the bottom of the Hudson alongside all the others buried beneath the waters dating back to the beginning of time?

We're silent for a moment as we watch the others.

"I feel like we're bonding. Who knows? Maybe we'll even be friends."

I almost choke on my beer.

"Yeah, I don't think so. Let's revisit this conversation when you're not pining over my wife." He turns to me, his beer bottle tilted to the side, and I realize he wants to make it a toast.

Oh, what the Hell.

The rims of our bottles clink, drawing River's attention to our truce. Her face lights up with a grin so bright it blinds my soul and kick starts my heart. Fuck, she's stunning. The fact that I contributed to her smile makes my chest swell with pride.

"You just got brownie points for making an effort with her best friend," Kai murmurs, a smug grin on his stupid face. "Remember that next time you're thinking about throwing me overboard." That gets my attention and an unexpected laugh bursts from my throat.

"Deal."

Day turns to night and when it's time for the fireworks, I stand at the back of the boat with my wife nestled in the security of my embrace while Lina and my mother stand right beside me. The show goes on for well over thirty minutes, the display of red, white, and blue prominent as the lights explode in the clear black skies.

"It's pretty, but between the air and noise pollution—all those poor doggies who have to suffer through this—the cons outweigh the pros." At Petal's words, my mother sniffs beside me as River shoots her hand out and squeezes my mother's in support. They both loved Bruce and when I found out he'd been murdered, I saw red. Ugo will pay for that, too.

It's almost midnight when we disembark and River and I make sure everyone has a car to take them back to their respective homes. Well, all except Freya, since she's decided to go home with her boy toy and I'm not paying for that shit.

Once everyone is gone, we thank the crew and head to our own town car. Well, it's more of a limo but whatever, I needed the space for my mother and Lina.

"She's lovely, River. How far along is she?" my mother asks as we slide into the back of the car, Enzo at the wheel watching us in the rear-view mirror.

"Six and a half months. Doesn't she just glow? I've always heard about the glow of pregnancy, but it's the first time I've actually witnessed it." River's love for her sister-in-law is awe-inspiring.

Before Lina has the chance to get inside, I take her in my arms and hug her tightly to me. She stiffens like my touch is physically hurting her.

"I'm sorry." My words are barely audible from the lump that's lodged in my throat. "*Mi dispiace, sorella.*" I repeat my apology in our mother tongue and rest my forehead to the crown of her head.

"Me too." She squeezes her arms around my waist for only a brief second before she sniffs and gets into the car.

When Enzo turns, everyone gasps. Everyone except for me. I'm livid.

"What happened to your face?" My mother's instincts to heal are in full effect. Enzo is like a child to her. From the bruise that's already darkening around his eye and the cut that's actively bleeding, I'm guessing a fist fight. The tip of his tongue darts out as he licks the drop off his lip and I notice his wince when he sniffs. Hmm, he may even have a broken nose. My gaze lands on his knuckles, his grip on the wheel so tight it's like the thing has personally offended him, and I shake my head in frustration. This is his M.O. when he's pissed off at the world. Picks a fight, gets his ass beaten even though he could easily avoid getting touched when fighting on a good day.

"Nothing worse than the other guy."

Motherfucker.

Chapter Seventeen
River

Nightmares still haunt my sleep most nights, but it's apparently my new norm and I'm dealing with it. It's my karma for the wrongs I've done, and I refuse to complain. I could have lost my family, I could have died, I could have been forced to endure what Lina did, so I'm choosing to be grateful for the good instead of focusing on the shit.

Marco has suggested I talk to Lina's new therapist, and I've considered it, well aware I'm being stubborn by refusing, but I don't think I'm ready to truly dissect everything like that with a stranger. I'd rather talk to my husband, to be honest.

We're still on high alert, with Nathaniel and Elizabeth basically ghosts in the wind, and Ugo fuck knows where—not even Stefano, the super ninja, or J's Reapers have found any of them yet, despite the brief glimpses of

Nathaniel and Elizabeth on CCTV around New York. They've been seen simply shopping, or buying a coffee, but never for long enough to catch up to them, quickly disappearing, as if they were just an illusion, without a trace. Marco is certain they're getting some outside help from the Greeks somehow, because there is no way they'd be able to avoid him like this otherwise.

He's trying his best to remain positive and not let his anger show too much around others, but I know he feels it. Finding and dismembering Ugo is at the top of his priority list. What happened with Lina plays on his mind more than he lets on, and I get it. It features in my nightmares often. So Marco's anger is all focused on that task for right now, which, for him, is as healthy as it's ever going to be.

As for me, I've been throwing myself into my work too. Only my work is the less-plotting-murdery kind. Sheryl has been amazing with the general office paperwork, Lily has been fantastic with the guys and girls I have working out of the club, and Mimi has been a rock for the dancers and staff inside the club. It's a well-oiled machine and I couldn't be prouder of how these women have pulled together to help me.

I may have only been physically out of the country for a few days, but my head has been fucked for weeks. It's all a process though. I'm not expecting miracles and am well aware that time is the only thing that can heal any of the wounds we've all gained from what happened. Although, I'm also aware that some things will never be truly healed, and some of the scenes I've witnessed are permanently burned into my mind.

It's been a month since our Fourth of July celebrations, and just a couple of weeks longer since all the revelations and shit. At least the slash on my face has cleared up faster than I thought it would. I mean, it's still there, but it's a Hell of a lot easier to conceal now.

Signing off an order for the downstairs bar is the last thing on my list of things to do today and I sit back in my soft swivel chair once it's done, breathing in the lavender scent of my burning incense. A lot of people think lavender is just for relaxing or aiding sleep, but it's actually really good for chasing the blues away and lifting spirits, getting rid of negative energies. Which is exactly what I need before I see Polly. She's always been a solid rock for me, in her own unusual way, and I don't want seeing her today after so long to be all about my problems and miseries.

"Mimi has just radioed up. Polly has arrived and she's downstairs in the corner booth by the stage." Sheryl's sing-song voice comes through the intercom, and I smile.

I really need to figure out a way to thank these women for what they've done and continue to do for me.

"Thanks, Sheryl. Now get your ass out of here. It's late and you've been here with me all day."

"Yes, Ma'am. I got a fuck buddy just waiting for my call. Over and out." She laughs, a loud and dirty kind of laugh that is impossible to not enjoy.

I stand after putting my paperwork into the right folders and grab my small over-the-shoulder bag as I pull my phone out. There are a couple messages from Marco waiting.

Husband: I miss your face. This meeting is dull.

Husband: Send nudes. *Winky face emoji*

I shake my head with a smile. My husband, the romantic. So I do exactly what he asked, sending him a picture of the nude lipstick from my bag before locking my office up and heading downstairs.

"Hey, Mimi. How are things doing down here tonight?"

She's at the bottom of the stairs, her favorite place to stand as it has the best view of the club, and she gives me a brief nod in greeting, continuing to survey her surroundings. And this is why she's an amazing head of security. I never get any of the weird feelings I used to get with Frank.

Ugh, just the thought of him sends a very non-exciting shiver down my spine.

"Good crowd in tonight, Boss. The extra people your husband sent are a little grumpier than I like for my staff here, but they're not affecting the atmosphere, so I won't complain."

The loud, thumping music rings out around the space but it's not enough to hinder a conversation, thankfully. If it was, I'd be permanently shouting in Mimi's ear when down here, seeing as the dim red hues of the lighting make it difficult to see super clearly.

"I'll have a word." I give her a wink and pat her shoulder reassuringly. She smiles as I walk away to find Polly.

Glamorous as ever, Polly is sipping from a martini glass, her hair up in a classic French twist, and her houndstooth skirt-suit neatly pressed. She's paired it with gold accessories, a chain belt, earrings, and even the handbag sitting next to her.

Her blue eyes light up when she sees me approach and she stands, opening her arms wide to pull me in for a hug. She's not usually a hugger, more of a European double-kiss on the cheeks kind of woman, but I go with it.

I am a hugger.

"My darling girl. How the Hell have you been?"

We sit and she pushes a waiting blue cocktail in front of me, getting comfortable in the soft plush red bench seat. The music switches to one of Lina's favorites and I half expect her to be next out on the stage, but she hasn't performed since... Italy, not that I blame her.

Instead, it's a group dance, and I love these. The synchronicity, the joy on their faces as they dance together, the beauty in their fluid movements. It's a sight to behold.

"River, darling?" Polly's concerned voice pulls my eyes from the stage.

"Sorry, I know that was rude of me. They're just mesmerizing."

"That they are. But that's not all, is it? I can see there's something going on with you. Come on. Talk to me." She takes a sip from her glass and focuses all her attention on me.

"Polly, we haven't seen each other for far too long. I'm not going to bother you with all my problems."

Her deep stare and raised brow says a thousand things...

I won't accept that for an answer.

You better talk to me or I'm going to force it out of you.

Stop hiding things.

My people-reading skills were honed from experience, but they began with the woman in front of me. I sigh, knowing I won't get away with pretending everything is all sunshine and roses.

"Okay." I pick up my own glass and have more than just a sip, preparing myself for what is likely going to be a difficult conversation.

Polly has been a part of my life pretty much since the moment my parents died. She gave me a chance, an opportunity, has helped keep me safe, and given me more advice than I know what to do with, so trusting her is easy. We may not be as close as I am with my family, for obvious reasons, but that's what she is. She's basically family. The kind that you see a few times a year, acting as though you've never been apart, then not seeing or speaking to each other again for a couple of months.

So, I tell her everything. From the Ambrosios, to Nathaniel, and even the whole, I'm actually really a Volpe mafia princess thing. She nods at all the right moments, not interrupting and allowing me to get the words out. I skip over what exactly happened in Naples, but she gets the idea: It wasn't pretty.

When I'm done, both our glasses empty, fresh ones waiting, I slump back in the seat, exhausted.

Polly takes a few moments, slowly sipping at her martini before resting her eyes on me.

"Well, that's quite a lot. No wonder you're away with the fairies. There has never been any reasoning with those Ambrosios."

"You knew them?"

"Of course I did. You don't get to be around New York City for as long as I have without knowing people, my girl." She's hiding something from me. It's not obvious, but I caught the small tick in her eye just now.

"Polly, what is it you're not telling me?" It's best to just be honest. I'm not about beating around the bush to get answers.

Her eyes widen at the question before her whole body deflates in a way I've never seen her do before. She's always so regal in her posture and this is new, which means that whatever she's hiding must be quite big.

Fuck.

What is it with all these big reveals?

Secrets are the devil.

"I knew your grandparents. Your grandmother was actually a very good friend of mine." Even though she's deflated, she still holds that air of grace about her, but there's also a little sadness behind her eyes.

"Well, I wasn't expecting that." I get a sinking feeling in my gut that almost tastes like betrayal, even though my brain is telling me otherwise. All of these years and she knew? "Why didn't you ever tell me?" I barely recognize my own voice, like a disappointed child finding out Santa was just a great big sham.

"Your grandmother made me promise to look out for you if anything ever happened to her. She knew the Ambrosios weren't trustworthy and thought making a betrothal for you with the Mancini family would deter them, but it only seemed to anger them, and well, you know what happened next." Polly reaches out, placing her hand on mine and squeezing her fingers in a show of support. "I almost told you a hundred times, River. But then something would remind me of what happened to your grandmother and your parents and I just..." Her eyes dart to the stage but she's not looking at the dancers making dreams come true, she's somewhere else, in another time completely. "I couldn't put you in that kind of danger. So, I watched you and made sure you were safe. Frank was supposed to be one of your safe keepers, but I guess I failed on that note."

I can't stay mad at this woman for trying to protect me. If I did, I'd have to put a giant cross to Marco as well and that's not happening. Ever.

"I get it, Polly. I really do. I just wish I'd been armed with the knowledge, you know? Like, having that information may have prepared me for all of this shit happening to me. I mean, these Ambrosios really have it out for me." Squeezing her hand in return to let her know it's all good, I shake my head at the thought of Ugo and Elizabeth wanting to kill me for something they'll essentially never have... Marco.

And don't get me started on Nathaniel. What's going on with that?

"Truth be told, the Ambrosios have always been a giant bag of dicks." She chuckles and sips at her drink again.

I laugh, because hearing something like that come out of Polly's mouth is like the Queen of England saying fuck. And the distraction is wholly welcome.

"You're not wrong, Polly. So, you only gave me a job in the club when I was seventeen because of my grandmother?" I'm not salty about it. Far too much has happened lately for this to be something I allow to bother me in any way, I'm just curious.

"I did. When I heard they had passed away, I sought you out, which wasn't easy, considering your parents rarely had a fixed address, and then you basically avoided the system with Everest. But I have my ways, as you well know. I never expected you to get into the escorting side of things, but I was never going to stop you from becoming who you wanted to be either. I just guided you a little along the way. Much like I do with all of my girls."

"Well, thank you, Polly." I hold my glass up to clink against hers in a toast of gratitude.

"I'm glad Eleonor got what she deserved, by the way. She's had that coming for years. Your face will heal, but her soul was always destined for the dirt. I remember the job for her husband all those years ago. It was just an arm candy job, where you had to look pretty and hang off his every word all night. He was purposefully trying to piss off his wife and it turns out he did a spectacular job, I guess. To the point where she killed him and played it off as suicide. She even went as far as to forge a suicide note that essentially said he felt so guilty for his open infidelity, he could no longer live with himself."

"How do you know all of that?"

"Research, darling. Even once a job is complete, you keep an eye on those big clients. I knew it wasn't suicide from the moment I read about his death online. Not with the way he had spoken to me. He planned more bookings, but obviously never got around to keeping them."

"Wow, I guess I need to up my research game. I've been trying to keep on top of the current client lists we have, getting to know them. We've recently opened up to new clients, but only after they've been vetted by me personally."

She smiles and it fills me with warmth because that's the kind of smile my mother would give me when I finished any task.

"Your grandmother would be so proud of the woman you've become, River Rose Fox-Mancini." We both drink, placing our glasses down as she takes a deep breath. "You do need to be wary, though. I don't know them personally, but the Ambrosio twins are known to be devious."

"Twins?"

"Elizabeth and Ugo are twins, but it's not a widely known fact among the families. No idea why they kept it a secret, but now you know."

Polly's dropping some bombs this evening.

"I'll be careful, I promise."

"Good. Now, you've been married to that delicious man for a while. When shall I expect a mini-Mancini on the way?" She wags her brows, encouraging me to answer, and I almost spit my drink out.

"Erm, definitely not any time soon. Petal is due in just over a month though, so I'm going to be an aunt. Which is perfectly good enough for me. I get to dote on the little thing and give them back again when I'm finished.

Win-win." It's that dreaded question I've heard about that all married women of my age get asked, and I don't understand why it's such a thing. Marriage doesn't automatically equal babies. We are simply two people who fell in love and got married, not in that order—okay, maybe not so simply, but whatever.

"Oh, yes. I remember you telling me Petal was pregnant. How is she?"

Nice swerve on the subject there, Polly.

"She's great. We met her doula the other day too, Lydia. She's perfect for them, actually."

"Evening, ladies."

We both look up and, to my surprise, standing there in slacks and a deep blue shirt, bottle of beer in hand, is Kai.

"Oh, hello, young man. You must be Kai. It's a pleasure to meet you. I'm Polly."

He looks a little taken aback at her forwardness as she offers him her hand, but it's only brief and he kisses her knuckles like she's royalty. He shrugs his shoulders at me like he has no fucking clue what he's doing, that dimple on his cheek more prominent now as he smiles; he's clearly done some face-scaping.

"River, darling, it's been a pleasure, as always. I'll see you again soon. Charles is waiting outside for me." I stand as Polly leans over to air kiss my cheeks.

"Are you sure you have to go?"

"Don't leave on my account, ma'am."

Kai and I speak at the same time and Polly chuckles as she ties a black scarf around her neck.

"It's okay. Eight in the evening for a woman my age is almost time for herbal tea and bed." She winks at me and I know damn well what she'll be doing. Waving, or more like wiggling her fingers at us, she heads toward the exit through the throng of tables.

"It's alright in here, Riv." Kai slides into the booth next to me and clinks my glass with his bottle.

"Don't get me wrong, it's great to see you, but what are you doing here?"

"Job in the city finishes next week and I got my divorce papers filed, so thought I should at least come in and have a drink at my best friend's club while I'm still here."

"Congratulations! You know you can still visit from Staten Island, right?"

"Yeah, but it's easier having somewhere to stay close by. Not a fan of the ferry after a few of these." He tips his beer at me and I laugh, because I get it. All that sloshing about is not a good mix with alcohol.

"How did you know I'd be here? It's not exactly working hours."

"You didn't answer your phone and I worried, so I asked your husband where you were." He smirks.

"You did what now?" My eyes could probably fall out of my head in this moment because that is not something I thought would *ever* happen. I know they did a bit of man-bonding on the Fourth of July last month, but woah.

"It's okay, Riv. We're cool. He told me where to find you, said you were having drinks with another old friend."

He's watching the stage as a trio of burlesque ladies begin a routine to *Fever*. I love when they do this one, the classic music with a good old fashioned dance routine always brings the girls great tips. Checking my phone, I see two missed calls from Kai and a couple of texts from Marco.

Husband: Fine, I'll take my own pictures tonight. *Winky tongue out emoji*

He's such a horny pre-teen sometimes.

Husband: Your hippy friend is on the way.
Husband: Have fun, wife.

I choose to ignore him, because I have no doubt he's already sitting in a corner of the club somewhere, watching over me like the possessive caveman he is. I'd berate him for it, because no man will control me in that way, but I also think it's kind of sweet—and I couldn't give two shits if outsiders believe that's a little fucked up.

"That shorter one is hot." Kai nods to the dancing trio on the stage with a grin.

"She's also married and has two kids at home."

"You know I've got a thing for married women." He laughs, and while I know he's joking around, I have to acknowledge the truth behind it, because I'm not a dumb ass. I'm aware of his feelings toward me.

He's not wrong, we are soulmates, but not in the way he believes we are, or the way I once thought we were. Soulmates can mean so much more than just lovers.

"Yeah, yeah. The brunette on the left is single though. Her name's Natalie if you want me to pass your number on."

"Seriously? Hell yeah."

We both laugh and I roll my eyes. To be fair, they'd be a good match.

"How are you doing, anyway, Psyche?"

"You really can't call me that anymore, Kai. But I'm fine. Coping, you know."

"Don't worry, I don't dislike Marco... too much. And you don't have to be brave with me. I'm here for whatever you need, okay?"

He nudges me gently and I know he's being genuine, the glint in his honey eyes is clear as day. Well, as clear as it's going to be in a dimly-lit club.

We spend the next hour forgetting about all the crap and watching the various routines on stage. Burlesque night is one of my favorites, the music so easy to get lost in. Spending this time with Kai is refreshing, a nice change from all of us as a group, and it only cements my feelings.

I love him with all my heart.

As my best friend.

CHAPTER EIGHTEEN

MARCO

It was late when Hippie Kai dropped by asking where my wife was hiding. My first instinct was to drop kick him and tell him to go look for his own damn wife. Then I remembered we have somewhat of a truce going on, which basically entails I don't put him six-feet under and he respects my marriage by not being a love sick puppy every time River is around.

I never promised I wouldn't have eyes on him, though. I trust only a handful of people in this world and he's not one of them, for obvious reasons. That said, I don't think he's a bad guy, per se. Misguided? Surely. A royal fuck-up? Probably. But evil? No. I've seen evil up close and personal and he's not it.

"You wanted to see me, Boss?" Enzo walks into my office at the hotel without knocking. On nights where River is at the club, I catch up at the hotel. Keeping the same hours as she does ensures that we have free time together.

When I lift my eyes to ask him where the fuck he's been for the last two weeks, I'm shocked into silence.

"What the fuck happened to you?" My question is logical. There's no way to ignore his swollen right eye and broken nose. Dropping my gaze to his hands, my guess is confirmed when I see his knuckles are cut up and so red they look like they're still bleeding.

With a shrug, he drops into the chair across from my desk and just stares at me, like that's answer enough.

It fucking is not.

I may be his boss but he's also my friend, almost a brother to me.

After a stare down worthy of a spaghetti western, he finally answers with an added eye-roll to boot. "There's a fight club in Jersey. I go there sometimes. It's no big deal."

Leaning back against my high-back chair, I steeple my fingers and rest them against my mouth. I'm reining in my anger, taking control of my temper, as I breathe in and out at regular intervals. Enzo watches me, his eagle eyes and sharp mind knowing exactly what I'm doing, yet he just sits back, head cocked and legs spread like he's expecting some young thing to walk in and give him a blowjob.

"So, here I am, debating my next move." My voice is low and even, my fury on a tight leash because I know he's dealing with what happened in Naples in the only way he knows how. Except, as much as it hurts to have witnessed Lina's rape, she's the one who lived it. She's the one who lost a piece of herself that night. "I could end you or I could be lenient. The jury is still out."

Enzo doesn't even flinch at my words. Death doesn't scare him. In fact, he probably welcomes it at this point.

"Lina—" I begin but Enzo cuts me off.

"Do not fucking bring her into this." The low growl he uses to address me surprises me. He's only ever spoken to me and my family with the utmost respect, but I've touched a nerve and his response only confirms my suspicions. He blames himself. He blames me. Probably blames River above all else and I'm going to have to nip this in the bud or else I'll be forced to kill him.

I stand, my palms pressing against my desk, my face devoid of all emotions as I lean in and remind him of who the fuck he's talking to. "I'm going to let that slide because I was there and I know why you're being a selfish asshole."

Enzo blinks, a semblance of his humanity coming back for a brief second before it's gone again.

"But, Enzo, you listen to me and you listen good. Lina…" I pause, hoping he won't interrupt again. I'm not above adding more bruises to his face for his disrespect. "She's not okay and you being gone for weeks at a time getting your ass beat like a fucking rookie is not helping. So, here's the thing." I straighten to my full height and slide my hands into the pockets of my dress slacks, my eyes boring holes into my second in command. "You either get your shit together or disappear completely. You choose right now. But just so we're clear, if you disappear you don't ever get in contact with my sister again or I will slit your throat myself." I'm hoping for the former. I'm really fucking hoping he'll get his shit together and deal with this in a way that won't push my sister even further down the hole of despair.

Time is suspended in those seconds we hold each other's gazes. He's weighing his options, it's clear in the tension of his jaw and the creases at the corners of his eyes. It's only when he flexes his knuckles, opening and closing his fists like he needs the pain to remind him that he's still alive and has a fucking job to do.

I wait. Patience has never been my strong point, but River has taught me that good things come to those who don't run into a burning building before assessing all possible risks.

"You need more bags in the gym at home. And maybe a sparring partner."

On the outside, I don't react to Enzo's words. I'll let out my breath later when I'm alone and realize how fucking close I came to killing someone I love. But the fact that he's just promised, in his own way, that he's going to pick up the pieces in a less dangerous way, gives me hope for the future.

"Done. Now, what do we know? What are the streets saying?" I sit back down in my chair and get my mind back to business.

"The Greeks are keeping Ugo in one of their safehouses in Queens. I don't think Yiannis knows, from what my sources are saying. This is Aleko's doing." Tapping the pad of my fingers to my lips, I digest this new information, opting for the less bloody scenario but not excluding painting the entire borough in red if that's what it takes to weasel Ugo out of hiding.

"I'm not surprised, to be honest. Yiannis is content with what he's got, but his brother has always been a greedy motherfucker." The Greeks and my family have always tiptoed around each other. Ever since Don Kastellanos, the brothers' father, put a hit out on my grandfather decades ago. He got too cocksure, thinking the Ambrosios would have their backs. They didn't, because they're fucking sewer rats to the core, choosing the safe camp and siding with our family. Old Kastellanos lost his head in a very Marie Antoinette moment because my grandpop was all about sending messages in the ways of the old country.

After the brothers took over, there was a round table of the dons, a peace treaty of sorts, and Yiannis had proven to be the reasonable one, whereas Aleko pulled at the bit, always demanding more. I guess the apple didn't fall too far from the rotting tree.

"I've got ears in place. One of their cooks is a second cousin to J's most trusted soldier." I remember that. My father had anticipated shit going south a few years ago and placed dormant spies all over The City, planting them in various big families. The useless fucks in the Ambrosio family did fuck-all to help us. If they hadn't been killed in the shoot-out in Naples, I'd end them right now for their lack of loyalty.

"Keep him close, I don't want another slacker on the job or worse, a double agent." But something nags at me about the Greek brothers and I realize that we've been communicating by proxy. It's maybe time to look each other in the eye and assess. "Do me a favor. Set up a meeting; me, the brothers, you, and a couple of men. Choose a date for next week."

"You sure about this? We don't have much leverage." Enzo is typing on his phone, probably getting the message out that I want to sit down with the Kastellanos clan.

"Not yet, we don't. But we will tonight. I want you to destroy their warehouse on the dock. The one where they stash their new arrivals. Make it big and showy. I want it on the fucking six o'clock news with every fucking talking head blabbing about it." Then I'll have my leverage. "Make sure they get my message."

Enzo pauses his typing and looks up at me, his eyes alight with the fire they've been missing.

"We get Ugo, they get peace." He nods at his own words.

"Yes. If I don't get Ugo, I will burn down every fucking warehouse they own across the whole of the five boroughs. And once that's done, I'll fucking kill them myself." Truer words have never been spoken.

I am Marco fucking Mancini and these pieces of shit fucked with the wrong family.

Foxy Wife: I'm about to head home, need anything?

Me: I need you to stay put, I'll be right there;

Foxy Wife: Okay, Caveman husband. Don't forget your club *baseball bat emoji*

Me: I bet you won't be smart-mouthing me tomorrow morning when your *peach emoji* is so red you can't sit down.

What the actual fuck am I doing?

I scroll through our text messages and realize I've been using a fuckton more emojis in our conversations than any don ever should. If anyone were to find out it would kill my street cred.

I can just imagine the conversations with the soldiers in the field.

Oh hey look, it's Don Mancini, be careful or he might emoji you straight down to the bottom of the Hudson.

Fucking ridiculous. Yet, here I am, chuckling at my peach emoji and thinking that a good spanking on my wife's delicious ass is my greatest idea today.

By the time I arrive at Rapture, I've got four different scenes I'd like to play out with River, one of which she's gagging on my cock while I devour her pussy and fuck her ass with her own dildo.

"Sir."

I nod at River's chief of security, giving her a grateful smile.

"Mimi, how are you?" We shake hands and, with a conspiratorial smile, she tilts her head toward the back corner.

"Good, sir, thank you. She's over there and he's been respectful as far as I know, so no beat down tonight."

I grin.

"Oh, the night is young, Mimi. The night is oh, so young."

River sees me before her little puppy does and I bring my index finger to my lips, not wanting to alert him. When I'm just behind him, I lean in and growl, "The last man to look at my wife like that stopped breathing. Forever."

Kai stills then shrugs. "Totally worth it."

It's a wonder I haven't made good on my promise but, dammit, the guy's growing on me. Although, I would never say it out loud and in front of witnesses I wasn't willing to kill myself.

"You'll have to excuse us. My *wife* and I have plans."

River chuckles, knowing exactly what I'm talking about since we were just texting about it, and Kai cringes because he's not a complete idiot and got my drift without any innuendos needed.

Standing, he hugs River and wiggles his eyebrows like he's won a set. The problem is that he's forgotten that I've already won the match and he's just watching the replay.

"Night, Kai, and remember, her name is Natalie and she would totally be into you." Patting his cheek like he's a good boy—puppy, not boy toy—River sways into me as I wrap my arm around her waist before leaning into Kai and giving him my final jab.

"Hippie-Kai-yay, motherfucker." River snorts at my play on words and when she looks up at me, I notice a spark in her eyes that I haven't seen in a long time. She enjoys this, me and her best friend sparring amicably.

"Har-har, Marco Corleone." Now my wife is outright laughing and I'm hoping it's because his joke was a big pile of shit.

"That's lame, Kai. You need to practice." I pull her away and we leave the club shortly after saying goodnight to a couple of members who stopped us along the way.

"Is this going to be a thing?"

Frowning, I look down at my wife just as we reach my car, the driver waiting at the wheel.

"What do you mean?" I open the car door, looking around to make sure no one is watching us.

"The film references and the banter between you two." Her words make it sound like it's a ridiculous idea, but her tone is so excited that I can't deny her this one thing she needs. Peace of mind that me and her family get along.

"Maybe. Depends on his level of culture. He'll need to up his game or I'll just get bored." I shrug and pull her into my side, pressing my nose to her hair and inhaling her sweet lavender scent.

"I love you, Marco Mancini."

"It's about time."

Chapter Nineteen

River

"Are you all ready for Marco's birthday tomorrow?"

Lina and I are in what feels like the millionth shop today and we've spent a small fortune on new shoes.

"I am. I can't say I'm looking forward to the whole mafia gathering thing in the evening, but at least I'll look badass in that outfit you made me buy." I nudge her shoulder with mine and we quietly chuckle as we take our seats at the table.

We're in the same restaurant as the last time we came out together and I have a sneaky feeling it has something to do with the blonde and buff chef—who is currently standing by the small bar area with a huge grin on his face as he watches Lina.

I feel slightly underdressed in my black denim cut-off shorts and heeled Timbs, considering this place is a little fancy—it doesn't give off casual cafe-diner vibes, that's for sure—but Lina's wearing jeans too, so I'm not alone.

The dirty blond makes his way to our table with two glasses of something pink in his hands. He has a natural swagger to his walk that I can appreciate would be drool-worthy to Lina. Her eyes haven't left him since we walked in.

"Alright, ladies? I'm not officially workin' today, but I'll make an exception for a chance to cook for you." He winks at Lina, who rolls her eyes with a smirk playing on her lips as he places the tall glasses in front of us.

I make eye contact with one of our bodyguards, Sam, letting her know this guy is nothing to worry about.

"You really don't have to. It won't make me change my mind."

"Oh, we'll see, sweetheart. Let Scarlett know when you're ready to order." He bows his head slightly, still grinning, before heading toward the kitchen through the double doors.

"Change your mind?" I raise a questioning brow at Lina.

"He's been texting me, insisting we have a date because I *need a cheeky Brit in my life*. And well, you know, I'm not exactly in a place where I want to be around men like that.

Enzo's been basically ignoring me and I've been basically ignoring Tyler." She shrugs, eyeing the menu and sipping at the pink thing Devon brought over. "Oh my God, this is delicious! You have to try it!"

Today is one of Lina's good days and I'm taking full advantage of this time with her, hoping it helps her in some way to feel a little normalcy. To be honest, it's good for me too, but seeing her like this is a major bonus.

"Mmm, yeah. This is nice! Tastes a little like grapefruit." I choose to drop the subject of her love life. It's none of my business and I know she'll talk when she's ready. We're not exactly in the right place for a conversation that could be a potential trigger for her. "Are you coming to the thing tomorrow?"

"I'm not sure yet. I'd like to, but... I don't know. We'll see. Anyway, what are we eating? Do you want to share a platter?"

"Why the Hell not? Let's go for it."

As we're finishing off the last of our food, Devon saunters over, now in his chef whites with the sleeves rolled up his heavily-tattooed forearms.

"How was it, ladies?"

"As delicious as last time, thank you. But don't pull that not paying thing on us again, okay?" I give him my best serious face, which currently consists of a smirk and two raised brows.

"Can't promise that, love."

I shake my head in defeat as his attention is back on Lina. I've got to give it to him, the man's a trier.

"You ready for me to take you on that date yet, sweetheart? Anywhere you wanna go, anything you wanna do?" He rests his hands on the edge of the table and leans forward, the veins in his painted forearms bulging, and I shake my head again. *He knows exactly what he's doing.*

"You really won't quit, will you?"

"Never." He winks at her again, blowing her a kiss before picking up our empty plates and taking them into the kitchen.

She's not outright saying no to him, which makes it clear that she likes him, but I can't deny her love-life is already complicated, even without all the other shit that's gone on. Lina laughs gently as he walks away and I love the small spark I see there. I kinda hope this Devon guy doesn't give up.

"Come on, you. The car's waiting on the next street over."

"I don't like him, you know?"

"Of course you don't, Gorgeous." I smile to myself as we head out and I leave cash on the table for our food, knowing we'd be waiting here for hours for no bill to arrive.

As we make it to the door, a huge, mammoth of a man is blocking our exit, dressed in a black suit with his arms folded across his chest. Two more huge men in black suits appear from behind him and I know this isn't good. The man on the left with a dodgy eighties-porn mustache steps forward, breaking their trio formation and pulling a gun from behind his back quicker than I can blink. The others do the same.

They're pointed at us and I'm not going to lie, I'm shitting myself, but also, I'm so fucked off with guns being pointed at me and feeling helpless.

"Got a message for Mr. Mancini."

"Well I think you must be confused then, because neither of us are Mr. Mancini." I trust that Sam and Ryan, our appointed security for the day, have our backs, because I'm all bark and no bite in the weapons department.

"Don't get smart with me, Mrs. Mancini. You tell your husband that we don't give a fuck about peace. We're not giving up Ugo."

At the mention of his name, I hear Lina inhale a sharp breath beside me and I grip her hand, squeezing it in mine.

"What in the actual fuck is going on here? Who the fuck do you think you are pulling a gun in my restaurant?" Devon saunters over, changed back into his slacks and deep-purple shirt, as if people holding guns up all around us is just a walk in the park.

Sam and Ryan are just in front of us, their own guns raised at the three intruders, at a stand-off because I presume no one really wants to start a shoot-out in the middle of Manhattan. The restaurant may be otherwise empty, and the mirrored windows basically blacked out from the outside in, but guns are loud.

"This has nothing to do with you, scum. If you know what's good for you, you'll fuck off back to the kitchen." Mustache guy looks bored as he barely makes eye contact with Devon.

With the guy distracted and feeling a little over confident—but fuck it—I quickly step forward, grip the guy's wrist, trying to grab the gun, and knee him in the balls. The gun falls to the floor, which is a massive fail, but he's now bent forward, clutching at his crotch and yelling out in pain. My hand is still gripping his wrist tightly, and I use the other one to yank his head toward mine.

"I don't do threats. And neither does my husband. I suggest you three scurry the fuck out of here because, as you can see, you aren't the only ones with guns." Then I let my knee meet his face, because it's right there, so why not?

"You fucking bitch!"

"Oh, so original." I push him away and take a step back, realizing Lina had followed my lead and now has one of the guys in a chokehold with his gun pressed against his head. Sam and Ryan have their guns both pointed at the largest man and he slowly lowers his, knowing he's absolutely going to die if he even tries to pull the trigger. Devon is still standing off to the side, a little pride on his face as he twirls a kitchen knife that appeared from nowhere in his hand.

"You'll regret this." Mustache guy spits out a little blood from his broken nose, gesturing for the others to follow him out.

"You've got to let him go now, sweetheart." Devon approaches and gently lifts Lina's arms from the man, letting her keep the gun but allowing the man to leave with the others. He trips the man up as he scrambles for breath and tries to hurry out. "Whoops." He laughs and brings Lina into him, wrapping his arms around her, and she lets him.

It's clear to see the soft and content look on her face as she's held by him after another fucked up life-moment.

Sam holds her fist out to me, a look of respect in her eyes, and I obviously bump it. My plan wasn't to drop the gun, and thankfully the safety was on and it didn't go off, but I think I got my point across.

I will not be walked all over.

Wearing a red knee-length pencil dress, I'm sitting beside Marco in the bar of his SoHo hotel. It's nearly the end of the evening and the capos have just finished paying their respects with birthday gifts for their don.

Ray "The Stinger" gave him a small case of cigars, "Babyface" Tommy gave him a new shotgun—who the fuck gives someone a shotgun for their birthday? Eddy "Snake-Eyes" gave him a bottle of super-expensive-looking whiskey, and J has just given him a large dagger. I watch as he pulls a penny from the hilt, flicking it in the air where J catches it one-handed. Each of them all do the whole respectful nod thing to each other and it's like some kind of strange ceremony.

Will my next birthday be like this?

Marco squeezes my thigh, leaning over to kiss my neck. "Shall we get out of here, Tesoro? One more toast and my duty is over."

"It's your night, baby. Whatever you want to do."

"I want you to call me baby again while I eat you out."

"Such a romantic."

"Always for you, Tesoro."

He pulls away and raises his whiskey glass, gaining the attention of all the capos and the few soldiers around the room. "Salute."

"Salute," they all respond, and everyone downs whatever drink they have left, cheering and slamming glasses down.

We leave the bar with lots of back patting and half hugs for Marco on the way out as they wish him a happy birthday.

"Why aren't we going to the exit?"

"We're in the new honeymoon suite tonight, Tesoro. It was the last room to be renovated and I want to christen it with my wife." He guides me toward the elevator and pushes me inside as it opens.

Before I have a chance to speak, Marco shoves me against the wall and his lips are against mine as the doors close behind us.

"I've been waiting for this all night." His words are whispered over my mouth between nips and licks. He bends and pulls the skirt of my dress up and over my hips while maintaining the bruising kiss as he rubs against my clit, finding me plenty wet for him already.

Two fingers are pushed inside my pussy, and I gasp at the welcome intrusion. He bends them just right, using his palm against my clit, moving his lips down to suck and nip at my jaw then neck.

My orgasm builds from the tips of my toes, growing up and through my stomach as he adds another finger. His other hand is in my hair, massaging my head and keeping me exactly where he wants me as his lips are back on mine, capturing my moans of pleasure.

It hits me a little unexpectedly when one of his fingers brushes against my asshole and my whole body shudders at the sensations. The vibrations of his chest against mine are addictive. Every time this man makes me come, it sends fireworks off in my brain.

The doors ping open and, luckily, there isn't anybody around as Marco lifts me and carries me out with my legs wrapped around his waist. We continue to kiss all the way down the hall, even while he uses the keycard to unlock the room.

I pay zero attention to the space around us, because right now I'm focused on my husband. It is his birthday, after all. We go through another door, and he places me on the bed before unbuttoning his shirt and unzipping his pants—I could watch him undress all day and never get bored of the sight before me—and I smile as I stare at the tattoo on his ribs. Now that I know what it means, it has a special place in my heart for my own personal stalker.

There is a silver dome over a tray on the table in the corner of the room and a tall can of whipped cream, giving me the best idea.

"Stand at the end of the bed for me, Husband." I get up and move over to the tray as he watches me with a lust-filled gaze, saying nothing, a smirk firmly planted on his face.

I strip off my dress, leaving me in fishnet stockings and nothing else, before picking up the can of whipped cream. Walking back over to the bed, I squirt a little in my mouth as I get on my knees in front of him, pressing the nozzle and watching as streams of whipped cream shoot out along his shaft. Like it's the best dessert in the world, I lick at the cream, moaning as I suck it all off, looking up at him through my lashes.

He looks like he's struggling to maintain any semblance of control as he takes a deep breath and holds my cheeks, encouraging me to stand.

"It's my birthday, Tesoro, and I'm hungry for my dessert." Once I'm standing, he switches our positions and pushes me back onto the bed, not wasting any time in spreading my legs apart. Somehow, he's got ahold of the whipped cream, and he squirts it over my nipples, down my stomach, and around my belly button, then he squirts some more along the inside of my thighs.

"Hands above your head, no interfering with my birthday treat."

I do as he says with no argument. My husband is a master with his tongue.

He slowly licks up one of my thighs, whispering the tips of his fingers along the outside, moving across my stomach and latching onto my right nipple. He sucks all the cream off before moving on to the other nipple, swirling his tongue around and gripping it between his teeth. My back arches off the bed in ecstasy as he tastes me all over, his hands constantly massaging and gripping at my hips, my ass, and my breasts.

Letting my nipple out of his mouth with a pop, his tongue trails back down my stomach. Then he begins again at my other knee and continues all the way up the thigh with cream still on it. When he reaches the top, he takes his time, licking my lips, gently flicking his tongue over my clit before sucking it into his mouth, hard, as he shoves two fingers inside me.

He holds me down with his other hand against my lower stomach, only adding to all the sensations as that hand rises and begins playing with my nipple. My second orgasm hits even quicker than the first and I can't help but yell out, "Oh, yes, Baby!"

"Good girl."

I feel him grin against my pussy as he laps me up, my clit pulsing like it has its own heartbeat. Then, he climbs up my body, lining himself up and planting his mouth on mine again, making me taste myself on him, and I love it, trying to top from the bottom, lifting my pelvis up to meet him and encouraging him to put his cock inside me.

"My birthday, my rules. Turn over."

"Yes, sir." I smirk and move to my front, my chest against the bed, and my knees underneath me so my ass is in the air for him.

"So fucking beautiful." His words are barely a growl as he lines himself up again and pushes inside me. His thrusts are powerful as he grips my hips, leaving the best kind of bruises as our bodies slap together with the most delicious sound.

He reaches around with one hand and grasps my breast, encouraging me to lift my back up to meet his chest. Kissing my neck and holding me tightly against him, he continues to thrust into me and our sweat mingles together, just as our sounds do as they echo around the room. He brings his hand up from my breast to collar my neck, his other hand moving around the front of me to play with my clit as he nips at my earlobe.

His heavy breaths and all the sensations are quickly sending me into orgasm number three and I never want it to stop.

"Come for me, Tesoro."

I don't need telling twice.

I explode around him, screaming out my release, and warmth fills me as he lets go at the same time. His movements become softer, slower, and our breaths become the only sound filling the silence.

"Happy birthday, Husband."

Chapter Twenty
Marco

After River told me about the Greek ambush at the restaurant and her security detail wrote up the report for me to have, I decided those fuckers needed a visit.

They refused. Apparently, they have nothing to say to me.

Today, however, I'm meeting with the Greek brothers after they realized I wasn't fucking around.

It would seem that their central shipping warehouse had faulty wiring, which explains the fact it's now burnt down to the ground. Completely unsalvageable.

"I don't trust them. Who's to say they won't put a bullet in our heads the minute we march in there?" Enzo is driving us, his white-knuckled grip on the wheel a clear sign of his emotions. For once, he's not beaten to a pulp. Only a fading bruise around his eye remains, which is fine. Black eyes are common in our world.

"They won't." I reassure, but he's not hearing me.

"And how the fuck could you possibly know that?" We're headed across the Queensboro Bridge, which seems like a complete waste of time.

"Why don't you take the Midtown Tunnel? It's a straight line from there." I know what he's going to say because we have this conversation every time we have business in Queens.

"I don't trust tunnels and I sure as fuck ain't gonna pay for them." Christ, he's impossible. "Now, tell me, why aren't you worried?"

Taking out my phone, I check the extra cameras we had installed since returning from Italy to make sure everything is quiet at the house.

"I sent Yiannis pictures of every single one of his warehouses, letting him know those *also* have faulty wiring." Enzo chuckles but it only lasts a second before his mask slips right back into place. "I need you to keep your shit together. Aleko is a crazy motherfucker and highly unpredictable, so I need you to be alert and clear-headed."

With a snort, he rolls his eyes like an annoying teenager. "When have I not been alert?"

"*And* clear-headed?" I raise a brow and allow the silence to gnaw at him. Since Naples, his brain has been muddy and I get it, but now is not the time to dive into his emotions.

"Fair point."

I barely hear his response but that's fine, I don't need any more than that.

Fifteen minutes later, we're pulling up at the docks with two SUVs behind us filled with our men. I may have taken assurances by instructing my men to place linear shaped charges on the steel bars of the warehouses in case we don't make it out, but that doesn't mean I'm going to go in without back-up.

Yiannis greets us outside, his arms open wide as he makes his way to us. From the outside, it looks like we're friends or family, but the tension between the two groups is palpable.

"Marco! It's been a long time." He offers a hand for me to shake, our eyes fixed on one another, with Aleko only two steps behind him. Physically, they look alike with their dark hair and eyes, although Aleko's are more hazel than dark brown like Yiannis's. Hell, we all share Mediterranean blood so, in a way, we could all be mistaken as family. But where Yiannis has an air of class about him—a nice suit and an expensive haircut—Aleko looks like he's been hanging out with bikers and ignoring his barber.

"Yiannis." I shift my gaze to his younger brother. "Aleko." I don't trust either of them but contrary to Yiannis, Aleko is missing the empathy gene and got a double dose of the narcissist one. He's a fucking menace to the human race.

"Come, come. Let's discuss business inside. I find the heat in this country to be unbearable. At home," he looks over at me as though we're about to bond over the fucking weather just because our two countries are a stone's throw away. "Our houses are built to withstand the hot days. Here, it's all about air conditioning."

He's not wrong, though.

As soon as we settle inside an open-plan office, Enzo stays standing at the main entrance while I take a seat on the loveseat, arms spanning the length of the back and legs crossed, ankle over knee.

"I don't appreciate your men threatening my wife, Yiannis." My voice is calm but deadly.

"We don't appreciate you giving us an ultimatum." My eyes fall on Aleko, who is against the wall, one leg bent with a foot pressed behind him, typing on his phone like we're not having a crucial meeting that could end in a massacre. With his head bent, the longer strands of his hair fall to about his cheek bones, right where his prominent five o'clock shadow begins.

"Hmm, right. Well, I don't take too kindly to your helping our enemies kidnap me and raping my fucking sister." I can't disguise the venom that seeps through my words, my hard stare boring a hole through Aleko's skull.

"You have to know, we had nothing to do with that." Yiannis frowns, shaking his head vehemently. When I look at his brother though, a small smile hitches at the corner of his mouth as he continues to tap out messages on his phone, his thumbs flying across the keyboard.

From the corner of my eye, I detect movement and I know Enzo saw it too, which means he's about to rip the guy's tongue out of his mouth.

I stand, intercepting my right-hand man with a palm to his heaving chest.

"I don't. But here is what I do know. Ugo and Elizabeth Ambrosio kidnapped me and my man, here, flew us to Naples, tortured us, then when shit wasn't going their way, Ugo raped my sister right in front of my eyes." Yiannis doesn't flinch, in fact it's as if he's looking right through me, like he'd rather be anywhere else but here. I'm not surprised, to be honest, I've been groomed my entire life to see this family as the enemy, the heartless monsters who had my grandfather slaughtered. However, right now, I need them because my hatred for Ugo surpasses my family feud.

When I look over to Aleko, I don't see an ounce of emotion in his features.

"You know we do not condone this kind of behavior," the older man assures me, but my jaw ticks knowing his younger brother has no such qualms.

"You, maybe, but Aleko surely doesn't give a fuck. Do you?" I'm addressing him now, my fury unmistakable.

"You're right, I don't." At Aleko's words I have to steel my spine and push Enzo in the other direction to avoid an all-out war right here and now.

"Yiannis, keep your dog on a leash or I will fucking end him right here and now." Okay, so maybe I'm not in complete control of my emotions.

"*Fkale zilikourti.*" Yiannis addresses his brother then turns to us. "Look, we can give you Elizabeth's location but we don't know where Ugo is. He's not in one specific spot and, to be honest, we don't really care. Our business with him is done."

I remain standing, hands in my pockets like I have not a worry in my world, and nod like I'm considering his offer.

I'm not.

"We think we know where Elizabeth is. It's Ugo we want." Enzo grunts beside me like a fucking caveman, which is exactly what he'll be when he gets his hands on that piece of shit.

The brothers have a short conversation in Greek while I watch their body language. Yiannis is firm, his stare unwavering and his mouth tight with displeasure. He doesn't like being in a position of defense. It's not a comfortable spot to be in. Aleko looks bored with his heavy lids and slouched posture.

The fucker shrugs like this whole fucking situation is an inconvenience to him but when he raises his dark browns to meet my grays, all I see is pure evil with his narrowed eyes and sardonic grin. I can't wait to kill this fucker.

"We'll find Ugo and give you his location. Elizabeth, too." He pauses, but I don't answer, knowing damn well there's going to be an ask that follows. "We hear the port in Naples has been taken over by the loyalists to the Volpe family. That's you, correct?"

He's got my attention now and I don't fucking like where he's going with this.

"Yes." I don't bother correcting him because I don't want to offer any information he may not have... like my wife's true identity.

"We need safe passage of merchandise through Naples so we can fan out from there to the rest of the continent."

I don't think it would be too difficult to arrange this but, deep down, I don't want to. I don't want to ask for a favor this early in the game and I sure as fuck do not want to give these assholes free access to my home country.

"That can be arranged. But no deal until I have Ugo."

Both brothers nod but I don't fucking trust that snake to not come around and bite me.

"Deal." They both stand, but only Yiannis shakes my hand in good faith.

I don't like it.

Staring right at Aleko, I point my finger and make sure he understands my words clearly.

"You fuck with me or my wife and I don't give a fuck what deal we have on the table, I will carve your heart out and feed it to you." And because he's a fucking psycho, Aleko licks his lips and makes a slurping sound in guise of an answer.

"You have my word, Marco."

I turn to Yiannis and nod at his words.

"Fucking better."

"No, River, you cannot name your gun."

We're at the shooting range in Midtown so River can feel safer handling a gun. She's still having nightmares about the shit that went down in Naples and, of course, the fact that she accidentally shot one of our own. Despite having apologized to him and offering him the moon and half the stars, she still has guilt sitting at the pit of her stomach. I figured if she knew how to handle a gun properly, she could at least be reassured if she ever found herself in the same situation.

God fucking forbid.

"Well, that's just stupid. It's an intimate toy, or whatever, we should name them." The gun I bought her is still in the box, she hasn't picked it up yet, but she loves the fact that it's a smaller gun she could easily conceal in her purse. Also, I had it custom made, which means my wife has a black and pink Ruger LC9 that she will learn to use here, at the range, until I feel she's ready to have it with her at all times.

"Tesoro, it's not a toy. Jesus Christ, woman, proper vocabulary saves lives." I pinch her chin between my thumb and index finger until her pretty green eyes are focused on me, only. "This is not a toy and you will be responsible with it at all fucking times. Am I clear?" She licks her lips and gives me a smile that instantly makes my dick rock hard.

"This whole teaching moment you've got going is turning me on. We should role play." I kiss her, hard, bruising our lips and sucking on her tongue.

"Behave." I release her and when she sticks her lip out to pout, I swear to fuck my dick swells even more. "I will spank that ass as soon as we get home."

"Promise?" Fuck, her grin is my entire life.

"Prometto, Tesoro. Now, let's get to work."

We go through the rules and etiquette at the firing range. The proper ways of holding a gun and placing it on any given surface. Once, she turned to face me with the gun pointed straight at my chest and I saw my entire life flash before my eyes.

It took her only thirty minutes to hit the target, another twenty to hit the center... once.

Progress.

When she started getting tired of the noise and the kickback, we cleaned our guns and secured them in the safe before going for coffee.

"You never told me how the meeting went with the cockadoodles."

I almost choke on my coffee, not just because the temperature should be illegal on the whole of the planet, but because my wife is a gem.

"The Kastellanos?" Wiping the drops of coffee off my chin, I can't help but chuckle.

"Whatever. Those motherfuckers do not deserve that I call them anything." She swipes three packets of sugar and spills them into her cup. I frown.

"First of all, that's a ridiculous amount of sugar to put in coffee, even if it's as disgusting as this one." She shrugs, not at all caring that I'm chastising her like a wayward child.

My phone vibrates in my jeans so I take it out and see Enzo has the address for Elizabeth. Good, now we're getting somewhere. When I look back up at my wife, she's frowning at me.

"What's wrong?" I'm on instant alert when she's not smiling.

"Nothing, I'm just waiting on two." It's my turn to frown.

"What do you mean?"

"You said 'first of all' so I'm waiting on the second of all." I chuckle again and watch as she takes a sip of her coffee, her face scrunching up seconds later. "You're right, it's disgusting, but we've got Stefano at home making the best coffee the world has ever tasted. We're snobs, don't forget that."

Fuck, I love this woman.

"Second of all," I lean in, take her hand in mine, and kiss her ring finger where her wedding band screams that she's mine. "You'll need to be punished for your language."

Rolling her eyes, she meets me halfway across the table and whispers like we're spies and this conversation is confidential. "Is it punishment if I like it?"

"Good point." With a peck on the lips, I sit back and fill her in on the conversation with Yiannis and Aleko.

"Al Caponos sounds like a real piece of work..." She's putting on a brave face with her jokes and sarcastic commentary but underneath it all, I see the shadows behind her eyes, the worry that lies in waiting there.

"Yeah, but we kind of need them, don't we?"

"So, I was thinking." I look up at her words, curious about her take. "What if, instead of going all mafia and shit, we report Elizabeth to some kind of international police?"

"Interpol?" I don't know how I feel about that. Getting any kind of police involved with our business is always dangerous.

"Yeah. I mean, she had you kidnapped and taken across international borders, right? And since she's an Italian national, wouldn't they have jurisdiction?" I think about it, but I need to speak with Stefano and my mother to get their take on this.

"I get that you want her to pay and I'm guessing dying is too easy, but my first concern is keeping our family—the entirety of it, from you all the way down to my soldiers—safe." I reach out, caressing her fingers and looking around to make sure we're still out of ear shot from the other three patrons in the coffee shop.

"Yeah, I know. Will you consider it?" She's the yin to my fucking yang so of course I'll consider it. Whether or not it's possible is an entirely different story.

"It depends." She frowns at my serious tone.

"On what?"

"On how many orgasms you give to me, tonight."

Chapter Twenty-One

River

Petal is basking in the atmosphere that is her Blessing Ways. She insisted we call it that rather than a baby shower because that's what her family has always done. The yoga instructor has just left after our guided meditation session and everyone seems invigorated by it with a renewed energy. Everyone except Freya, who is moaning about how her thighs hurt.

Lianna and Becca—Petal's sister and her wife—are bringing out the special chair they made from natural materials for Petal to sit in as we create our circle in the clearing of trees around us. Marie, Petal's mom, holds her hand in the air to signal for us all to pay attention, and I check beside me to make sure Lina's still enjoying herself.

"It is a blessed thing to welcome new life into the world. If you could get out the beads you each brought with you, I shall begin the Labor of Love necklace with mine. I'll pass it around so you can add your beads. Even before birth, this new life will absorb our positive energy, knowing they are loved forevermore." She passes the twine to me and I add a rose quartz bead to symbolize the strength of unconditional love for the baby before handing it to Lina.

Lina adds a Black onyx to help speed labor by bolstering stamina and strength. After asking me for my advice on what the Hell she needed to do for this Blessing Way, we paid a visit to Crystal Gardens.

I smile as Lydia, the doula, adds a malachite stone bead. The perfect one for her to give as it's also known as the midwife's stone. Lianna, Becca, Ginny, Freya, and a couple of women from Marie's coven all add their beads before it makes its way back to Marie. She ties off the end and goes to kneel in front of Petal, presenting her with her new necklace to wear during labor.

Petal's big brown eyes tear up as she stands to hug her mom. "Thank you, Mom." Marie moves away, and Petal addresses us all as a group. "Thank you, everyone. It means so much that you could be here to celebrate this new life. I feel so blessed by each and every one of you. Now though, I wanted to play a couple of silly games that I asked my sister-in-law, River, to prepare."

I guess I'm up.

I grab the large bag I brought with me, which Lina helped me put together, and pull out a small notepad and pencils for everyone. Placing them in front of me, I reach back inside the bag for the first game props.

Melted chocolate inside cloth diapers.

However, I may not have thought this through properly. The chocolate in each of the diapers has been mashed up and melted, and at the time, the smell was strong and it was a gooey mess. Now though, the chocolate has solidified, making the contents of each diaper look like solid little lumps of authentic, well, mess.

"Okay, everyone come and grab a pad, pencil, and a cloth diaper. There are ten diapers in total and the aim of this game is to guess the name of the chocolate inside. They are numbered one to ten, so once you are finished with the one you have, pass it along to someone else until you have written down something for each diaper. When we've all got ten, we'll sit back down and I have the answers. Whoever guesses the most correct will win a lollipop. I've also marked the vegan and non-vegan ones, so feel free to help each other out a little with those." I watch as each lady approaches to get their items and the groans of disgust mixed with giggles begin immediately as they peek inside the cloth.

Freya parks her ass beside Lina, no doubt trying to get her to give her the answers because she's a sore loser. The thing is, Lina doesn't know which chocolates I put in each diaper, so Freya is shit outta luck.

I've got to say, the melted Snickers bar and the Reese's peanut butter cup look rank. *Perfect.*

I smile to myself as Petal's little doll face lights up with excitement and joy at the sight of everyone mingling with each other, smelling and tasting the diaper treats.

"Can you give us a clue on number five, please, River? We literally have no idea on this one," Ginny asks, holding it up with a mock look of disgust on her face.

"Ooh, I just had that one. It took me forever, but I know what it is!" Lianna tries to look over Becca's shoulder for the answer, but Becca holds her pad close to her chest. "Nah ah, Sugarlump. Figure it out yourself." She kisses her on the head and moves to grab another diaper.

"I will say this, they're all chocolatey goodness and I have unmelted bars in my bag of wonders for afterward." I shrug my shoulders and laugh as a whole load of yum noises echo around me.

The way Freya is cozying up to Lina isn't sitting well with me but Lina's smiling so I'll leave her to it for now. Today is a big deal for her to be around so many people.

She didn't make it to Marco's birthday gathering and I understand that; there were a lot of men in an enclosed space. When Petal extended the invite for today to Lina, she practically jumped at the opportunity. She's as excited about me becoming an aunt as I am and I know she'll be over the moon when she finds out Petal is planning on asking Lina if she'll be an honorary aunt.

"Finished!"

"Ooh, nice."

"Nooo."

"What? Already?"

"Me too!"

"You're joking."

"Me three!"

"Nearly there."

It's like everyone is talking at once as they rush to finish so we can get to the answers, because they're all dying to know what's inside those diapers. We all sit again while I read out the answers, pulling out a bar of chocolate for everyone to match each one. Nobody gets them all right and it's hilarious listening to what some of them have written down.

After handing a smaller bag with all the cloth diapers inside to Marie—she's thankfully washing them before handing them over to Petal—I explain the next game.

"Lina and I have prepared a few vegan meals, perfect for Baby. We're going to call you to the middle in pairs where you will both sit on these chairs, blindfolded, and feed each other as much as you can."

We all make a lot of mess, laugh until our cheeks hurt, and bond in a way only a group of loving women—and Freya—can. Petal's glow is almost iridescent as she grins, vegan chocolate pudding dripping down her cheek from one of the games as she claps her hands together, watching her mom and Ginny chug from baby bottles.

I step away from the circle when I see Marco's name calling on my cell. He's with Ev and Kai, having a man baby shower—or just drinking beer and smoking weed, if I'm being honest.

"Hey, Baby. Ha, get it? Baby?" I chuckle down the phone at my own lame-ass joke.

"Tesoro. How fast can you get here?" His breathing is heavy. Something feels wrong.

"What's wrong? I can leave now, let me just tell Pe—"

"No. Don't tell them why I'm calling. Not yet. Leave two of your guards behind for the girls and bring Sam with you, Tesoro. Ti amo, with everything I am. I'll be right here." He hangs up without waiting for me to say anything else and, if I had to guess by his tone, it's because he was crying.

Now I'm freaking the fuck out. My heart drops to my stomach and a pit of dread begins to fill my insides. There's a reason Marco needs me to come alone, leave Lina and Petal here with the others having fun, and I'm not sure I'm going to like the answer.

So I do something that feels so wrong; I lie to Petal.

"Hey, Gorgeous, I've just got to go back to your place and get a couple of things I left behind. I won't be long. Okay?"

"Oh, babe, you really don't have to. Everything you've done already has been amazing."

"Nope, I'm not done yet. I'll be back." Without hanging around for a response, I squeeze her tightly and move over to Lina, who still has a Freya-shaped cling-on basically attached to her hip. "I'm heading home real quick to pick up a few things. I'm taking Sam with me, but the others are still here for you. Okay?"

I expect her to ask me why I'm going or if she can come with me.

"Yeah, that's fine. See you soon, Riv." She barely pays me any attention, continuing her conversation with Freya.

The pit in my stomach grows bigger and I find Sam, relaying the message to her and the others before running as fast as I can to Ev and Petal's house. It's quicker than waiting for Sam to bring the truck around and navigate the roads.

It takes me ten minutes before I can see the house. I have a side stitch and am close to collapsing, but Marco sounded desperate, so unlike he's ever sounded before.

I round the corner of the drive, pushing through the side gate, and my knees buckle when I see the reason Marco called.

No!

Chapter Twenty-Two

Marco

An hour earlier...

When River asked me—more like begged with my dick in her mouth and my balls in the palm of her hand—to celebrate the baby shower with her brother and best friend, I was not amused. The only guys I've ever bonded with were a billionaire playboy, a legit psycho, and a guy with questionable morals who enjoys doing my dirty work.

Yet, here I am, drinking organic beer with a couple of hippies and watching them consume the equivalent of a small tree in dope. I don't smoke, or even drink to excess, because losing control—especially of my inhibitions—doesn't sit well with me. I must admit, though, this is nice. The warm weather isn't suffocating today. The light breeze coming in from the harbor is just enough to cool us down. The trees offering their shade helps, too.

At first, the place was full to the brim with Ev's friends and coworkers from the market. Lots of music and laughter, good food for all tastes and preferences. At the risk of sounding like a complete snob, this is my first cookout that doesn't involve a staff serving top-of-the-line Angus steak. I may even prefer it this way. Minus the throng of people. I didn't know anyone and it made me uncomfortable. Not because I wanted to be the center of attention, but because with the unknown comes the possibility of danger.

Now, though, with only Everest, Kai, and myself left at the house, I feel truly privileged. Not the social or financial kind, but the more important type of privilege... family.

For the first time in my life, I'm not the most important man in the room, or back yard, to be exact. I'm just a guy hanging out with his brother-in-law, telling stories and getting some dirt on my wife.

"So, when I was..." Ev leans his head back, facing the sky with his eyes closed before he snaps his fingers, "Ten! Yeah, cause that's when we had that dog with one missing paw. You remember that, Kai?"

Kai just nods, a goofy grin on his face. A year ago, I would have sneered at him and his intimate memories of my wife but tonight, jealousy toward Kai has no place. River is mine and I am hers and no matter what his puppy heart is feeling, he knows deep down that he lost her a long, long time ago.

"So, yeah, when I was ten, River was babysitting me because our parents were all out doing adult shit… I don't know, it doesn't matter." Everest has been trying to tell this story for the better part of fifteen minutes and he's still not past the beginning. My beer is already warm and I don't even know what River did that was supposedly so hilarious.

"Dude, you digress." Kai tilts his beer at Ev, who taps the necks together and grins before nodding.

"Right, right. So, River's making dinner and at the time we were vegetarians but not yet vegan. To be fair, we didn't consume a lot of—"

"Ev, the story, dude." I chuckle as Kai cuts off Everest so he can finally tell this fucking story.

"I'm giving context, man. But yeah, okay. So, River decides to make pasta, but she had homework to do so she thought it would be easier to put the spaghetti in the oven." I almost choke on my next swallow, my Italian blood draining from my face.

"She did what?" My question is barely audible and I wonder if I made a mistake… maybe River isn't a Volpe after all. She's an alien.

"Yeah, bet you wish you didn't marry her, now, huh?" I narrow my eyes at Kai but he just laughs, which sends Everest into a laughing fit as well.

"Continue, I'm sure she salvaged this. Probably invented something great."

Fuck, I hope so.

"Nah, man. She put the spaghetti on a platter like she was cooking frozen french fries, set the oven to like, six hundred degrees, and let it cook until smoke started floating out the door." He's having a hard time talking, what with the laughing and coughing.

"Shit, Ev and I were playing outside with the dog when the fire alarm started screeching like a motherfucker. When we ran inside, River was standing on the kitchen table trying to turn off the alarm instead of turning off the fucking oven." They're both heaving with laughter at the memory, but my mind is still on the poor pasta that lost its life that day.

"Needless to say, we ate cereal for dinner that night." Ev calms down and goes quiet.

"Fuck, the kitchen was a mess from the smoke, remember that?" Kai also goes quiet.

"Yeah, we pinky swore to never tell my parents." I have no doubt they're both thinking about their parents and the few memories Everest has of them.

I know what it's like to lose a father and, as much as it hurt, I was older and living in a world where bad people have good people killed. I also still have my mother. These two only have each other and there's a melancholy beauty to these kinds of friendships. A brotherhood beyond blood.

"Anyway, moral of the story? Do not let River cook, man. She'll destroy your heritage." They both nod at Ev's words and I agree. Not to mention our chef would keel over with a pride-induced heart attack.

"Duly noted." We drink to that before changing the subject.

"Are you nervous about the baby?" I'm curious about this. Ev and Petal are still quite young and I can't imagine being their age and expecting.

"Not even a little, man. That kid is going to be so loved and appreciated. We're opting for the simple life, nature-based and nurtured with love and understanding. Petal wants to homeschool just like we all were, but we'll see. The public school in our district is pretty cool with lots of nature-based activities. They let us farmers come in and teach them how to care for plants and vegetables. I don't know... we'll see. If we have, like, three or four kids, then we could homeschool since they'll be together but if this kiddo is an only child, I want him or her to have a social life, too."

I listen to Everest and wonder what River and I would do. We haven't talked about children much besides the casual "we'll see" conversation. In fact, when I really think about it, she has a tendency to avoid the subject and hop onto something else.

Making a mental note to ask her about it later, I stand and walk to the cooler where the beer should be.

"Fuck, let me grab some more. Here, take the last one and I'll bring out a few more." Ev stands and heads for the kitchen.

"Five bucks says he passes out on the kitchen table for ten minutes." Kai grins as he looks inside through the open back door. Ev is walking around the kitchen doing God knows what and making lots of noise doing it.

"On the table?" Why would he do that?

"Yeah, pot makes him tired but he only needs like a ten-minute nap, then he's all good and ready for another." Kai's chuckling then turns serious eyes on me, his tone losing its lightness.

"I may joke about being in love with River, but I need you to know something." Clearing his throat, he takes a deep pull from his beer before he continues. To be honest, I'm not sure what he's going to say but I'm hoping it's not something that'll piss me off. The evening is going too well for me to pummel his face for disrespecting my marriage.

"Lay it all out." I sit up, my elbows resting on my knees as I hold the neck of my beer bottle between my thighs, my eyes fixed on Kai.

"I've never seen her happier, even with all the shit she went through back in June. The way she looks at you? She never looked at me like that." I've got a little lump forming in my throat knowing that what he's saying to me can't be easy.

"I'm sorry that you have to see that but I'm definitely not sorry that she's mine." We both nod and he sits back, relaxing.

"As long as I can keep her as my best friend, we're all good, man." The muscles in my shoulders loosen and I lean back on the Adirondack chair, eyeing him from across the circle.

"I don't have a say in that. Her choices are her own, I just make sure that people who hurt her... well, can't anymore." His eyes widen at my admission but he tries to hide his reaction by grabbing the pretzels from the side table.

"Fair warning." Kai is interrupted by something that sounds like a diesel engine roaring to life in the kitchen. We both turn to face the door, then each other, before laughing.

He was right. Everest is lying on the kitchen table, face down, arms hanging from the side, snoring like his lungs can't get enough air but his nose refuses to accommodate safe passage.

"Jesus Christ, is he okay? How does Petal sleep with him snoring like that?" Thank fuck it's not hereditary because I'd have to take drastic measures if River had that problem.

"Ear plugs."

I nod.

"Okay, I've gotta piss." Kai stands and, before heading inside, walks over to me, his hand out like an olive branch.

I stand, because peace is achieved eye to eye.

"Take care of her." All humor is completely gone as our hands clasp and we lean in for a side hug and a clap on the shoulder.

"Until my dying breath." I do not make my vow lightly. I will always protect River, even if it means sacrificing myself to do it.

"Good." We stare at each other for a couple of seconds, signing a treaty with just a handshake and a nod, then we finally break apart and Kai walks away.

This truce is going to make River so incredibly happy, I can't wait to see the smile on her face. It's been her greatest wish, that her best friend and I find a common ground so she can feel comfortable and relaxed at family gatherings.

That said, it won't keep me from busting his balls once in a while. After all, he's the dumbass who let her go.

Standing, I decide to stretch my legs by taking a stroll around the property while Kai takes his piss and Ev sleeps off his joints. This area is quiet, barely any cars rolling down the street. The house isn't on the water, but it's close enough that I can smell the salt of the ocean. The sun hasn't set yet even though it's nearly eight at night, but the oranges and pinks in the sky are breathtaking.

It's the last peaceful thought that I have as I stand under the thick branches of the willow tree. Everything after that happens in slow motion, like a movie on the slowest setting.

The side gate on the other side of the yard clanks open, a dark figure casting a shadow across the grass.

Everest announcing he's awake and ready for another just as he reaches the doorjamb and takes two steps.

Kai slapping his two hands on his best friend's shoulders and squeezing with a wide grin taking up his entire face.

These are the things I notice as I simultaneously reach for the gun at my ankle, aiming it at the figure across the large space from me.

By the time I get one shot, two others have already gone off, the *pop pop* of a silencer making it impossible for neighbors to be alarmed.

My head snaps to the side just as another *pop* sounds off. Kai pushes Everest to the side, landing on top of him like he's shielding him from the intruder. Adrenaline courses through my body as I pull the trigger two more times and see the figure drop to the ground.

Kicking the discarded gun to the side, I crouch beside the guy who is now actively bleeding all over Ev's lawn and press my fingers to his artery. I'm met with a steady pulse so I slap the guy a couple of times to wake him.

I've got fucking questions and I want them now.

"Who sent you?" The guy smiles, blood smeared across his teeth, pupils dilated like the devil.

"Your mother." I don't have time to deal with this motherfucker and just as I'm about to punch him in the face, I notice the tattoo on the side of his neck.

The Kastellanos symbol, a brand for their soldiers, of the letter K in an incomplete circle tells me everything I need to know. Rising to my feet as quickly as I can, I put another bullet right between his eyes before running to Kai and Everest.

There's blood everywhere.

The stairs, the wooden footpath, the green grass.

Kai rolls off of Everest, his entire front painted red, Ev's back and head soaked in blood.

"Are you hurt? Are you okay?" I'm slapping Kai, who looks dazed and a little out of it.

"Check on Ev. I'm... I'm fine. Check on Ev." I don't believe him but my need to make sure my brother-in-law is still alive is stronger than my doubts.

"Everest. Hey, buddy, talk to me." He's passed out cold, a large gash along his hairline tells me he ate the ground with the full force of Kai's weight behind him.

Careful not to hurt him any more than he already is, I check for bullet holes by lifting his tee shirt so I can stop the bleeding.

There's so much of it.

There's nothing there, but if I didn't know his shirt was originally yellow, I'd think it was a bright red. Still, there's nothing along his back or shoulders. No holes, no sign of entry or exit, which means he took it in the front and maybe the bullet is lodged inside.

"Fuck!" If that's the case, I need to turn him over so I can stop the bleed.

"Kai, can you help me turn him over by holding his neck steady?" I'm looking around, trying to find a piece of wood or something that could hold Ev's neck steady, but there's nothing.

Fuck it, I can't let River's brother bleed out. I just can't face her or Petal and tell them he's gone because I couldn't save him.

"Kai, man, I need your help." Annoyed, I turn to Kai and see him leaning against the stairs, his hand holding his side, blood seeping between his fingers, over his pants, and onto the ground.

Oh, fuck no.

Unfocused eyes look at me, a small, regretful smile at the corners of his mouth, as Kai licks his lips and tries to talk.

"Is he okay?" His words are barely a whisper and the brick in the pit of my stomach grows heavier with every second that passes.

"I... I don't know. Kai, you took the bullet." It's obvious, but for some reason, saying the words out loud urges me into action.

Ripping my shirt off, I ball it up as tight as possible and press it to Kai's wound, trying to stop the bleeding, or at least slow the outpour.

"Don't you fucking die on me, man. I swear to fuck, I will never forgive you for that." Kai chuckles at my words and I ignore the trickle of blood that seeps out of the corner of his mouth.

"You need to tell them I love them."

Motherfucker.

"No. *You* fucking tell them that you love them!" I pull out my phone and it slides out of my hand, the blood making my fingers incapable of getting a good grip.

"Fuck!" I point at Kai and growl. "You fucking hold that shirt to your side and keep your blood inside you. Do not fucking piss me off." Behind us, Everest groans, slowly turning over, his hand going to the gash on his head making him flinch.

Wiping my hands on my jeans, I dry them enough to be able to use my phone. Enzo answers immediately.

"Get the fuck over here. I need J, her men, for a clean-up and a doctor right fucking now!" I hang up and just as I reach Kai with a towel that was hanging over the back of a chair, I hear Everest gasp and curse.

"What happened? Fuck, Kai! You stupid motherfuck-er." With unsteady steps, Everest stumbles over to Kai and leans in to help stop the bleeding.

I run inside and get a glass of water for Kai, thinking I should keep him hydrated.

Then I make the most difficult call of my life.

"Tesoro. How fast can you get here?"

It feels like an eternity by the time River arrives, but as my eyes scan her from top to bottom, making sure she's okay, I notice her chest heaving, her nostrils flaring and her legs trembling. She ran here, her adrenaline and fear pushed her to be here as quickly as possible.

"Oh my God. Marco! Are you okay? What's going on?" I watch my wife as she takes in the scene.

There's a dead body at her feet, making her beautiful face frown in confusion. Everest and I have laid Kai on his back as we try to keep pressure on his wound and pile on blankets to keep him warm.

"Marco?"

"I'm here, Tesoro. I'm here, Baby." Fuck, I hate this for her. I hate that my world is causing her pain once again.

Her eyes fall to Kai and she gasps so loud I'm afraid she'll pass out.

"Kai! Oh gods, no! What happened?" Falling to her knees, she doesn't know what to look at first since her brother's forehead is still wide open with a serious gash that needs stitches.

"Everest?"

"I'm fine. I'm fine. Fuck, just... keep him awake, Riv. Keep him awake." Everest is hurt and doing everything he can to keep his shit together as we both do what we can to keep Kai alive.

The signs, though, are not reassuring. He's pale, pupils dilated, lips barely able to close.

"Kai, sweetheart, don't close your eyes. Look at me." River is kneeled over him, her hands on his cheeks, her face only inches above his as she keeps him focused on her.

"We called for someone, we just need to keep him alert and alive until they get here." I'm not sure who I'm trying to reassure, maybe everyone.

"Kai, hey. Look at me." I bend my head to give them a little privacy as Everest begins to silently cry beside me.

"River?"

"Yes, I'm here. You need to stay awake, okay? Can you do that for me? Just, just stay awake okay? Help is coming." Fuck, my wife is so strong. Her voice barely breaks even though I know she's dying inside.

"My Psyche."

River hiccups, but manages to chuckle.

"I told you, you can't call me that anymore." But who are we kidding? In this moment, he can call her anything he wants.

"I know..." His words are just air at this point, but he's fighting to stay alert and I can't help but respect his will to live. "Marco... we... shook on it." Fucking Hell. I'm grinding my teeth, trying not to lose my shit.

"Shh, don't try to speak. Keep your energy and you'll tell me everything later when you're better." River bends again and kisses his forehead. "Marco, why is he so clammy? He's going to be okay, right? He's going to be fine?" Panic is starting to take over, her fingers on his face trembling, her back heaving from the sobs she's desperately keeping at bay.

"Just keep him awake, Tesoro. Help is on the way." I don't have the heart to tell her she needs to say goodbye. I just can't.

Screaming gets our attention as we all look over to the top of the stairs where a very pregnant and very distraught

Petal is holding on to the door frame with everything she's got.

"Sunshine. I'm okay, I'm okay. See?" Everest rises to his feet, slowly making his way to his wife. Needing to calm her down. This cannot be good for the baby.

"River?"

"Yeah, sweetie. I'm right here."

"I know... I fucked... up."

"Shh, Kai. Please."

Lifting a weak hand to cup River's face, blood covering her cheek and neck, he closes his eyes for a brief moment before he continues.

"I fucked up... with you. But it's how... it's how it was supposed... to be." Goddammit. He's saying goodbye, he knows.

"No. No, no, no. You are not doing this, Kai Briggs. You are not allowed to die. Do you fucking hear me?" He smiles at her, blood running down his cheek from the corner of his mouth. I'm still using my entire body to apply pressure but when I see blood trickling from his ear, my jaw aches with how hard I'm keeping my emotions in check.

"I have... loved you... my entire life. But..."

River shakes her head, whispering "No" over and over again, tears now streaming down her face, over her cheeks and down her neck.

"You are... so happy. Stay... happy, Riv. Be ama... zing."

"Well, I will be, you goof. And you'll be here to witness it." She says the words but they are resigned; flat and watery from her tears.

She bends down and kisses him on the mouth and I can't look away as their tears mingle over their lips, sobs racking over her chest. They whisper words I can't hear but I feel their intensity in my bones.

My hands are soaked with his blood, the towel and my shirt doing nothing to keep the hole from bleeding. But I try. I try everything I can to keep my wife from suffering more than she already has.

"Kai, please, please, please. Don't go. Don't do this, please." Next to me, River is howling with grief as I feel his body slack away. His muscles give under my touch and I know.

I just know.

Chapter Twenty-Three
River

"Kai, please. Oh, God. Marco, do something, do something!" I'm helpless. There's nothing I can do. My words are a desperate scream as I try really hard to keep myself together... and do a really bad job of it.

There's so much blood. And Kai's so pale, so cold, and his gaze slowly moves from mine.

"River, sweetheart."

Marco's speaking to me but it's barely registering, my eyes locked on Kai's honey orbs. They're unfocused, he's not moving. *Why isn't his chest moving?*

"No no no no no no no. Kai, come on... please... please come on, Kai. Stay with me. Please... oh gods, please."

Marco leans over and gently pushes Kai's eyelids down, his head bowed in grief.

No, this isn't happening.

It can't.

No.

"Kai Briggs, wake the fuck up. Marco, do something. Please..." I can't finish.

Sobs wrack through my body and I hear a wail from Petal, Everest's cries just as loud.

"Tesoro."

"No. We can do something. There has to be something we can do. Marc—" I'm slapping against his chest, shaking him, urging him to help me, but I know... I know it's too late. Marco sits beside me as I continue to hit him, screaming for help, for justice, anything. Then he grabs my wrists and pulls me into him, tightly wrapping his arms around my body.

I can barely breathe through crying. My cheeks are wet with tears, my throat sore from screaming, my head pounding through the pain, and my heart breaking for my best friend.

It's too late.

He's gone.

Everything happens so quickly and all I can do is watch through blurry, tear-soaked eyes as I remain curled up in Marco's lap on the ground next to Kai. I can't leave him.

J arrives with a few of her soldiers, cleaning up the body of the guy responsible for this in silence.

"Marco, we need to call the cops, but you, River, and Lina, can't be here for the story to work. I need to prep the brother with what to say to the cops a—"

"*The brother* is Everest. He has a name." I hiss the words to Enzo against Marco's chest, unable to push any kind of softness into my tone. All emotions have fled my body. Except pain. That one's hanging around and building a city in there.

"I'm sorry, River." Enzo has the sense to look genuine as he dips his head in apology before continuing his report to Marco. "I need to prep Everest with what to say to the cops. All they need to know is that a random shooter came by and left again. No motive, no reason, no suspicion."

"Sounds good. Thank you, Enzo. Leave some people behind to keep an eye out, get some security cameras put in aro—"

"No. Petal won't like cameras everywhere."

"I don't give a fuck, Tesoro. Their safety is a priority and that means security cameras."

Even I can't argue with that and I sag further into his hold, losing the will to argue. He rubs a palm up and down my back and I take a few stilted breaths every now and then as my body calms from all the tears. Not that I think it will ever calm fully.

A piece of my soul has just been cruelly ripped away, forever.

"Is Lina already in the car? I haven't seen her."

"She stayed behind for a little longer with that Freya girl, but I just received word that she's on her way back, alone. Rough ETA is five minutes."

"Okay, do what you need to do. Thank you, Enzo."

"Where are Petal and Ev?" I look up to Marco, my body numb to everything around me, but I have a need to support my brother. Kai was his best friend, too.

"They're inside, Tesoro."

I want to go but that means leaving Kai outside on his own, with strangers moving around and cleaning up blood splatters that don't belong to my family. I can't leave him alone.

"Okay."

This might be selfish of me but Ev will understand. He wouldn't want Kai to be alone either.

As if divine powers are at work here, Petal and Ev slowly walk out through the front door. My brother's face is swollen from tears but the gash on his head has been stitched up. I heard Enzo tell Marco that part of the story Petal has to give the police is that she was focused on stitching up her husband before calling the police because Kai was already...

I can't even think it. A lone, fat tear slips down my cheek, its saltiness adding to the dried-up mess that is currently my face.

Marco's hold on me loosens, like he knows I need to go to my brother, and I do. We hold each other up and let fresh tears fall. Sniffing, I do the best I can to steel my spine and reassure Everest that we can get through this, but I fail miserably. My words are unable to come out without me breaking down.

"We can get through this, Riv." Ev's words echo my thoughts as he gently pats my back and I'm so fucking proud of my brother right now. I know he's breaking inside as much as I am but it seems he's been taking notes on masking his true feelings to help make others feel better.

"I love you."

"I love you too." My tone is pitchy, much like his, but nothing stops us from saying what needs to be said to one another.

Petal is cuddled into Marco's side as they stand beside us and I know all this can't be good for the baby, I just can't seem to find the right function to help anything though.

"Come here, gorgeous." I open my arm to bring Petal into our hug and we stand there for I don't know how long. This seems good enough for now. It's all I can offer them.

"Marco, you guys need to get going. We can't hold off calling the cops any longer."

"Grazie, Enzo." A warm palm lands on my shoulder and Marco whispers into my ear, "We have to go, Tesoro."

I don't want to leave.

Ignoring him, I squeeze Ev and Petal a little tighter.

"I would do anything in the world for you but we really need to go, Baby."

Petal pulls away first, nodding like a voice of reason who understands exactly what she needs to do. I never wanted any of this for them. They don't deserve an ounce of the pain they're suffering. I make a vow to remind myself to have a talk with Ev about the whole Volpe thing soon. It's not that I've been keeping it from him but it's difficult to find a good time to talk about your whole family living a secret life.

It was difficult enough to tell them about mine.

With her arm around her husband's waist, Petal gives me a sad smile. "Beautiful girl, you know everything happens for a reason. And as shitty as this is now, you know we all have something to learn from this." Petal swearing is always a shock, but hearing it now only hammers home what she's trying to say. "We'll find a way through this." She squeezes Ev's side as tears trickle down his cheeks and steps forward, grabbing my cheeks and kissing my head before moving back into her husband's side.

Her strength is astounding and I nod as she and Ev head back inside. Enzo is hovering behind us, silently urging us to go and get into the waiting car.

But I can't do it. As the front door closes behind Everest and Petal, my knees buckle beneath me. I fall to the ground, Marco moving quickly to stop me from hurting myself, and gently grip Kai's hand.

"I can't leave him alone, Marco. I can't..."

"I know, Tesoro."

He doesn't say anything else as he slides an arm under my knees, the other across my back, and lifts me. My strength has been zapped away and I don't even have the energy to fight him. I know he's doing what he needs to, which is why I wrap my arms around his neck.

Kai's body slowly gets farther and farther away from us as Marco walks away with me in his arms. It's one of the most painful moments of my life and I'm going to allow myself the time to suffer this loss.

For once, I'm going to rely on the man who loves me with all his heart and let myself break.

If only for a little while.

Chapter Twenty-Four

Marco

River fell asleep in the car on the drive back from her brother's house. No doubt, her body crashed into protective mode from the inconsolable sobs that racked her entire body as her head rested against my shoulder.

The only thing I could do was wrap my arms around her shaking shoulders and squeeze her against me as tightly as humanly possible.

Once we arrive home, I carry her sleeping body into our bedroom and lay her down on the couch in the corner of our large bedroom. Her face is blotchy, eyes swollen, even with her lids closed, lips puffy and wet from her tears. Worse than everything is the fact that, just like me, she's covered in Kai's blood and I can't let her see that when she wakes up.

Making quick work of undressing myself, I send out a quick text to Stefano asking him to bring me a garbage bag.

We're not keeping these clothes. If I could, I would burn them to ashes. Hell, if I could I would go back in time and shoot that motherfucker before he ever got the chance to take out his gun.

Enzo is keeping me informed of any news he may have in real time. He knows me well. I need information to stay sane and I refuse to have nothing for River the minute she wakes up.

A light knock distracts me from my wife's sleeping form. Taking the bag, I thank Stefano. Before I can close the door, he stops me with a hand on the knob.

"Come sta la signora? Cosa posso fare per aiutare?" A soft smile graces my lips at worry swimming in Stefano's eyes. River has become like a daughter to him and wanting to do something to help her makes complete sense.

"If there's anything, I promise I'll let you know." Stefano nods, bows his head slightly and steps back.

"Si signore."

Every piece of clothing on me, save for my boxers, is in the bag, yet I'm covered in blood nonetheless. River stirs on the couch, her breath hitching, and my heart breaks for her all over again. The mind is a fascinating thing. It's our superpower but also our worst enemy. It can change the world for the better and, in the blink of an eye, can just as easily destroy it.

Right now, River's mind is protecting her by allowing her to sleep so her consciousness isn't working against her. Yet, from the frown on her beautiful lips and the crease right between her eyes, I'm guessing she's dreaming about what happened. About Kai. About the incredible loss she will be facing as soon as wakes up.

My only job as her husband is to make sure that when she breaks, she does so in my arms, where she's safe.

In our en suite, I get the towels ready on the counter while I run the shower, making sure the temperature is exactly how she prefers it. I'm walking back to where she lies, ready to undress her and wash the blood off her body, when I hear what I can only describe as literal heartbreak. A whimper escapes her slightly-parted lips just as a sob breaks free from her throat. Her fingers grip her shirt, stained with the memories of her best friend. Even in sleep, she feels the loss of him.

Fuck.

As I sit on the edge of the couch, I run a finger down the side of her face. Her scar is barely visible—another consequence of this life I chose for her—but I know it's there. I watch her as her eyes dart right to left in rapid movements behind her lids. She's not at peace. In fact, she's struggling all alone in the depths of her unconsciousness.

"Tesoro, wake up, Baby." My voice is soft. I don't want to startle her but I will if I have to. "River, open your eyes, my love." I bend and place my lips on hers, ignoring the blood that remains from when she kissed Kai goodbye.

Finally, her eyes flutter open and, for a blessed second, she's forgotten that her world is upside down. For a brief moment in time, she smiles at me like I'm the reason her world is perfect. For just this fraction of time, she's content all over again.

The transformation soon follows and with it, the frown, the immediate tears blurring her bloodshot eyes, the destruction of a piece of her soul.

"Tesoro, come. Let's take a shower together." I undress her, not wasting any time as she stares at me but doesn't see me, I don't think. Once she's naked, I slide my arms beneath her thighs and shoulders and carry her, like my beloved bride, to the bathroom. The shower is large enough for us to be comfortable, with a bench along the entire far wall. I sit her down and unhook the shower head so she doesn't have to stand. Her knees would give out, I'm sure.

With every passage of water, more and more blood stains the tiled floor as it circles the drain like a bad Halloween movie. River just stares at it, unmoving, as it turns from transparent to crimson, then back to transparent. Like the cycle of life itself.

"He's gone." Her whisper is as painful as a screech. It pierces my eardrum with all the pain it holds.

"I'm sorry."

We wash in silence after that and before long, we're in bed where her body curls around mine, begging for protection from reality.

One day turns to three and, while River allows herself to wallow in her loss, I make sure the arrangements are made for Kai's funeral with constant guidance from Petal and Everest.

I've asked them to join us at the house, needing to keep them safe. I expected them to refuse but, to my relief, they agreed it was a good idea for them to stay together as a family unit. Freya refused our offer, blaming me for Kai's death.

She's not wrong, but that doesn't mean I can ignore the fact that she's his wife and needs support in this tragic time.

To my surprise, Lina offered to stay with her. She insisted, actually. The only reason I agreed was because I sent five men to guard Kai's house.

Until we know exactly what the fuck is happening, I won't take unnecessary risks.

"What day is it?" I turn my head, then my entire body, until we're face to face, chest to chest, lying in our own personal bubble as my thigh rests between hers, the top warmed by her hot pussy.

"Monday. Tomorrow is the funeral." My voice is low, even, so as not to send her spiraling.

"Oh." She blinks and new tears well in her eyes, but she closes her lids and wills them to retreat. "How is Petal?" My wife, always worrying about others.

"She's resting, keeping herself busy by choosing flowers and the place for the ceremony. I suppose a church is out of the question?" I'm trying to lighten her load and my reward is a faint smile flashing across her lips, but just as it greeted me, it's gone again.

"We have to cremate him, it's what he wanted. We're going to need candles and Marie should lead us in prayer."

I make a mental note to let Petal know but I'm distracted by River's sudden change in mood.

Straddling my hips, she circles my wrists in her fingers and, with a strength I didn't think she had, pushes my arms up and above my head. I arch a brow at her, making sure she knows what she's doing, my dick going instantly hard at the sudden position.

"I need this." Leaning in, River captures my mouth with hers and grinds her pussy over my steel-hard dick. I feel selfish for even thinking about sex but I know what she's doing. She's seeking an escape and I'm her rabbit hole.

"You know I won't... I *can't* deny you, Tesoro."

"I'm counting on it." Chest to chest, she lifts her hips and before I can take my next breath, I'm inside her, deep and tight. We both exhale like our problems have lifted from our shoulders and our lives are lighter somehow.

"Fuck, yes." River riding my cock is a thing of beauty. The slope of her neck tense from the effort. The rise and fall of her chest as she fights every breath she takes. The swell of her tits as they bounce in tempo with our desperate fucking. But when I reach her eyes, they're hidden behind her lids, her head tilted back, her mouth facing the ceiling.

This won't do.

I get that she needs to escape but I refuse to let her fuck me, her husband, without being fully aware that we're fucking.

Hell no.

With little effort, I disentangle myself from her hold and flip us around until she's on her back—eyes wide and pupils dilated with her growing need—one hand at her throat squeezing the indifference right out of her.

"I get that you're hurting, Tesoro, but when I'm inside you, nothing else comes between us." Her breath catches as I plunge my dick back inside her and pump my hips enough times to feel her pussy soak my shaft. "Do you understand?" She smiles, a real one this time, and for a moment, I see my wife again.

"Si, signore." Her words, spoken in my mother tongue, only make me want to dive inside her harder and faster. River reaches back with one hand, holding herself on the headboard while her other settles on my back, her nails digging into my skin and ripping it open.

I welcome the pain, it means we're alive. It also means that she's here, with me. It's all that really matters.

When I kiss her, we moan into each other's mouths, breathing air into each other's lungs. Giving life to one another in the best way we know how.

"Give it to me, Tesoro." She knows what I want. She needs to give it to me, needs to feel alive while I rip it from the depths of her soul.

"Marco!" Her body flies off the mattress as I fuck her harder than I had anticipated today or even next week. I figured I'd give her time but I was wrong. The longer she falls into despair, the harder it will be to pull her out.

So I fuck my wife with every muscle and every tendon in my body. I fuck her with my heart *and* my dick. I take her orgasms and make them mine and, in return, I lift her up and out of her madness.

"That's it, Tesoro. Come all over my cock, Baby." I feel her warmth making me slicker inside her and that image makes my balls contract until I come so far inside her I wonder if she can taste me.

Falling into each other, I breathe against her neck as she wraps her arms around my shoulders.

"I love you, Marco. I feel like I should tell you this every day. Every minute."

"You should. Never hold back, Tesoro. Life is short." I almost regret the words as soon as they're out but her watery smile tells me she was already thinking the same thing.

"It is and I'm glad I get to spend mine with you."

Later that day, we are all eating in the living room, River on my lap so I can force feed her myself, Petal lying back against Everest, settled right between his spread legs as she regails us with her favorite stories about Kai.

The more I learn, the more I realize he wasn't such a bad guy. He just made stupid teenage decisions and had no idea how to fix his mistakes.

"He saved my life." Everest practically whispers the words, like speaking them somehow makes him guilty for being alive.

"His sacrifice will not be forgotten, Bear. I promise, his soul will bless us every day with his kindness." Petal's words linger in the room as we all take in the selflessness of Kai's actions, which made sure that their baby, my niece or nephew, would not grow up without a father.

"Boss?" Our silence is interrupted by Enzo's urgency, which only means one thing... he has news.

"Excuse us." Ever since the other night, I refuse to be more than a few feet away from River, which means I take her with me everywhere. Physically carry her if I have to. But today, she stands, taking my hand as we follow Enzo to my office where I settle into my chair with my wife curled up in my lap.

Enzo closes the door and, without any kind of greeting or introduction, announces loud and clear. "Nathaniel has been leaving us clues as to Elizabeth's plans and Ugo's whereabouts. We just didn't know until I caught something on one of my cameras today." This information gets our attention as we both sit up and focus on every detail Enzo throws at us.

"What do you mean, he's been helping us? I thought he was buddy buddy with Elizabeth?" River's tone is clipped and she is *not* amused. "And how did you miss the clues? I don't understand." This is the first time since our wedding that I hear the tone of a leader, the disappointment when one of your team fails to get you the results you need. She's speaking like a woman who holds power.

"We... I got caught off-guard. I wasn't expecting him to be on the right side of history." He's standing with his hands on his hips, head bowed like a kid who's being reprimanded by his school teacher.

"How do we know it's not a set-up? I mean, if we follow his directions we could get ambushed, get our men hurt." I don't know why hearing her talk about "our" men makes my dick hard, but judging by the way she looks over her shoulder and at me, I'm guessing she felt that.

"We don't. But... we had a couple of soldiers check it out and they spotted Elizabeth entering and leaving an apartment building in the financial district. The exact address on the note." Enzo's responding to this authoritative side of River, keeping eye contact with her instead of seeking me out. There's no need for me to intervene because she's got this.

"Okay." She turns to me and I see the questions in her eyes. "What do you think?"

Fuck, I love this woman.

Taking in a deep breath, I allow my fingers to trace idle circles on her thigh as I voice my opinion.

"Personally, I don't fucking care if he's helping old ladies cross the road and doing their grocery shopping. He laid his hands on my wife without her permission. End him." Enzo nods but doesn't turn to walk out, waiting on River, who holds my stare.

She doesn't agree with me. I can read it in the slant of her brows and the downturn of her lips.

"Tesoro?"

"I want to speak with him." She's not addressing Enzo, she's asking without, in fact, asking a question.

"It's risky, I don't like playing with your safety, especially not now." My hands grip her tighter, closer to me.

"I need this closure, Marco. I need this." We hold each other's gazes and the intensity of her stare tells me how true her words feel to her. "Elizabeth can burn in Hell for all the shits I give but Nathaniel... well, I need answers."

"Then that's what we'll do but, Tesoro, I'll be there. I won't allow you to be alone with him." She lifts a brow at me like my threat means nothing so I remind her of my stubborn ways. "Don't make me punish you for disobeying."

"It's not punishment if I like it."

She may not be one hundred percent but my River *will* be back in full force. No doubt in my mind.

CHAPTER TWENTY-FIVE

RIVER

Two days ago, I said the most heartbreaking goodbye to my best friend and helped to see him off into the Summerlands. Marco is skeptical about my beliefs in reincarnation and life after death, but he doesn't belittle me for it. He's been supporting me every step of the way, encouraging me to have faith in my beliefs because they give me hope. And that's essentially what we all want in this world. Whatever we believe in, we all just want a little hope.

Grief covers such a wide range of emotions. It's not just sadness. There's no one way to behave and there's no time limit to how long it can last. It can, however, make a person do things they wouldn't usually think about—like going all mafia queen and storming across the ocean to try and save her husband. And now? Well, now I'm about to walk into a warehouse—thankfully not the same one as the massacre—with Marco at my side, gripping my hand as tightly as I'm gripping his.

"You sure you want to do this, Tesoro?"

Do I want to face the man I thought I killed who is partially responsible for all the shit I've had to endure? Not really, no. Do I *need* to?

"Yup." I pop the *P* for added effect. My head is moving up and down, like one of those nodding dolls, but my feet aren't moving.

"We can go back to the car and drive home any time you want. Enzo's here, he can deal with Elizabeth, and would gladly do so."

Elizabeth is also in one of the rooms inside this building, separately from Nathaniel, and I don't know why I thought doing both of these things today would be a good idea, but I'm committed now.

"I'm ready, Baby. Let's go." Full of false confidence, I push open the shiny red metal door.

A chill hits me as we step into a long, windowless hall, the heat from outside gone, but it's actually welcoming. My faux-leather pants were a style choice rather than a 'wear something weather-suitable' choice. It makes me feel better to pretend I'm playing a part today, that I'll be sliding that good old mask on after my conversation with Nathaniel.

"Just remember, Tesoro, I'm right here with you. Always." He pauses outside one of the many doors, grips my face with one hand, and presses his lips against mine in a searing kiss. Then he lightly taps my ass as he twists the handle in front of us.

It's a small room, the walls are gray, and Nathaniel is sitting on an uncomfortable-looking metal chair, his hands cuffed to the table in front of him. His hair is in need of a trim and he could do with a shave, but other than that, he looks like every other time I've seen him. Casual light-blue T-shirt and all.

I'm not sure what I was expecting, but it wasn't this. A mixture of emotions course through me at the sight of him with his head down, looking at his hands.

Marco stays silent behind me, my steady sentinel, and while I *could* do this on my own, his presence is a constant reminder that I don't have to. If I close my eyes, I can picture his fisted hands as he tries real damn hard not to interfere.

Nathaniel takes a deep breath and slowly moves his head up, his eyes glancing over my shoulder briefly before making their way to mine.

"Skittles…"

The word is whispered and all it does now is send a chill through me. Nothing like it used to when Nathaniel was just Candy Aisle Guy.

I don't know how I'm supposed to feel about seeing him… alive. I mean, I should be ecstatic that I didn't actually murder him, my conscience is clear, and I should also be livid with him for everything he's been a part of with his mother, but none of those emotions are there. Instead, I'm just numb.

"How are you here? How is this even possible? You died, I saw you die." My voice is small, barely loud enough for my own ears.

"It's a long story." The last time I saw him, his handsome face was contorted with pain and hatred. Anger and blame. But here and now, all I see are the features of the man I met in my favorite Italian grocery store. I thought it was kismet, some kind of gift from the universe. In some ways, he was. He brought me Marco.

"We've got nothing but time, Nathaniel." Sitting feels wrong, like I'm having a good time with the guy. That's not my goal here. I want answers, no more, no less.

"Skitt—"

"Don't you fucking dare, Nathaniel Reed. You don't get to call me that anymore. "You lost every privilege and any friendship I was willing to offer you when you tried to fucking rape me!" My voice has slowly grown louder so that I'm now shouting, tears stinging my eyes. I guess I'm not so numb to my emotions, after all. "You lied to me, over and over again, trying to get revenge for your mother when, in actual fact, it was she who killed your dad. It had fuck all to do with me. I was her scapegoat and you allowed her to manipulate you. Then you went and lied some more—and I'll say it again because I really want to hammer home how fucking sick this is—before you tried to *rape* me in my own apartment!"

My breaths are heavy and I'm trying my damndest to keep those tears at bay because I am not going to waste any of them on him.

"Ski—"

I raise my brow in a 'are you fucking kidding me' gesture and he quickly amends what he's about to say.

"River, I'm sorry. I—"

"Pfft." I can't help myself.

"If I could take it all back, I would do it in a heartbeat. I wasn't in my right mind. It's no excuse, but I found out my mom had been drugging me. With what, I have no idea, but it affected me mentally. I thought I was going crazy but it turns out my mom had a lot to answer for. I didn't know she was responsible for my dad until recently either, and..." He pauses and inhales deeply, tears beginning to pool in his eyes. "And my wife. I know it's no excuse, I really do, but I was blinded by my grief."

There's that funny old word that means so many different things to each person in this room. Even though what he did and how he acted with me is unacceptable, sick, twisted, all the things, I kind of understand it. Especially considering where I'm going when I've finished with him in this room.

"I really did love you, River. And I'm so fucking sorry. So, so fucking sorry." Some of those tears escape, slowly sliding down his cheek before he puts his head in his hands in shame. He's full-on crying now, his head in his hands as his body shakes through his sobs.

These are the moments I wish I wasn't so empathetic. Seeing him like this is making me lose all the numbness I thought I didn't want. Turns out, feeling numb was better than feeling like complete shit for so many reasons. Makes me want to cry too.

"I don't blame you for what you did, either. You said no. I should have listened, and for that I'll always feel shame, but I really am sorry, River. So sorry." He lowers his head again as more tears fall, and for what it's worth, I believe him.

I'm not ready to let him know that though. Truth be told, his suffering makes me feel better, which is totally fucked up, but at this point, it is what it is. His suffering still doesn't negate my own.

"I need to know what happened. How are you alive?" The fact that he isn't being salty about me basically leaving him for dead has me a little confused. Being in this room for so long, around Nathaniel Reed, Marco at my back, has my emotions growing with every second that passes, making me wish for the lack thereof that I had when I walked in.

"Well, I was in a coma for about three months, so I don't know exactly, but my mom told me the Ambrosios' inside man brought me to her. She paid private doctors and basically made a hospital room for me in her house. I swear, I didn't know what they all had planned, Elizabeth was so kind to begin with..." He trails off, as if his memories are much better than the present... which I'd have to agree with, considering he's currently chained to a table in tears, accused of attempting to rape the most dangerous man in the world's wife.

The mention of that family's name causes me to inhale a sharp breath through my nose to contain my rage toward them.

"I-I'm just... so sorry. Words can't convey how sorry I truly am, for everything." His tears continue to fall, harder now, and he holds his head in his hands again. This time, his body shakes and it's almost heartbreaking to see him sob like this... almost.

The need to ask him more questions is overpowered by my need to deal with the second part of the reason I'm even in this warehouse. I've been emotionally battered recently and all this is doing is reminding me of things long passed. Things I want to begin to move on from.

While I'm positive that this conversation will eventually help to soothe some of my internal wounds, closure and all that, it hasn't happened yet.

"I'm sorry things had to turn out the way they have, Nathaniel, and I appreciate your apologies. I'll take them into consideration, and I might one day forgive you. But as it stands, I have my closure, and I hope you have yours. The best thing for you to do would be to find another state to live in and never let me or my family see your face again."

Fuck, all that was difficult to say, but I'm thankful for my experience as an escort because it's given me the confidence and skills to fake it when I need to.

Without waiting for Nathaniel to stop sobbing or say another word, I turn and walk out of the room, straight past Marco. If I stay in here for a moment longer, I may just break down in tears too.

Marco's voice is low and deep as I move past him, but I hear him all the same.

"She may be generous with her forgiveness, but I sure as fuck never will." Then he follows me out, closing the door behind him and pinning me against the wall, his hands on the sides of my face and his hips keeping mine in place. "I'm so fucking proud of you, Tesoro." His lips are on mine in the next second, but it's not the bruising and frantic kind of kiss I've grown accustomed to, it's soft, gentle, and slow.

"Nathaniel mentioned the Ambrosios had an inside man. Did we know about that?" I didn't want to show my concern in the room with Nathaniel because that could have been considered a weakness.

"We did, Tesoro. J dealt with them. Now, are you ready for part two? Or do you need a break?"

After many long discussions, we agreed Nathaniel would be allowed to go free before today, but he will be followed, watched, and made to leave, living as far away from us as possible. Elizabeth, however, is not so lucky. She's waiting in one of these other rooms too, only her fate is somewhat different from Nathaniel's.

I made a promise to that bitch on the day she came into my house and offered to help me find Marco, and keeping that promise is exactly why I need to lock my mask in place, be someone else, because this is not something I would ever do. But it *is* something a vengeful mafia queen would do and, in this moment, that's who I am.

"I absolutely am not ready, but I also don't break my promises."

His eyes are full of what looks like pride as he smiles down at me, rubbing soothing circles into my sides with his thumbs.

"Okay. Enzo messaged about two minutes ago to let me know Lina has finally arrived now too."

"Good." I nod. Having Lina here was important to me and I know it'll be important to her too. After all, she lost so much more than any of us that day and Elizabeth played a huge part in all of it.

Trouble is, it's been difficult getting Lina to do anything other than hang around with Freya lately. It's not something I'm comfortable with, I'm actually kind of worried about her, but I also know she's as stubborn as her brother when she wants to be. This means she is likely to push back at anyone telling her what's good or bad for her.

However, that's not an issue today, it seems. She's here and I'm looking forward to giving her a hug.

Marco leads me through to another room closer to the entrance and my mood is instantly lifted when Lina stands from the deep-blue sofa and rushes toward me. She's still too thin, the weight she's lost is not worse, but also not any better. My comments on that are staying firmly inside my head though, because now is not the time.

"Hey, Gorgeous."

"Are you ready for this?" I give her the same look Marco gave me out in the hall, my arms resting on her shoulders. There's something new stirring in her light-gray eyes, something darker than before, but I'm not going to question it because I understand it and I don't blame her.

Somewhere along the line, Marco and I discussed Elizabeth's fate, going back and forth on our decision. Ultimately, we are responsible for an entire community that is depending on us making the right moves. Getting Interpol involved was just too risky for our liking. At the same time, my soul doesn't need another black spot on it so I wanted to give her one last chance to persuade me to let her live.

"Ready as I'll ever be." She pulls a gun from behind her back, I assume it was in her waistband, and cocks it, holding it up beside her head. She looks like a total badass, in black hotpants and a black crop-top as she moves from foot to foot in her black sneakers.

I turn and Marco is right there, holding out a large dagger for me. After my mishaps with guns lately, I figured I was less likely to damage myself, or anyone around me, if he kept a hold of it until I needed it.

"Come on, ladies." Marco holds the door open and gestures for us to exit, then he leads us down the hall to the end.

The stench of piss hits me as we walk inside and it's nothing like the room Nathaniel was in. Elizabeth is in the middle of the cold and empty space, her hands chained high above her head so she's practically hanging. Her red hair is limp, hanging over her face as her head droops forward. She has her back to us and Marco slowly moves around to face her.

Enzo is in the far corner of the room, arms folded across his chest, glaring in our direction. A brief flash of pain zips through his eyes as he rakes his gaze over Lina but it's quickly masked by the well-practiced stern thing he has going on.

"Wha-what's going on?" Elizabeth lifts her head slowly, stuttering her words, seemingly confused. "Wh-where a-am I? Is that-that you, Marco?"

He says nothing. Hands in the pockets of his suit pants, legs shoulder-width apart, every bit the strong and powerful man I have fallen in love with.

I grip Lina's hand and walk her around to face Elizabeth, whose eyes widen when they catch sight of the accessories we've chosen to bring with us.

"You know exactly where you are and what is going on. So, Elizabeth, what do you have to say for yourself?"

The scared and confused look quickly disappears, replaced by malice and hatred. I knew the cunt was faking it... again. The only injury she sustained while being kidnapped and brought here was a punch in the face from J—who was really pleased with herself for holding back and not ripping her apart.

"You can't do anything to me. You wouldn't dare. And you," she turns her attention to Lina, "You're just a pathetic waste of space. The spare Mancini." When she's finished her ridiculous tirade, she spits, barely missing Lina's foot as she steps back.

Quickly raising her gun, Lina shoots Elizabeth in the kneecap, and the scream that follows is excruciating. I'm not here to listen to the villain's speech this time, I'm not here to find out her reasoning for anything. She means nothing to me.

"You fucking bitch!" Spit flies from Elizabeth's mouth as she shouts out her insult and I know I need to follow through on my promise, for my own peace of mind more than anything.

"I made a promise, one I was willing to ignore because I'm not an evil sadist like you clearly are."

"Your promises mean shit-all, whore." Her tone is venomous and I can't stand to look at her fucking face anymore.

"You're as original with your insults as your brother."

I put my face as close to hers as I'm willing and hiss my next words at her.

"This is for Kai... and for me."

Extending my arm, I slash out with the knife in my hand to Elizabeth's throat. Again, I fuck it up.

Instead of the clean slice across the throat that happens in movies, I must have misjudged the length of the knife, because it's now lodged halfway through her neck. It looks like I was trying to slice her head clean off and only got half way, and I kind of want to puke at the sight, but I did it.

Letting go of the knife, I leave it where it is, happy that I did what I came here to do... slice the cunt's throat. Although I've more like butchered it, but ya know... minor details.

I want to watch the life drain from her eyes, but I don't think I'm quite that fucked up yet. Much more of all this shit and I probably will be though.

I move over to Marco and he immediately wraps an arm around my waist, pulling me into him and placing a gentle kiss on my forehead.

Gunshots go off as Lina goes to town on her, not wanting any part of her body to touch Elizabeth's—hence the use of weapons today. She said she'd love to have beat the shit out of her but Elizabeth wasn't worth the effort or exertion required to do that.

Nobody ever talks about the smell of blood and guts in the movies, but it's rank as fuck. It's invading my senses and I think I'm ready to leave this all behind me now. I'm ready to take off my mask and be with my husband, run my club, spend time with my family... all the things that give me life.

So I take a line out of Marco's book, kissing him gently on the lips and looking him straight in the eye.

"I love you, Husband. Let's go home."

Chapter Twenty-Six

Marco

"Get me Kastellanos on the phone." My tone leaves no room for questions and Stefano learned this quickly under the rule of my father. In times like these, his guidance would have probably saved us a lot of fucking misery, but here we are. Trial and error.

No more.

It only takes seconds for my desk phone to ring and the Greek accent to echo around my home office.

"To what do I owe the great honor, Don Mancini?"

I have neither the time nor patience to deal with his underhanded pleasantries.

"Thirty minutes, Switzerland." I want him in a neutral meeting spot, a place of his choosing so he doesn't feel vulnerable. What he doesn't know is that I know every fucking spot he likes to use because my enemies are watched twenty-four-seven. It's how we stay on top. Hell, it's how we stay alive.

"Business or pleasure?" What he's really asking is if he needs to bring men for his protection.

"It all depends on you and your brother, Kastellanos." I don't have a bite in my tone. In fact, I sound rather bored with this conversation.

"Very well. Brooklyn docks, at the old abandoned brick factory." I know exactly where he means and, although I figured he'd want to stay in Queens where his men would be easily available, I'm not surprised he's chosen this place. After all, everyone knows the younger brother likes to dabble in the MC life when being Greek mafia gets too boring for his psychopathic ways.

"Thirty minutes." I'm only twenty minutes away but I'm guessing he's about ten out. He thinks he has the advantage. That's a mistake for those too fucking arrogant to live.

"Where we headed?" Enzo is ready to go, dressed all in black, with what I'm guessing are three guns on him and a couple of knives. The guy does not fuck around.

"Brooklyn docks." As soon as I've spoken, he's on the phone barking out orders as we close my office door, beelining for the front entrance.

"Where the fuck are you going, Marco?" River is like a ninja wife, one second you're alone, the next she's right there, smelling the bullshit from across the fucking house.

"I have a meeting. I'll be back for—" I don't have time to finish my phrase before she makes her displeasure known.

"If you say you'll 'be back for dinner', I will stab you in the balls, husband of mine. I'm not your trophy wife sitting at the dining room table, waiting for you to come home. Fuck that shit." I pause, my eyes meeting Enzo's gaze as he tries in vain to hold back his laughter. Before I can tell him to save himself, he's running out the front door and shutting it behind him for good measure.

"Hmmm." I turn, oh so slowly, until I'm face to face with my wife. She's nothing less than stunning when she's riled up and ready to fight for our marriage. It makes my dick hard as fucking steel. "That's three, Tesoro." I raise a brow, urging her to challenge me. I could probably get in a quickie before I meet with the Greeks.

"Jesus fucking Christ, Marco." So many things sound wrong about that expression.

"I'll have to add one more with a side of taking the Lord's name in vain." I take a step closer to her until we're nose to nose. Her chest is rising and falling, her indignation at my nonchalance making me harder by the second.

"Not *my* Lord." Ah, my little pagan is playing dirty.

"It's still disrespectful." My palm is out and my fingers are around her throat faster than she can anticipate it, giving me the advantage. Without losing eye contact, I push her into the wall and lick a slow, tortuous path across her parted lips before whispering in her mouth. "If you needed a rough fuck before I left, all you had to do was ask." She knows exactly what I'm doing, but she loves every fucking move I make. It's our game, it keeps us on our toes.

River pushes her hips into mine, no doubt feeling her effect on me. Hell, her mere presence makes me hard. Gripping the hem of her dress, I lift it up and push her panties aside, one finger thrusting inside her soaked pussy.

"Tell me where you're going, Husband." Her sultry voice is like a siren's song, irresistible and mesmerizing. My hips are moving to the rhythm of my finger as she unzips my pants and wraps her hand around my cock.

"Kastellanos. We have a meeting." As soon as the words are out of my mouth, I regret my rookie move. Her teeth sink into my bottom lip, the copper taste splashing across my tongue as the cool air replaces her hot palm around my cock.

"Well, you better get back home safe, then. No one comes until you're walking back through those doors." Then she walks away, leaving me smirking at the wall.

River - 1

Marco - 2 blue balls.

At least it's motivation to get in and get the fuck out in Brooklyn.

"Everyone in place?" We're almost at the site as Enzo checks our men's location around the docks. It feels like a sting operation, like we're fucking cops or some shit.

"Yes, sir. We've got about twenty-five soldiers waiting on your command." J's voice rings out in the cabin of my Escalade just as we pull into the dock yard. I have no doubt Yiannis has his own men around the perimeter, he'd be a fool not to, but those guys are covered by my men. The difference between Yiannis and me? Rage. Pure, unadulterated rage boiling in my veins.

Enzo steps out of the car first as I take in our surroundings. Water on one side, a red brick building on the other, the faded white lettering at the top telling the story of the good old days when shipyards were the city's bread and butter. Once Enzo is standing at the front of the car, leaning against the hood, eyes scanning every fucking inch of the place, I see the brothers coming out of the building.

"Marco, my friend." Fucking hypocrite. We're friends like hyenas and lions are fuck buddies. Never gonna happen.

"You disappoint me, Yiannis." His smile morphs into a frown at my tone and my words.

"What do you mean?" Yiannis doesn't take another step, his gaze hardening and his shoulders tensing. Behind him, Aleko leans against the building in his usual bored position with one leg bent, foot propped against the bricks. I'm not stupid enough to think he's not paying attention. In fact, by the tension in his neck and the rise of his brow, I'd say he's on high alert.

"We had a truce, didn't we? So imagine my surprise when one of your men shows up at my family's house and kills my friend. Who was your target, Yiannis? Surely, you weren't that upset with a construction worker that you had to murder him in public." I slide my hands into my slacks and scrutinize his every move, every tick and shift of his eyes.

My gaze bounces behind Yiannis to his brother, who suddenly seems more interested in the conversation. Like he might have a vested interest in the result.

"Ah, right. The botched job. You killed my man, yes?" I cock my head to the side, surprised he'd cave so quickly without even pretending to feel remorse for having Kai killed.

"Yes," I nod, my eyes fixed on his every move. "Two bullets."

"Well, then, we're even." I can't help but laugh at his words. Except there's no fucking humor in it.

"How do you figure?"

Enzo comes up to me and whispers in my ear, hiding his mouth so no one can read his lips.

"J said we're all good." I nod at his words but my eyes are following every one of Yiannis's moves.

"Well, for one, you didn't keep your end of the bargain, Marco. That's not good business." He's talking about the port in Naples and he's right, I haven't kept my end of the bargain because not only do I not trust this motherfucker, but he hasn't handed over Ugo.

"I told you I'd put in a good word, but the men there don't answer to me. I'm guessing whatever you're transporting doesn't fit their morals, but you haven't kept your end of the bargain either." Aleko pushes off the building and makes his way to us, his Docs stirring the dust with every step he takes until he stands shoulder to shoulder with his brother. He can't be more than twenty, maybe twenty-two, but the steel in his eyes holds a thousand stories of gore.

"Right, right. You did say that." Yiannis turns to Aleko like he's asking for confirmation. "He said that, didn't he?" Aleko crosses his arms and I don't miss his hand going to the butt of the gun on his shoulder holster.

"What were you trying to transport, Yiannis?" I don't want to get distracted. I need to know if I should warn the Naples family about any trouble they might encounter.

"The nectar of life, Marco. The reason wars are waged and men are killed." My molars get a workout as I grind them hard enough to make my jaw ache.

"Don't speak Aristotle to me. What the fuck were you trying to pass through Naples?" Yiannis doesn't respond right away, giving me enough time to see the corners of his lips turn toward the sky, his pupils constricting into tiny pin pricks.

"Young, virgin pussy. And a few virgin boys too." No sooner his words are out, my gun is too. In fact, every single person on this loading dock is aiming a gun at someone.

But that's not what has my attention. It's not the reason I haven't given the order to blow this whole fucking meeting to pieces.

What has me freezing with my gun aimed at Yiannis, is the fact that Aleko has his gun aimed at the same person.

His own fucking brother.

"Aleko, my brother. Don't be such a fucking pussy." Yiannis raises his gun, probably thinking his men would follow his lead. Just as his gun is halfway up, Enzo gives the order and every one of the Kastellanos around us goes down.

Including Yiannis.

It's like watching a real live Cain and Abel show, except I have no fucking clue why Aleko turned on his own damn brother. The guy is psycho, I can't imagine he draws the line at human trafficking.

My gun is pointed at his head, his men dead all around, and he just grins as he looks down at his older brother before spitting right over the bullet hole between his eyes.

"My moral compass may be skewed, but children as sex slaves is a hard pass." Then, like he doesn't have a care in the world, he flicks a business card at my feet and walks away, speaking over his shoulder. "The Kastellanos are dead. Do with the territory what you will."

I stand corrected. Psychopaths do draw lines in the sand.

I'm still watching Aleko walk away when Enzo picks up the card, reading it out loud.

"What does it say?" Lowering my gun, I turn to my second in command only once Aleko is no longer visible.

"It's Ugo's location." It's my turn to grin.

Gotcha, motherfucker.

We're in our car, heading for Ugo's hideout in the heart of Brooklyn, as Enzo orders J's crew to get their asses over there right fucking now.

Fifteen minutes later, we're screeching our tires on the driveway, surrounding the beat up house as we ride on the burned lawn—evidence of years of neglect.

Rushing out of the car, my gun locked and loaded and giving zero fucks about neighbors and witnesses, we run into the house ready to shed blood.

But just like every other fucking time, the place is empty.

"Goddamn, motherfucker!" I punch a hole in the wall and turn to J, who's holding a coffee pot.

"It's still hot."

Bastard was tipped off.

Chapter Twenty-Seven
River

S omehow, Lina persuaded me into believing that going for a run with her would be a great mind soother. "It'll be freeing," she said. I'm pretty sure she was taken over by the devil, who clearly hypnotized me into agreeing, because it's anything but freeing.

Freeing my lungs from my body as they try to escape the torture I'm putting them through, maybe.

Truthfully, the reason I'm doing this is because she's rarely at home lately and I hoped we'd be able to talk about what's been going on with her. I didn't account for the whole running thing making that damn near impossible.

When we left the house, crossing over the road and finding a route through Central Park—with our trusty bodyguards following at a safe distance, of course—I tried to speak, to ask questions, but her responses were minimal. I found myself making a lot of effort and my only reward was a lack of oxygen. Lina even went as far as popping an AirPod in. I mean, she offered one to me so we could listen to the same thing, so it's just a case of accepting what she's offering for now.

With her being home, I'll see if Stefano can whip us up some snacks for a movie night. Hopefully that will help her open up some more. She won't get to choose all the movies, because I may be grieving for a different thing than Lina, but I'm still grieving too. This movie night is for both of us.

Lorde begins to play through the tiny earbud in my ear, *Glory and Gore*, and, for the first time in too long, I smile. If there was a soundtrack to my life—and Lina's—then this song would definitely feature heavily.

My thoughts wander and Lina slows down to match my pace, but only a little. I can walk for miles in my heels but make me run and apparently I'm useless. The last time I ran was on the day Kai passed, almost a month ago, but I didn't really give the whole running thing much thought then. My focus was on my destination and the way Marco's voice shook.

Briefly squeezing my eyelids together, I lightly shake my head to remove the visions of blood... so much blood... Kai's blood. It's something I compartmentalize for later, when I can cope with those feelings in the arms of my husband.

Considering Marco is a dominant, controlling, and kinda possessive asshole most of the time, he's been amazing through all of this. He encourages me to talk about all the things on my mind, the good, the bad, the ugly, and he asks me about my life before him, wanting to hear about the memories I have—Kai included. The night of Kai's funeral, I expected Marco's jealousy to shine through as I recounted the time Kai broke his wrist when he fell out of a plum tree. Kai was determined to pick the biggest one because he said I deserved only the best and, even though Marco made a joke about Kai needing to compensate with big plums, it wasn't in bad taste or with any malice.

Marco's understanding and complete devotion is like nothing I ever thought I could have. I saw it in my parents when they were alive. They were so in love, going as far as to run away and live like hippies together. They argued, they had disputes, but at the end of the day, they were always laughing together.

Saying I love you every night and making sure my husband knows how much I appreciate him and am grateful for him is my newest ritual. If anything good has come out of all this shit, it's the closeness and trust it's given me with Marco.

My ass begins vibrating, because of course my phone is in the back pocket of my leggings and not in one of those fancy arm-band things Lina has. I manage to pull it out and unlock it without dropping it, my pace now basically at a brisk walk, not even close to a run anymore.

"Hey, Ev. I'm kinda in the middle of a run with Lina, can I call you back?" I could've let it go through to voicemail, but I'm using the phone call as an excuse to pause, resting my palm on my knee as I bend forward to catch my breath.

"Riv, Sis… It's happening. What the fuck do I do? I'm gonna be a dad, Riv. A fucking dad." Everest's voice is shaky, scared, and excited beyond belief.

I squeal down the phone, completely unlike my usual self, but this is a big deal. My brother's baby is ready to make an appearance. "Oh, Ev! I'm so happy for you both. First, how's Petal?"

"Oh man, sis, she's so amazing." He sounds in awe and my pride is beginning to overflow.

"Is Lydia there?" Making sure the doula has arrived, or is at least on the way, is a priority. She'll keep a cool head and help take some of the pressure off of them.

I can see Lina making her way back to me after realizing I'm no longer right behind her. She gestures to the phone with a questioning look and I gesture to my stomach the way you do when you talk about a baby bump before pointing down between my legs while Ev is speaking.

"Shit, no. I need to call her now."

"I'll be there soon, little brother. Stay calm for Pet, I love you."

"Love you too, Riv." He hangs up, no doubt to go and call the doula to help coach them through the natural birth.

"My brother's having a baby!" My squeal of excitement is unavoidable, and my cheeks hurt from grinning so widely.

Lina's face is a picture of amusement as she raises a brow at my statement, so I clarify... not that I need to, but ya know. "Petal's having the baby, she's in labor."

"Oh my God, that's great!" A little of the happy spark that Lina's been missing is now in her eyes, along with that beautiful laugh of hers, and I want to bottle it up for her so she can keep it forever.

"Yup, which means I've got a niece or nephew to go and meet and can't do running anymore." I fake pout, because it's obvious I've been hating every second of this. She knows I'm here for her though, and that's good enough for me—even if this has felt like torture.

Saved by the baby.

"You know we've got to run back to the house, right?" Lina smirks.

"Ah, fuck."

Ev was a panicked mess when we arrived, unsure of his role in all this and feeling entirely useless. Lydia assured him that he wasn't the only father-to-be to ever feel like this and that his role would really kick in when Baby is born because his Petal will need the rest.

Marco poured him a glass of the expensive whiskey he brought with us and has taken him outside, arm around his shoulder, leaving me inside with a grunting Petal.

"Hey, Beautiful." The smile on my face is so big my cheeks are close to aching, but I'll take all the hurt in the world to be a part of this.

"He-hey, Gorgeous." Petal's words are spoken through pants and even through childbirth, this woman never fails to amaze me. Her big brown eyes are full of light, her smile wide, and her cheeks pink from exertion. She's in their large bedroom, homemade dark-wood furniture all around, and she's sitting up in the middle of their bed. Plastic sheets rustle under the towels beneath her as she tries to find a comfortable position while Lydia dabs her forehead with a cooling muslin cloth.

"What do you need?" The latest contraction has stopped so I move forward into her open arms, pushing all my love for my sister-in-law into the hug.

"I'd love an orange." She laughs as we pull apart and I shake my head.

"One orange, coming up."

"How's my Bear?"

I pause before I get to the door, grinning at how Petal is *still* thinking of others, even in the middle of childbirth.

"He's good, Babe. I'll send him right on up with your orange, okay?"

She visibly relaxes a little more, leaning back on the pillows and sipping at the glass of water Lydia hands her.

The guys' voices are coming from the kitchen and I can hear laughter, so they must be finished with their man-chat outside.

Ev's shoulders aren't up by his ears anymore and the worry in his eyes has faded, replaced by a determination that makes me smile again.

"The lady would like an orange. Post haste!" I clap my hands, raising my eyebrow, and Ev moves like lightning.

"I guess I better get back upstairs then. My wife's having a baby." He straightens his back, grinning like the Cheshire Cat and grabbing an orange from the counter. On his way out of the kitchen, he kisses my forehead as he passes me and I sigh. Content for the first time in too long.

I know it won't last but it also won't be gone forever. The things that have happened will always have happened, the people I've lost will always be gone, but there will always be moments like this one. Moments when happiness is no longer just a dream to strive for, but a living breathing thing.

"Are you okay, *Tesoro*?" Marco's hands slide around my waist from behind me, pressing into my stomach as he rests his chin against my shoulder.

"Yeah. I really am. *Ti amo, marito*." I rest my hands over his and twist to look at him, kissing his head softly. I feel the movement as his eyebrows rise, hopefully impressed that I'm beginning to learn some Italian. I'll admit, I'm picking and choosing phrases I like rather than trying to learn the whole language, and "I love you, husband" seemed like one I should learn.

Thank you, Stefano.

"*Ti amo anch'io, moglie.*" His lips against my shoulder are like a balm to my soul but an almighty yell from upstairs quickly rips us out of the moment.

"What the fuck?" Marco's eyes are wide, questioning, then there's a knock at the front door before I can answer him.

I've been around women giving birth before. As a community of hippies, everyone was a part of everyone's lives, so the yelling and screaming feels natural to me. Although, I can tell by the look on Marco's face that he's genuinely worried something's going wrong, he's completely open to taking my lead on this.

"Hang on, Baby, I'll get the door."

His low growl on my way out of the kitchen tells me his shock has waned and I grin to myself once more.

I love today.

"Hi, I'm the midwife, Imogen. Lydia called and said it's almost time, so here I am!" The tall older woman was obviously cleared by Petal by the way light practically shines from her. She may as well be doing jazz hands with the way she's presenting herself, showing me her medical badge and identification, and I think Petal made the perfect choice.

"Of course. Come on inside, the mommy-to-be is upstairs, first door on the left." I move aside, allowing her to shuffle inside. "Would you like help with your things?"

"Oh, no. I'm used to all this, thank you. But if you could keep our water supplies replenished, that would be amazing." She heads on upstairs and the screams get louder as she opens the door, muffling them again as she closes it behind her.

Two hours later, the screams that had become persistent, have now stopped. My heart is beating a mile a minute as I sit on Marco's lap, curled into him as we wait for the news. I want to rush up there and find out everything, but Marco helped me realize that Ev and Petal need to do this part on their own.

There are now footsteps from overhead, after ten minutes of what felt like silence, then a door opens and the most beautiful and heart-wrenching sound I've ever heard brings a tear to my eye. But I hold that sucker back.

"Aunty River, Uncle Marco, would you like to come upstairs and meet your new nephew?" Ev's voice is full of so much pride, it's getting harder to keep my tears at bay.

I have a nephew.

I tap Marco's chest too many times for it to be normal in my excitement, standing quickly and grabbing his hand, dragging him up the stairs with me.

Petal is all covered up and resting back against the pillows and cushions, a serene smile on her tear-stained face, and Ev is sitting beside her, a bundle of blankets in his arms. I have no time to waste on pleasantries with Lydia or Imogen right now, although I'll thank them profusely for helping them through this later.

My focus is on the bundle.

Ev looks up as I approach, still dragging Marco behind me. I sit beside my brother, on the edge of the bed, and lean into him to get a better look at the baby. His tiny eyes are closed, his little fists up by his mouth and his button nose. And I'm in love.

My nephew is officially the best baby in the world.

"I'm so proud of you both. He's adorable."

Marco's hand is on my shoulder as we sit for a few moments, in awe of what they have created.

"I want to name him Briggs. Briggs Denali Fox." Petal's voice is so light, it's barely a whisper, and her words almost let loose the waterfall that's threatening to fall from my eyes.

"I love that." Ev kisses his wife's head as a tear slides down her cheek, but she's so happy, it's contagious.

The baby's name is something I'll definitely cry about later, in the comfort of my husband's arms right before he fucks me to sleep. But for right now, I want to bask in the happiness that is this new life. The fact that Petal wants to call him Briggs reaffirms our beliefs in a way. We've lost a life to gain a new one, and while that is completely tragic, it's also got a beauty to it. It's like the universe is reminding us to be grateful for what we have while we have it, to never take anything for granted because it can be gone in an instant. While on the other hand, we need to be grateful for new beginnings, new opportunities to be better, to *do* better.

Everything is precious and baby Briggs just became the most protected and loved baby in the whole of New York City.

Marco sits in a chair beside the bed and I get comfortable on his lap as Ev passes Briggs over to me for his first Aunty-cuddle. He's so light and delicate, I'm afraid I might break him, but I sit back into Marco's chest, my eyes fixed on the cute bundle in my arms.

"We'll be back when we're finished in the bathroom, Riv. Is that okay?" Ev is helping Petal out of bed.

"Of course it is. Take as long as you need."

Petal looks longingly at Briggs as she leaves the room, practically pushed out by Ev, and the midwife and doula have gone downstairs to do whatever they need to do.

The room is so quiet except for the occasional noise coming from Briggs, and when I say they're the cutest noises in existence, I'm not even exaggerating.

"This could be us one day." Marco's whispered words in my ear make my eyes widen in shock and I turn to look at him, trying to figure out how serious he is. There is a slight fear in the way his brows are raised, as if he thinks what he's saying is what I want to hear.

It's not.

"Nope. Didn't you hear how much pain Petal was in an hour ago? Crotch goblins are not for me. The good thing about a nephew is that we can give him back to his parents when we're done."

The relief in his expression as his shoulders drop at my answer is kinda funny, and I can't help kissing him lightly before he answers.

"Thank fuck for that."

"Language, Mr. Mancini." I wink at my husband, mischief in my eyes. "I'll have to punish you for that later."

Chapter Twenty-Eight

Marco

It's late when we arrive at the house, our ride home filled with quiet contemplation about the new addition to the Fox family. A tiny, fragile, human is now the center of attention in Everest and Petal's world and I have no doubts that Briggs will be the happiest of all children.

I'm just not ready for that. I'm too fucking selfish to share River with anyone, not even my own kid. I would, of course, if that's what she wanted, but I can't say I'm ready to step aside and share her heart.

Although...

"Close your eyes, Tesoro." With a frown and wrinkle of her nose, River turns toward me and blinks.

"Why?"

"Close. Your. Eyes." I use my stern voice when she continues to question my demands.

"Oh, I didn't realize I was dealing with dominant Marco. I thought sweet, caring Marco was still here." With one hand on the door handle and the other on the small of her back, I lean in and trap her bottom lip between my teeth before whispering, "Stop being a brat and obey."

"Obey, pfft, don't push your luck, Mancini." I allow the corners of my mouth to curve up while I wait for her to do as I ask. Or demand. Same thing.

"Fine, my eyes are closed. This better be good." I have no doubts she will lose her mind at how good this is going to be.

"I promise, you'll thank me profusely. On your knees. With my dick in your mouth." She snorts and I grin. She thinks I'm kidding.

I'm not.

As soon as I open the door, Stefano is waiting with River's gift in the palm of his hand and a crinkle at the corner of his eyes. He likes it. He approves of my present.

Once we're inside, I stand in front of my wife and hold out my hand for Stefano to pass me the fragile gift before I whisper a kiss across River's lips.

"Tesoro, this will never replace what we lost, but I hope it will fill a corner of your heart with love where pain resides. Open your eyes." Blinking, she looks at me, a small frown forming before her eyes fall to the palm of my hand and land on the ball of fur that lies there, eyes wide, tail wagging.

"Oh, my fucking gods, Marco. You got me a tiny Bruce?" Her eyes well up immediately, her lip trembling with happiness and probably a little sorrow at the loss of my mother's long-time companion. But when she looks back up at me as though asking for permission to pick up the little fur ball, tears track down her rosy cheeks and spill across her mouth.

"Well, I don't think we can call him Tiny Bruce, it might give him a complex."

"Yeah, we need to find a name." She picks him up like he's crystal and capable of breaking with too much pressure and brings him to her lips, kissing his ridiculously small muzzle. Now, I have to admit, the thing is cute as fuck, but as soon as his miniscule tongue starts lapping at River's mouth, I decide to put the brakes on that shit.

"No, no, Tiny, there's no licking my wife. Get your own damn wife. Then you can lick whatever you want." River looks at me as her hands go to his ears. At least, I think it's his ears, all I really see is a globe of fur.

"Do not call him the *T* word." She brings him back to her mouth and starts kissing him all over. Then I remember why having children wasn't a priority. I suppose I didn't take into account that she could love this guy and ignore me.

"He needs a name." Leaning toward me, she meets my lips with hers, aiming for a tender kiss, but I'm not having it. My hand darts out, my fingers curling around the short strands at the back of her head as I brand her with my mouth, a kiss so hard and full of deep-seated heat that it makes my dick instantly hard.

"He does. But I need to fuck you more than he needs a name." Careful not to crush the little guy, I bring my lips to River's ear and chuckle. "I hope you're ready to potty train him." Stepping away, I wink at my wife as Stefano chuckles beside me, taking his leave.

"Marco! You gave him to me, it's your job to train him. Plus, you're the big dominant here, he'll listen to you." I cock my head to the side as she juts out her bottom lip and pouts. As if I'd fall for that.

"Oh!" Mischief dances in her eyes, her entire body vibrating with excitement. "I have the perfect name."

Deep down in my gut, I have a bad feeling about this. The little brat that likes to come out and play is teasing me, and I'm certain the next words out of her mouth won't make me happy.

"All right, let's hear it." Her wide grin and wide eyes are scaring me.

"Polo."

I pause, frowning.

"Polo? Why would you call..." *Oh, fuck no.*

"Yes!" She sees the exact moment I realize what she's planning on putting me through for the foreseeable future.

"Fuck. No. This is not happening. I am putting my veto on this bullshit, right here. Right now."

"Yes! Come on! That way I can call you both at the same time. Marco! Polo!"

"Stefano!" I call for him but my stare is solely on River.

"Signore?"

"Would you mind taking him for a long walk? I need some privacy with my wife." It's my turn to grin like I have plans to destroy her.

"Si, of course." River pouts as she hands over a whining little puppy, but the way she licks her lips as she watches me, I know she's anticipating my next move.

When the front door closes, I grin and lean into River, the front of my body pressing against her, pushing her across the room until her thighs hit the dining room table.

"You know what this means, right?" My tone is low and dark as I watch her watching me.

"Hmm, I'm guessing I'll have a hard time sitting tomorrow." By the glint in her eyes, I'm guessing she doesn't mind the consequences of her actions.

"Interesting choice of words, Tesoro. Hard." I lick a hot trail from her collar bone to her jaw, tasting the saltiness of her skin. "Hard like your head when you're being stubborn. Like my cock every time you're near me. Like this table where I'm going to fuck the sass right out of you."

"Like the pounding I can't wait to get." This woman...

Fucking Hell, she's perfect.

"Exactly like that."

I spin her around and push her down on the table, head turned to the side so she can see everything I'm about to do to her.

With a quick flip of the wrist, I pop off the button of her jeans and slide down the zipper before I push the denim to the floor, leaving it there at her ankles.

As she begins to step out of them, I slap the perfect globe of her ass hard enough to make her grunt.

"Did I give you permission to move?" The dark tone of my voice makes the hairs on her lithe body stand straight, turning me on even more. "Spread your ankles as far as they can go."

"It's not much." At her words, I slap her other cheek.

"Did I give you permission to speak?" Her smile grows on her profile, her one visible green eye fixed only on me. She doesn't answer but she raises her arms to the opposite edge of the table and lays herself out like a feast, only for me.

As I kneel at the banquet of her delicious cunt, I slide her thong off as I go, my face only inches from the apex of her succulent thighs. I make her wait, blowing warm air across her lips and reveling in the soft tremble of her muscles. The anticipation is sometimes better than the orgasm itself.

With my fingers pressing against the flesh of her thighs, I bring my mouth to her pussy and devour her like it's my last meal. I lick and bite without any self-control, that part of me disappears whenever she's around. She's both my greatest strength and my most terrifying weakness. I've accepted that, just like she's accepted that her body is mine to bend and to punish. To praise and to bruise.

"Goddamn, you taste like a good girl who likes to do bad things." My face is now wholly between her legs, my tongue so deep inside her pussy it can feel her cum easing from her walls. Squirming and moaning, her small cries bouncing off the oak table and dancing in my ears, I reach around and flick her clit as my free hand grabs her ass cheek and squeezes hard enough to redden her skin.

"Come on my face, River." Pushing her ass back against the wooden surface, thrusting as hard as she can, she groans as I push a finger inside her ass and pinch her clit hard enough to get a primal reaction from her. "That's it, Tesoro, show me what you need."

As she explodes over my tongue, I lap up every ounce of her pleasure, drink in her most intimate gift. Take it all in and make it a part of me.

Because that's what this is. Every time we fuck and every time I feast on her cunt and come inside her, we share ourselves with the other.

Before she can take a breather, I'm pushing my own jeans down, my aching cock out and my tip pressed against the entrance to her pussy, eager to get a piece of her. I grab onto her hair and pull her head back until her upper body is arching enough for me to have access to her addictive mouth.

"Taste yourself." My lips descend on hers and, just as my tongue demands access, my cock thrusts fully inside her. I don't make love to my wife. I fuck her exactly how she deserves it: long and hard, rough and demanding.

The table screeches against the tile floor with every on-slaught of my hips slapping against her ass. We're cheek to cheek now, my voice broken with the effort of feeding her my hungry cock.

"I wish I could go deeper. I wish I could fuck you so hard there's no coming back from it. No pulling out, only driving inside you." We're both grunting, the sound of our skin slapping, our cum mixing.

"We're... not," River struggles with her words, exhaling them with every battering thrust of my hips against her ass. "Ever... coming... back." My lips latch onto her neck, sucking the skin with violent intent, marking her with my mouth and bruising her with my love. "From... this."

As her walls squeeze my shaft with her impending or-gasm, I switch my hand from her clit to her throat and pull her as close to me as I possibly can. "Come, Tesoro. Fly away with me."

We're both haphazardly dressed, barely hiding our bits when Stefano returns with—fuck my life—Polo. River has traded her off-the-shoulder sweater for my button down, claiming it's as long as a short dress and much more digni-fied than walking around in her thong.

I had to agree. However, I'm also guessing by the way her gaze travels up and down my torso and abs, she just wanted the view while we took a break in the kitchen for some sustenance.

Polo takes about three lifetimes to run straight—I use these words lightly because he neither runs nor goes in a straight line—toward us. His tiny paws have a hard time adhering to the tiled floors so he spends half his energy on trying to stay standing.

River kneels on the floor, patting her thighs and encour-aging him to come to her, and when he finally attempts to jump on her, he just slides right back down. Taking pity on him, she scoops him up and brings him to her chest, where she rains kisses down on him. His little button nose sniffs everything about her, probably imprinting her scent for future reference.

I know that's what I did. Imprinting.

Once he's done licking her cheeks and nose, he yawns like it was the greatest effort he could possibly make and immediately conks out in the palm of her hand.

"Wow, I wish I could just fall asleep like that." I turn to River with a brow raised and a smirk sitting firm and proud on my lips.

"Oh, Tesoro, you barely get a word out before you're fast asleep when I fuck the fight right out of you." She snorts then shrugs. I get no arguments from her because there aren't any viable ones out there. "What do you want to eat?"

Her gaze falls to my cock, already half-mast and eager to continue our games from the dining room. "Well..." Her words trail off and her deep emeralds burn a searing path all the way up to my lips before landing on my steel grays.

"Food, River. I'll feed you my cock after you've eaten actual food." Her fake pout doesn't bother me, it's her bratty side trying to get what she wants, despite what she needs.

"How about popcorn?" Taking a page from her handbook, I roll my eyes at her and give her my back. "What? Popcorn is food."

"It's *junk* food. You know what, forget this. Go shower, I'm taking you out to dinner."

"But it's like..." From the corner of my eye, as I'm putting away all the ingredients I had pulled out of the fridge, I see her awaken her phone and check the time. "Nine at night."

I pin her with a look that I hope exudes my power in this city. "I am Marco Mancini and you are my queen. In this city, we eat whenever the fuck we want."

"Nice try, baby. This is Manhattan, everyone can eat whenever the fuck they want." Biting her bottom lip, she takes a step closer, pressing her delectable body to mine and kissing her way up my chest and throat. "The real question is... what about Polo?" Goddamn, I hate that name.

"Stefano can watch him."

"But..." Her gaze falls to the tiny bundle of fur breathing heavily with occasional twitches of his ridiculously small paws, then brings her begging eyes up to mine. River Fox-Mancini doesn't play fair. In fact, she's using illegal tactics to get her way. The worst part is that she knows damn well that she'll get the last word. "He's going to miss us."

I kiss her crown and tip her head up with my fingers at her chin. "He goes where we go. How's that?" Her smile lights up my soul. Our lips meet, soft and teasing, warming my skin with every lick from her tongue. I could do this all fucking day or night.

"Thank you, Husband."

"The world for you, Tesoro."

Thirty minutes and a quickie later, we're headed down to the front entrance, where I stop at the door and watch her bend over to fasten one of her heels. I'm tempted to lift her dress up and fuck her again, but at one point I'm going to need to take her to dinner or else not even my name will get us an open kitchen. Only once she's ready and right before she scoops up Polo do I let my devilish grin show.

"Oh no, you're up to something." Eyes narrowed and lips pursed, she cocks out her hip and waves me off. "Go on, give it to me."

"I'm glad you said that because I absolutely want to give this to you." Opening the box in my hands, I grin as her gaze falls on the silicone balls nestled in the velvet interior.

"It's like déjà-vu." When our gazes meet, my chest burns exactly the same way it did the first time I dared her to wear the eggs at our dinner date. And just like that first time, she walks up to me, takes the device, and carefully inserts them in her cum-filled pussy.

Because contrary to the first time we did this, her lube is… me.

Epilogue
River

So that's my story—for now, of course. It's the story of how I found my twin flame, which was a Hell of a journey, and I won't lie... I'd change a lot of things that happened if I could. But it's the fate that the universe chose for me. They were the lessons I needed to learn along the way.

My heart is broken, but it's being healed by a man who loves me more than life and by my own pure determination to not allow the tragedies of my past define me. It won't be an easy ride, but I'm here for it all the same. I'm no longer trying to do everything alone. The world isn't on my shoulders and Marco reminds me of that every day.

The things that man can do with his tongue, his fingers, his cock, the toys... oh, the list goes on. Let's just say, as I'm sure you've gathered by now, I'm a very lucky woman.

I'm his lady in the streets, and his freak in the sheets.

And he is mine in every way a person could belong to another.

I promise you, reader, I'll look after him and do all the things, all the time... I won't let you down!

I'll always be grateful for my forever one.

For now though, even though I have my happy ending, I still need to keep an eye out for Lina. She's not okay and that isn't anything to be ashamed or afraid of, so I'll remind her at every opportunity how amazing she is and how I'm ready to talk about anything and nothing, whenever she's ready.

Remember, it's not shameful to ask for help sometimes.

Ugo is still on the run—just saying the fucker's name makes me want to vomit—but I know he won't be able to hide forever. Hopefully, Lina will get some kind of closure when we finally bring him in. But that's Lina's story to tell...

"Tesoro, are you ready?"

"Yeah, be there in a minute."

Time for me to go, we're taking Polo for a short walk around Central Park. Although, Marco will probably end up carrying him most of the way around. His tiny legs only go so far before he's ready for a rest... in Marco's arms. In fact, that very image is my cell screensaver.

So, don't forget my mantra if you're in need of a confidence boost...

Repeat after me:

"I am a badass bitch."

Go on, your turn...

You're awesome.

Thanks for sticking around for my happy ending!

For Lina's Story, read Kings of Kink next!

Then, The Reapers Duet (One Kill & One Love) are J's story...

THE BLONDE ONE

Book 6… The Escort series has been such a wild ride with Brunette. So much so, we've decided to carry on. Lina's story is next, plus we have plans for a couple of other characters. Feel free to message or email us with your guesses! One whole year ago, Brunette and I decided to join forces and write a dark and dirty series based on an escort and her exploits, what it has turned into is a massive story of growth. We've grown with her, and we hope you appreciate the actual real-life tears we've put into these words for y'all.

Thank you to each and every one of you for giving River—and N.O. One—a chance.

Marco may have done some questionable things, but in the end, it's always been her for him. If you find someone willing to burn the world to ashes for you… keep them!

This book in particular covers some sensitive topics, and we hope to all the Gods that you never have to experience those things, but if you do, please know, you never have to be alone. Help is available, please speak to someone. Do not stay silent <3

For everyone who has been a part of this journey with us... you're freaking awesome. We could name you all, but we've been kind enough to make some of you into characters already ;) and Brunette is naming a bunch of you beauts in her bit!

For Lina's book... we're taking a walk on the #whychoose side! Did you figure out who all of her men are yet...?

We hope this book leaves you feeling beautifully satisfied and also eager for more; we love to see those reviews, they give us absolute life!

Ciao, Bellas!

P.S. These aren't the only places you can go to for help... they're just a couple we have found we thought could be useful <3

UK Website for help: https://www.sarsas.org.uk/

USA Website for help: https://www.rainn.org/

THE BRUNETTE ONE

Jayzus, I cannot believe The Escort is finished. Six books in ten months is insane but I can't imagine doing it any other way.

We haven't done it alone, that's just impossible.

First, we've had Lily Wildhart's support from the get go...in fact, she's the one who suggested we write together. (Thanks, Lils, you're amazing!).

Even though he quit many, many times, David never really gave up on us. Thank you for sticking around, Pot Stirrer. We love your face.

Our Alpha and Beta readers: Zoe, Sam, and Lydia...what the ever living fuck would we do without you? Nothing, that's what. Thank you!

To Gabri for making sure Marco's Italian was perfect. Anything less would have been a travesty. Grazie, cara!

For The Forever One, we chose to reach out to Candi Kane PR and we can't thank her enough for the work she's done with this release. Thank you, thank you, thank you!

And of course...our stories wouldn't have the same impact without our gorgeous covers. Thank you a million times to Bailey Grayson for designing them.

Finally, to Sam O'Neill working behind the scenes to make sure we don't fuck up royally. You are the sprinkles on our rocky road ice-cream cones. Thank you so much for keeping us in line!

This project started exactly a year ago, when I approached Blondie, hoping she'd be wild enough to join my crazy train. Turns out, she's all balls to the wind and loves a challenge as much as I do. We talked and talked, video chatted and texted for hours and hours until we knew exactly how we wanted River's character to feel. How we wanted you to see her.

River is all us.

She's you, hurting because life has been knocking you down.

She's also you, taking charge and walking through doors of opportunity because that shit doesn't come along every day.

She's you, protective and fearless when it comes to family.

She's every single one of you, protagonists of your sexual needs and desires.

She's kind yet fierce. Brave yet vulnerable. She stumbles, sometimes scraping her knees, but forces herself to stand right back up and keep on going.

River is your mother, your sister, your best friend. She's the woman you call when you need someone to bail you out but also when you need a comforting hug.

River is the woman I want to be when I grow up. Also, I'll take Marco any freaking day of the week.

Here's the good news, we're not finished with you. In fact, we have lots of plans that involve breaking your heart and putting it all back together again.

That's right...we're planning on giving your Lina's story and this time, you don't have to choose, you get the whole damn package. Tyler, Enzo and... well, make sure you download Kings of Kink (aka KOK) and find out who the new addition to her love life will be.

So, when all is said and done, you the reader, are the reason we can keep going. So, thank you for putting your reading pleasure in our care. We promise not to break your hearts (too much)... only to bruise it (a lot).

Books by N.O. One

Dark Contemporary Romance

The Escort Series (MF)

The Rich One ~ https://geni.us/TheRichOne

The Kinky One ~ https://geni.us/TheKinkyOne

The Filthy One ~ https://geni.us/TheFithyOne

The Broken One ~ https://geni.us/TheBrokenOne

The Almost One ~ https://geni.us/TheAlmostOne

The Forever One ~ https://geni.us/TheForeverOne

The Christmas One ~ Prequel to The Escort Series

KOK – Lina's story (RH)

Kings of Kink ~ https://geni.us/KingsOfKink

The Reapers Mafia Crew Duet – J's story (MF)

One Kill ~ https://geni.us/TheReapers1

One Love ~ https://geni.us/TheReapers2

The Psycho Trilogy – Remember Aleko… Sons of Khaos (MF)

Psycho Hate ~ https://geni.us/PsychoHate

Psycho Love ~ https://geni.us/PsychoLove

Psycho Reign ~ https://geni.us/PsychoReign

A Night To Remember Auction – A shared world (MF)

Once Upon A Sale ~ https://geni.us/OnceUponASale

Books in the Auction Shared world by other authors ~ https://www.amazon.com/dp/B0CLKVXLXJ

Sons of Khaos – The Standalones

Bear Hunt (MF) ~ https://geni.us/SOKBearHunt

Meat Grinder (Poly with MF and MM)

7 Deadly Sins – A Shared World

Gluttony

Next Door

The Assassin Next Door

Dark Paranormal Fantasy Romance

Society Of Soulkeepers

Hack (MF) ~ Book 1 of The White Horse Duet

Hex (MF) ~ Book 2 of The White Horse Duet

If you'd love to get in touch or find out more about our books, please feel free to stalk us in all the places and join our newsletter.

www.author-no-one.com

If you'd love to get in touch or find out more about our books, please feel free to stalk us in all the places and join our newsletter.

Here is our linktree: https://linktr.ee/n.o.one

BOOKS WE THINK YOU SHOULD READ

Dark Romance

DATE WITH THE DEVIL (MF) ~
HTTPS://GENI.US/DWTD

Contemporary

THE UCC SAGA
DISHEVELED ~ HTTP://AMZN.TO/2ARPBXP
DISARMED ~ HTTP://AMZN.TO/2MYVXNN
DISCARDED ~ HTTPS://AMZN.TO/2VWTRPF
UCC BOXSET ~ HTTPS://AMZN.TO/3LJVEPE

STANDALONE
THE WISH ~ HTTPS://AMZN.TO/2FTIKQB

Rom-Com

THE WOOLF FAMILY SERIES
SCREWED ~ HTTPS://GENI.US/SCREWED
SCREWED UP ~ HTTPS://BIT.LY/3IBFWKB
SCREWED OVER (COMING SOON)

Supernatural

SOUL GUARDIANS SERIES
REPRISE ~ HTTPS://BIT.LY/3CT9NPE

Eva LeNoir
Fun Flirty Romance

BY LILY WILDHART

Dark Romance

The Saints of Serenity Falls series (RH)

(You will find crossovers from The Escort series by N.O.
One in the Serenity Falls series by Lily Wildhart, and vice
versa!)

A Burn So Deep ~ https://geni.us/burnaltcover

A Revenge So Sweet ~ https://geni.us/revengealtcover

A Taste Of Forever ~ https://geni.us/tastealtcover

Website & Newsletter: www.author-no-one.com

Facebook: https://geni.us/Facebookauthor

Facebook Group: https://geni.us/FierceReaders

Instagram: https://geni.us/Instagramauthor

Goodreads: https://geni.us/Goodreadsauthor

Bookbub: https://www.bookbub.com/profile/n-o-one

Linkedtree https://linktr.ee/n.o.one